M. L. WHITE

Realm of Darkness

Copyright © 2025 by M. L. White

All rights reserved. No part of this publication may be reproduced, stored or transmitted in any form or by any means, electronic, mechanical, photocopying, recording, scanning, or otherwise without written permission from the publisher. It is illegal to copy this book, post it to a website, or distribute it by any other means without permission.

This novel is entirely a work of fiction. The names, characters and incidents portrayed in it are the work of the author's imagination. Any resemblance to actual persons, living or dead, events or localities is entirely coincidental.

M. L. White asserts the moral right to be identified as the author of this work.

M. L. White has no responsibility for the persistence or accuracy of URLs for external or third-party Internet Websites referred to in this publication and does not guarantee that any content on such Websites is, or will remain, accurate or appropriate.

Designations used by companies to distinguish their products are often claimed as trademarks. All brand names and product names used in this book and on its cover are trade names, service marks, trademarks and registered trademarks of their respective owners. The publishers and the book are not associated with any product or vendor mentioned in this book. None of the companies referenced within the book have endorsed the book.

Second edition

ISBN: 9798899713293

Cover art by SeventhStar Art

This book was professionally typeset on Reedsy.
Find out more at reedsy.com

To my wonderful children,
You three are my whole world.
Love, Mom

Prologue

Momma was sick.

Real sick, and there wasn't anything I could do for her. I was only 15, and no one would hire a kid to work, even in the crummy Kingdom of Odemark, but I had to do something. She was all I had left.

Papa died some time ago, and we were forced out of our cottage due to a lack of money. After we ran out of things to sell, Momma was forced to do unspeakable things to try and provide food for us. The land was desolate, and it was difficult to grow anything here for some reason. People called me the son of a whore and wanted nothing to do with us. I was in quite a few fights before the King's men began to get involved, and I had to ignore everything for fear of getting locked up. *Then where would Momma be?*

Day after day, I'd search out a cure for my mother, only to turn up empty handed. There was one highly sought after doctor in the kingdom, but the King kept the physician and his family hidden away at the castle. No one could approach him, and I was stuck trying to figure it out on my own. I couldn't even find herbs to make a healing concoction as nothing grew out here.

It frustrated me to no end being entirely powerless to help her. I hit brick wall after brick wall, wearing nothing but rags with no shoes. Most in the village looked at me like I was just a disease they could catch. I stole what I could, but it was getting harder and harder to steal anything nice. The Kingdom of Odemark was under a high tax by the King, so there were very few valuable things left to take.

The King and Queen lived in luxury though. Their surrounding land was lush and green, and they had no problem growing food. With the tax staying high, it kept the entire kingdom in check as the King would sell food to families that could afford it. If you didn't have money then other arrangements could be found, and many kids were sold to serve the royal family, giving their own families a monthly supply of food, while the child worked his or her life away.

No one understood how the King was able to cultivate the land, but there was always rumors he had a Lightspark under his control. According to legend, they had the ability to heal whatever they touched, whether it be a person or the land. No one ever saw proof though, so it stayed nothing more than a rumor. You would think he'd use them to heal the rest of his kingdom though instead of just his home, but the trade wagons would come and go constantly, so I guess it didn't really matter what happened to us. As long as he was fat, rich, and happy, that's all that was important.

Sadly, the King's men would not even speak to me about Momma, and I had nothing of value to barter for medicine that might be able to save her. If I joined the rations program, then she would have no one in the village to care for her, and still no cure for whatever ails her. I was stuck, and I hated them for it. A King should care for his people, even the ones who were insignificant like us. The citizens of Odemark just seemed to accept it too, and no one seemed to see the mistreatment of the people.

Or at least I never noticed.

Most just seemed grateful for the food, I suppose. The neighboring kingdoms were all in desolation too as the land was dry and infertile everywhere in these parts. At least in Odemark, they had a chance to keep their families alive and mostly well fed. They had to deal with the Nightlocke though. That was the downside.

"Arthur?"

My mother's soft voice pulled me from my thoughts. It was dusk, and we needed to hide for the night. I turned to Momma, whose brown eyes pleaded with my own. I knew she was in a tremendous amount of pain, yet she reached for me anyways. Her small frail body was getting easier to move with each passing day. While I knew I was getting stronger as I grew into the man I was to become, I also knew it was because her body was failing her. *She was withering away right in front of my eyes, and there was nothing I could do for her.*

I walked over, picking Momma off the cobblestone floor. She fell against me, and I fought away tears as I looked down to what used to be a strong woman. *She was dying, and I couldn't save her.*

"Shh... Momma. I'll hide you from the shadows. Don't you worry."

She laid her head on me as I walked further into the alley. We came upon a makeshift shed of sorts, and I had pried the lock off the door weeks ago. It let in some light, and as long as we were gone by morning, and I remembered to put the lock back on the door, the owners were none the wiser. I slid down the wall, pulling out a stale chunk of bread I managed to steal earlier today from my pocket. I placed it in her hand, giving it solely to her.

Her hands were weak, and she tried to push it back. "I cannot take this, Arthur."

I gave her a look before forcing it in her hands. "Momma, eat. I already ate my portion earlier."

I lied, but I wasn't about to tell her that. She gave me a sad look before taking a small bite. I sighed in relief, knowing it would give her some strength and maybe another day with me. I know I was being selfish as I'm sure death was something she was ready for, but I just couldn't let her go. I needed her, and I couldn't be alone just yet. I wasn't ready to lose her.

She ate about half before passing it back. I tried to make her eat the rest, when she shook her head softly.

"Arthur, I can't. I'll lose what I ate."

My heart broke, and I set the bread aside. *She can have something for breakfast in the morning then,* I thought to myself, but she gave me a stern look.

"Do not be so stupid as to feed the rats, son. They're just as hungry as we are. Eat it before they do," she said firmly, and I stared at her hard. I felt like I was taking from her, when she insisted I eat again.

"Arthur..."

I sighed, giving in. "Yes, Momma."

I ate the small piece in two bites, and my stomach hurt something fierce as it hit my belly. Almost like it would have been better to skip entirely, but I knew I needed it. I had not eaten for the entire day as it was. I craved more, and I forced myself not to focus on my stomach. It was difficult, so I stared through the cracks of the shed door, hoping for something to distract me. I had seen the shadows fill the alley many times since we found this spot, and while we heard the screams of the victims it found, I had never actually seen the violence it brought. Tonight, it seemed different though. Normally, the night was unusually dark, but tonight it was fairly clear. You could actually see the stars in the sky, which was something that hasn't happened in years since the Nightlocke first appeared in this area.

No one knew who the monster was, but the trail it left behind was gruesome. I looked at the castle off in the distance. I always imagined what it was like living in a place like that. The King had two boys near my age, and I had seen them before when they went through the kingdom in their fancy carriage. It was hard not to envy them. Not a speck of dirt on them, and they were most definitely well fed. They each had shiny silver swords that hung from their belt, and I wish I had my old one again. My father taught me how to wield a sword before he passed, but I didn't get much practice before we lost everything, and I had to sell it. I wondered how different my life would be if my father were still alive? I missed him greatly, and I knew Momma did too.

My heart began to race as the castle started to darken until suddenly you could not see it anymore. *This had never happened before...*

"Son, what is wrong?" Momma asked, seeing my fear.

"I don't know. Shadows have covered the castle, Momma," I replied, but my eyes were glued to the sight before me. She gasped and began rocking back and forth in fear. For some reason, the Nightlocke was at the castle tonight. We could hear the screams of the King's men from here, and Momma and I dare not move. It felt like an eternity passed before the ground shook violently, and a horrifying scream pierced the air.

It sounded unholy and in complete *agony*. It screeched loudly throughout the land, and I covered my ears for fear my eardrum would blow from the sound. The black shadows bolted from the castle then and began to spread throughout the land. It was horrible on a normal night, but tonight something was very wrong, and the Kingdom was about to pay the price for the Nightlocke's wrath. I held my breath as the black shadows shot down the alley we were hiding in and forced their way inside the shed.

The black shadows hit me square in the chest, and I gasped. My heart stopped as I lost my vision and fear quickly spread throughout my body, knowing we were it's next victims. I couldn't see anything before me as the shadows completely engulfed the two of us. I prepared myself for the nightmares to come or the violent death they always gave, but as quickly as they came, they left us in peace. I was immediately at Momma's side, but she seemed alright as well.

I was baffled as to why it left us alive until I noticed a mark on my wrist. It looked like a black hood, much like what the assassins who frequently passed through the Kingdom would wear, and it was tattooed on my left wrist. I quickly hid it from Momma's view as I held her, trying to calm her racing heart. I didn't know what that mark meant, but I was determined to keep it a secret. I would be lynched if anyone found out. I had heard of men being marked by the Nightlocke, and I wondered if this is what they were talking about. Everything grew quiet and calm then, like nothing had even happened in the first place.

"We must never speak a word of this, Arthur," she whispered, and I gave her a slow nod. It was bad enough we were outcasts, but if anyone found out we had been spared by the shadows, they'd kill us. No one would believe we were not working with the Nightlocke, and they'd take us escaping as a sign that the shadows claimed us as one of their own. Especially if they saw this mark.

Anxiety grew inside, and I felt jittery over it all. Despite the start to our night, it stayed quiet and peaceful. I fully expected more, but nothing ever happened. I stayed awake, watching over Mama for as long as I could manage, but somehow I fell asleep.

The whole village was abuzz about the night before. I awoke to the loud chatter from the streets outside, and I slowly stretched my arms out. I slept in a horrible position, and my back ached something fierce. *It was time for a new spot,* I thought to myself as I stole a peek outside. My eyes widened when

I realized how late it was. *I slept in...* I've never made this mistake before, and I scurried to get the two of us out before the shop owner came out.

"Momma, we overslept! We need to move now," I said as I quickly shut the door. I turned to face my mother, when I realized she was still asleep.

"Momma?" I said as I gently shook her. Nothing. I checked her pulse, and her heart was still beating, but she wouldn't wake. The owner spoke just outside, talking to one of his employees now and panic crept in.

"Momma! Wake up!" I said in a hushed whisper. My heart twisted in fear when she still wouldn't wake, and I dug my hands in my hair as I tried to figure out what to do. The shop owner drew closer to the shed, and I shook her hard this time. No matter what I did, she wouldn't rise.

I hauled her up into my arms, my heart thundering in my chest. I carried her out of the shed, and the owner spotted me. He and his employee shouted angrily, throwing rocks at the two of us, and I did my best to shield my mother. He nailed me in the side of the head though as he shouted at me to never return or he'd kill me. I believed him, and I ran like mad getting Momma to safety.

"Momma, please wake up," I whispered gently, tapping her face once we were far enough away from the alley and that horrible man. My chest constricted. I couldn't catch my breath as I tried to figure out what to do. *This can't be happening!* I thought to myself. *I can't lose her!*

I didn't know what to do as she lay lifeless in my arms. She was breathing still, but it was labored and weak. I began shouting at anyone that passed by for help.

"PLEASE! My mother won't wake! Is there anyone that can help me?!"

I'd do anything for Momma, but no one would listen.

The streets quickly emptied as no one wanted to help, and I gritted my teeth in anger. *I hate this kingdom! I hated everyone in it as well.*

"It's no wonder the Nightlocke chose you people," I bellowed to nobody listening. "You all deserved his torment!"

I walked Momma to the castle, deciding to bravely ask for their assistance, but I froze when I saw the land. Their once lush, green land was brown and desolate, just like the rest of the land around here. Bodies lay everywhere, and what was left of the King's guard were attempting to clean them up. The fallen were bent in multiple directions, with their eyes and mouth wide open. I noticed some didn't even have eyes left, and my stomach threatened to revolt. I quickly turned away before they noticed me and made my way to the tavern instead.

It was late in the afternoon by now, and Momma still hadn't woken up. My arms were shaking, but I couldn't bring myself to set her down. I held her close as I stomped my way inside the tavern. *I'd risk the lashing I'd get for coming into a place like this, if I could get Momma help.* The second I stepped inside, the man behind the bar started yelling loudly, and everyone's eyes were upon us.

"Did you not learn your lesson before, boy! Get that corpse out of here!" he shouted as a violent anger filled my core. I have never felt this aggressive before, but I embraced it now.

"She isn't dead, but she needs help! Please!" I shouted back as some of the men in the room stood abruptly. I lost some of my confidence once they came for me though.

"We all know that woman is sick because she's a whore! Don't you dare bring her in here!" the man shouted back as the others faced me.

A burly man stood before me and took a glance at Momma in my arms. A split second of hope filled my heart before it shattered entirely when he struck me across the face. Momma and I dropped to the ground. I gritted my teeth together and scooped Momma back up. As I reached for her, the wrapping I had around my wrist dropped, and the men stumbled backwards.

"He's been marked!" one of them shouted as fear gripped my heart. *I was a dead man now.* I quickly covered my wrist again as everyone backed away from me. I scooped Momma up, bolting from the tavern before they could stop me. I could hear the owner shouting, "Catch him! We can't let him escape! Who knows what the shadows will turn him into!"

Heavy footsteps thundered after me as I fled the tavern. I cursed myself for foolishly turning to my fellow citizens for help, knowing full well they wouldn't show us any basic human decency. As I ran, I realized that I had nowhere to go. No family, no friends, no home. I had nothing, so I raced towards the only place I knew I would not be followed... The Forbidden Woods.

I shot through the dark thick foliage before I finally stopped to catch my breath. The angry villagers halted at the tree line, and I knew their superstitions would keep them there. My lungs burned in agony as I watched the men shout obscenities at me. These woods were filled with wild beasts and scary creatures. The trees were so thick that it didn't let any sunlight in. It was an invitation to the Nightlocke as well, but I was safer in here than I was out there. The men stayed at the treeline, watching to see if I would come back, and my shoulders slumped forward. *I could never return to the Kingdom now. Momma was going to die in my arms, and I was going to be alone until something found me in these woods. Some man I turned out to be.*

"Do you need help, child?" a deep voice said from behind, causing me to jump out of my skin. I didn't even hear him creep up on me, and I stared hard at the man before me. He was tall, with long dark hair and dark eyes. He wore a equally dark cloak, and I spotted a sword clipped to his waist. My eyes narrowed. *Did he live here? No one survived these woods, so how was he here?* I took a step backwards and watched his eyes drop to the movement. He gave me a vile smile, cocking his head to the side.

"What choice do you really have, child? You cannot return, and your mother remains comatose. How exactly do you plan to survive in the Forbidden Woods?"

The man's words struck me because I knew he was right. But I had heard of trickery much like this before, but I looked down at Momma and then at my wrist. If I didn't try something she would surely die, and I was a dead man anyways. The Nightlocke would find me at sundown, when he was finally allowed to emerge into our world again. I didn't want to, but he was right. *I had no other choice.*

I finally found my voice, "I need help."

He smiled again before gesturing to the woods behind him. I noticed black tattoos vaguely on his left arm, and my eyes narrowed. His left hand and wrist were wrapped due to an injury, but he shifted his cloak around himself again before I could see more.

"Come. I live not far from here, and I might be able to help her," he said as he started walking further into the dark. I hesitated before forcing my feet to move. I followed the strange man, despite the warning bells going off in my head. We soon came upon a small cottage, and he guided me inside. It was a small and rather plain looking cottage with loads of herbs hanging from the wall. It smelled rather funny here, but I had no idea which plant it was coming from, and I wasn't about to ask. In the center of the room was a large table with mortar and pestles filled to the brim with different concoctions I didn't want to know about. The man had loads of weapons all scattered about the room as well, making hairs on the back of my neck stand tall.

"Lay her down here."

The man gestured to the open table on the left side of the room, and I carefully laid Momma down where he said. I stood in front of her protectively as I watched him mix something together at the other table. It smelled vile, and I was regretting trusting a man I just met in the Forbidden Woods of all places. I felt stupid, and I stepped in front of him as he approached Momma with the mixture. He simply cocked his head to the side again, and we stared at one another in silence for a moment.

"This will help her sickness. It is her only chance," he said quietly, but I didn't move.

"What is it?" I asked him, trying not to let my voice shake. This whole place freaked me out, and my entire body screamed for me to run.

"Just different healing herbs," he answered, offering me the cup with his bandaged hand instead. It looked dark under the wrapping, and my brows furrowed as I took the bowl. He pulled his hand back, softening his gaze to the point he looked nearly *broken* for a moment before he blinked, and the emotion was gone. I held the bowl in my hand, looking inside before turning back to him again.

I didn't know what to do. *Was this the answer I was looking for? What if he really was just trying to help, and I let her die because I was too afraid? Maybe he was just an outcast like I was and maybe we could actually help one another?* I couldn't stop the overflow of questions filling my head, and I slowly turned to Momma, who's breath labored even more. She wasn't going to make it through the night, and I sighed, caving into my decision to try.

"Please work," I whispered as I lifted Momma's head. I poured the mixture into her mouth carefully. I set the cup down, watching whatever it was work through her system. I let out the breath I'd been holding when color returned to her skin, and her breathing leveled out. I nearly sobbed as her condition improved, and her eyes began to flutter.

Suddenly, Momma began convulsing horribly, and her skin turned to a pale grayish color. I watched in horror as her cheeks sunk in, and her skin shriveled up. Her bones stuck out like someone was sucking her life from her body, contorting and twisting in an unnatural way before her breathing finally stopped, and she laid there in a crumpled heap. My heart stopped as I stared at my dead mother before, knowing it was because of whatever I just gave her. A loud booming laugh sounded behind me.

"You stupid boy! You should know better than to trust a stranger from the Forbidden Woods. But thank you for the show though! I had been deprived of entertainment for quite some time," the man laughed again, and my jaw locked. I clenched my hands into tight fists as fury rushed through me.

All the anger I had buried resurfaced, and the mark on my wrist burned as the rage became overwhelming. I grabbed the large knife on the table, diving towards the man before I even registered what I was doing. Every awful thing I had heard about my mother over the years rattled through my brain. All the pain and suffering came bubbling forward. Everything that was *unfair, unkind, and awful* flooded my memory, and I screamed.

The knife plunged deep into his chest, and we both fell to the floor. His dark eyes went wide as he gasped for air, but I just wanted him to suffer for what he did to Momma. I was determined to make him pay for what he did, and I pushed the knife further, twisting it until his warm blood covered my hands. He suddenly smiled and fear gripped my heart as it registered in my head what I had done. I flew off his body and stared at my hands. His blood was black, and my body began to shake uncontrollably. *What had I done?!* My eyes widened even further as dark shadows slowly began to escape his body. I couldn't breathe when I recognized those shadows.

This was the Nightlocke.

"Finally. I am sorry they chose you, boy, but I cannot live with what I've done to my Julianna. The burden is now yours," he muttered softly before taking his last breath.

The black shadows slammed painfully into me, filling me to my core. A tremendous power flooded my system as his memories flashed before me. It took me straight to the night the castle was attacked. I watched the Nightlocke cut down knight after knight, searching for something. His memories rushed through me, and I caught a glimpse of a beautiful woman with long blond hair and shackles on her feet, dead in the throne room. I felt his agony and horror seeing her lifeless body.

A thick black substance surrounded the wound on her stomach, and I realized the Nightlocke killed her. I could feel his rage towards the King and Queen, who stood off to the side fearfully. *He accidentally killed this girl, the one he loved, in the process of trying to kill the King. He was too unstable and struck her instead.* He reached for her, touching her skin only to get burned. He hissed as the pain engulfed my own hand, and I screamed in agony. The Nightlocke shook with rage, and I felt the darkness consume him entirely. He screamed as he emitted a burst of darkness into the room striking the Queen. The Nightlocke wanted revenge for what was taken from him, and he made sure to return the favor.

I felt his overwhelming guilt, and the madness that came with the shadows after that. The pain was too much for him to bear. It was his screams that filled the night, and he sent his shadows out, searching for another capable of holding the dark. His shadows marked me, and he plotted right then to provoke me into killing him using the only thing I had left... My mother. His memories continued to flood my system until I saw his earliest memory of the shadows choosing him.

I stumbled as the last of the shadows hit me at full force, and his memories became nothing more than a foggy dream. I stood in his cottage entirely alone. The power within seemed to love my anger, and I clenched my fists together, embracing the darkness.

He killed Momma because he wanted to die. He was after *me*, and Momma was nothing more than collateral damage. *This is all my fault,* I realized, feeling the tremendously heavy guilt hit me in full force.

The guilt built in my system, and I raised my hand as the shadows seemed to answer my every desire now. They burst forward, destroying every bit of the Nightlocke's home around me. I let my anger pour out, screaming as *everything* broke apart.

I was numb by the time I stood in the rain that coated the entire woods. The home was leveled, nothing more than a pile of broken wood around me, and I forced myself to take a deep breath. Slowly, I turned to Momma. My heart broke seeing her corpse lying on the table still, and I dropped to my knees, screaming out in pain this time. I sobbed then. *I had failed her. No, more than that... I killed her.*

A screeching wail came from deep within the woods, and I knew I couldn't stay here for much longer. I was alone, but not for long, and I didn't want to stick around to meet anyone or anything else. I looked back at Momma once more, and slowly got to my feet. *I couldn't just leave her here.*

I carefully picked her up, trying to figure out where to take her that would be safe from the creatures that plagued these woods. I felt renewed and strong because of the darkness inside me. I was no longer malnourished or weak, and that dark power inside me that pulsed through my veins. So strongly that I no longer felt scared about what lived in these woods.

Somehow, the shadows inside knew exactly where to go, and they tugged me forward. I took a step forward, then another, and vowed right then that I would come back. I would bring brutal retribution and suffering upon *all* who refused to show us mercy or kindness. I was going to kill and torment all those who put me and Momma in this situation. Everyone who was cruel was about to pay a tremendous price. As well as the King, who brought the wrath of the Nightlocke upon us in the first place. The corners of my mouth rose as the darkness sang within me. I was eager to exact my revenge on the Kingdom of Odemark.

They had no idea what was coming for them.

Chapter 1

"Run children! Run into the pantry, and do not come out! Do you hear me?!"

A tall servant girl shouted at me and my sister. Someone was attacking the castle where we lived. We were all frightened, and I couldn't find my father. All we had with us was this servant girl, who wasn't much older than we were.

"What's happening?" Amarna asked. I clung to my sister's hand as loud wails pierced the halls. There were screams everywhere, and the candles flickered. I was terrified they'd go out, and we'd be left in the dark completely.

The girl glanced behind her before pushing us again. "It's the Nightlocke! You must run now! Don't stop!"

Amarna took off running where we were told, and I struggled to keep up with her.

"Wait! What about Thomas? And Liam? We must help them!" I shouted as she dragged me into the pantry. She forced me inside, shutting the door behind us. My sister struggled but managed to topple a large crate in front of the door before shoving cloth into the gap beneath it.

"There is no time for them! We cannot..."

Suddenly, screams filled the air, and we heard loud clashing. It sounded so close now, and I clung to my sister terrified. I was afraid for my father and my closest friends, the princes.

I prayed they were okay.

There was a loud sound, followed by the loudest screeching wail we had ever heard. It didn't sound human, and we covered our ears as it was deafening. The whole place shook violently.

I screamed for my dad.

What was happening?!

I stirred awake as the bright sun filled my room. I slowly rose in my bed, catching my breath. It had been a long time since I had that nightmare, but the memory was still so fresh. It felt like it was yesterday, even though it was nearly seven years ago.

Today was another day and a chance to help my family. I lived in the Kingdom of Odemark with my father and sister, and honestly, we were very fortunate compared to most. My father was a fantastic healer and had moved our family here when I was but a babe at the request of the King. I grew up in the castle, becoming fast friends with the Princes, while my father worked solely for the King.

As a child, we lived on the palace grounds, but when the castle was attacked by the Nightlocke, everyone was forced to leave. After losing his wife in the attack, the King had stopped trusting anyone for quite some time, but who could blame him? I couldn't imagine losing someone so close to me in such a violent way.

We went from a fine house on the castle grounds to a small apartment behind one the stores in the kingdom. Although, we were on the verge of losing it. I very rarely saw my best friend, the youngest Prince as my father wasn't called to work as much after that. My father was having a difficult time finding work period as he could not grow the herbs he needed to assist *anyone*. He was becoming useless, and I could see the struggle and worry on his face. Something deep within me needed to fix that, and I had finally found a way to do it. Now that I was 17, I could volunteer myself for service to the King full-time, and by doing this, I could provide monthly rations to my father and sister.

I couldn't explain it, but I *needed* to do this. I've always had a strong desire to help those in need and was drawn to the land. I wanted nothing more than to help cultivate it again because then I could help everyone, but I was not a Lightspark. So I did what I could. My chest always burned when I saw someone in need, and if I did not assist then the pain would grow worse. I learned to listen to it early on.

I was okay with my choice to serve the King though. My family would have enough food to survive, and the extra money they'd have would allow them to keep the house. The pain would stop then, and secretly I missed my friend a lot. Working at the castle would mean I could see him again. The last time I had seen him was months ago. Even at a distance, I could see he had grown into a fine young man. The thought of seeing him again made my heart skitter in my chest.

Thomas Einer was incredibly handsome with blonde hair and piercing blue eyes. He always wore this mischievous smile that made me weak in the knees, but it was foolish to entertain these thoughts. While the Prince was allowed to marry whomever he wanted, regardless of class or station, Thomas would never choose me. I was becoming poorer by the day, and I was not as extravagant as the young women that would come to visit with the royal family. Still, it was hard not to fantasize about it. At least for now, I could work for however long I wanted and could always opt out of the program if I chose to.

I forced myself to leave the bed and quickly grabbed new clothes before giving myself a quick sponge bath. My long dark brown hair curled on its own, coming midway down my back. Most needed expensive products and equipment to get what I had, but I didn't have to lift a finger. My sister Amarna said I was lucky, but I always shrugged her off.

My vivid green eyes were just like my mother's as my father repeatedly told me. She died when I was little, but I honestly don't remember her very much. My sister got most of her looks and was drop dead gorgeous compared to me, but only I got her eyes. That was something that always made me smile.

My sister had plenty of suitors poking around, and since she was of age to marry, my father would entertain each one and hear their offers for her hand. No one really paid me any mind, but I really didn't want any of them either. My small frame made it difficult to be seen sometimes, and that was the biggest part that weighed heavily on me. I didn't like being invisible, but most of the men who came around only saw her. I was very short unlike my sister, who stood nearly a half a foot taller than I did. It was hard not to be envious of her as she turned heads wherever she went. I knew Amarna would find a great match for her someday, while I'd be lucky to even get an offer.

I ignored those depressing thought and dressed quickly in my pale blue dress. Once I was ready for the day, I took off the shutters on the windows, letting in the much needed light. Light to keep the darkness away. The Nightlocke still plagued this land, but ever since the attack on the castle, the monster had changed. It doesn't always kill its victims like it used to but those left alive are never the same. They have lost their minds, forever plagued by whatever happened to them in the night. It saddens me because there's nothing I could do to help them. They'd become lost souls. Minds permanently warped by the horrors the Nightlocke brought upon them. I wish I could bring them peace.

The ones the Nightlocke does kill all end up the same. They'd end up nothing but skin and bones like someone had sucked them dry. It was gruesome to see, and those were just the ones we found. A great many just disappeared, never to be seen again. No one has ever seen the monster since that fateful night, and I had no desire to ever meet him.

Amarna slept in and never once stirred as I left our home. I already knew what my father would say if he knew what I was doing, but I needed to do this on my own, and they'd only try to stop me. I made my way to the castle, passing the bustling dirt roads filled with horses and carriages. The kingdom was still hanging on despite the horrors it saw, and it was their drive that pushed me to continue with my plan. If these people could continue to survive like this, then I could give away my freedom for my family temporarily.

I approached the guard's men, who stared at me through the slits in their helmets, giving them a kind smile.

"I'd like to apply for the food program, please," I said confidently.

The one on the left gave me a nod before opening the side gate. I stepped through to find a very cross looking man standing over a stack of papers. He motioned me forward before sitting at his desk. This overweight man with thinning gray hair wore a long robe that was tied in the center and smelled strong of tobacco.

"Are you here for the food exchange?" his high pitched voice asked, and I nodded my head. I put my hands behind my back, slightly nervous now that I was here.

He grunted. "Sign here, and then put the name of whom you wished to receive the rations. Times have changed though, and most of the food is brought in from other kingdoms because of the shortage. The King is working on an alliance with a far off kingdom, but until it is finalized the rations will be halved for your service. Do you understand?"

I nodded again as I finished writing my father's name. *Food was food.* As long as they could stay alive, I was happy to work here. I handed back the paperwork, and he abruptly stood from his seat. The cross man circled me, studying me closely, as if getting an idea of what use I could be for him.

"We do not have a Lady anymore, so for now you shall be in the kitchen. You have to the end of the day to sort out your affairs before you are to report here at dusk to begin your duties. You will live here at the castle and shall remain working until the King gives you permission to leave."

My eyes widened at that. *That wasn't how it was before.* My anxiety rose, and he noticed the alarm on my face.

"Like I said child, things have changed, and the King now owns you. You may request your freedom, but you will remain a servant unless he allows you to be free."

I gulped, not realizing I signed my entire freedom away just now. The deep burning feeling surged forward in my chest, insisting I follow through with this plan, and it has never been wrong before. *I am helping save my family by doing this, so this cannot be a bad thing. Right?*

"You will be allowed four hours of freedom each week to visit family, but it is *your* responsibility to report back on time. Failure to do so means you will not be allowed out the following week, and continual tardiness could result in your arrest. You will get your uniform when you return, and you may pick up a rations bag on your way out. We find it usually softens the blow when you tell your family. Now go, and I will see you at dusk."

He sent me on my way after that, and one of the knights tossed me a medium sized bag as I made my way back through the gates. They slammed the metal gates closed after I stepped out, and the weight of what I had done rested on my shoulders.

The scent of food filled my nose then, and I took a small peek inside. My mouth watered at the sight. *Apples, cheese, and fresh bread! I haven't had real bread in such a long time!* I was ready to devour it whole, but I refused to take even a crumb before showing my father. I shook the bag carefully to see what was underneath, and it looked like something was wrapped up at the bottom. *It must be meat of some sort,* I thought. *But there were some carrots and other vegetables as well.* I knew I'd be able to make a decent stew for them before reporting for duty.

I quickly closed the bag, hiding it close on my person and ran like mad back home. I didn't want to give *anyone* a chance to rob me before I could give it to my family. That or just asked for help, and I'd be forced to give them some. I wasn't trying to be selfish, but I needed to feed my family too. If I helped everyone that needed it, even just a little, I'd have nothing left to give my family by the time I'd get home. I bolted into my house, shutting the door behind me quickly, startling my father and sister.

"What in God's name is the matter with you?!" my father asked. I turned to face him and cringed as I saw him adjust the belt on his pants. He was slowly withering away and losing too much weight to be considered healthy. His once dark hair was graying too, but it was hard to feed a family when your job is obsolete.

My sister's nose scrunched up something fierce before she eyed the bag. "Is that food?"

I carefully set the bag on the table and started unloading it. Their eyes widened, and I could see the hunger in them.

"Where did you get this child?" my father asked, reaching for the apple. He seemed almost shocked that it was real before setting it back on the table. My father was a great man, and I knew he would not eat before us. I handed him back the apple, and then gave one to my sister before making my way to our counter. I unwrapped the meat and a slab of roasted beef fell from the package. I carefully shredded it before tossing it into our large pot.

"Kymra, where did you get all this?" my father asked again. His voice sounding stern this time.

"I started a rations deal with the royal house," I said quietly, before reaching for the carrots. My father's eyes went wide.

CHAPTER 1

"You did what?!"

"Kymra..." my sister said, covering her mouth as her voice trailed off.

"Father, it's okay. I wanted to help..."

"Kymra, it's slavery! You just sold yourself to the King!" he shouted angrily, and I winced.

"I'm allowed to visit once a week, and I'm confident the King will free me of our deal when the time comes. Thomas and Liam are there at the castle too so I will not be alone, but we needed it, father."

My dad grunted and opened his mouth to protest but snapped it shut instead. He rubbed his face in frustration, and I continued to chop the vegetables. I needed to do something as my anxiety was building under his intense gaze. I added water to the pot and what little dried herbs we still had left before setting it over the fire.

"Kymra, time's have changed. The King is not the same man we once knew. Not since..." Dad's voice trailed off, and I vividly remembered the attack he was referring too. I pushed those thoughts away, turning back to my family.

"Father, you and I both know Amarna will receive a wonderful offer of marriage, but I more than likely will not. I'm not as pretty as she is nor am I as graceful but this... This is something I can do to help us. Please, don't be angry with me," I replied, dropping my head as shame coated my face.

I tried not to admit to others how I felt about myself, and I refused to tell him anything about that strong desire to help everyone I talked to. I couldn't explain it even if I tried, but something compelled me to always put others first. To assist those in need, and I wouldn't make a good match even if I wanted to. The only way to survive in Odemark was to be selfish, and I just couldn't do that. I wouldn't harm anyone because... *I couldn't.* There were always mouths to feed and always someone in need. My future match would not approve of all this charity work that I couldn't help but do.

My father walked over to me, wrapping his large arms around my small frame and held me close. Soon, my sister joined in.

"Kymra, you are as beautiful as your mother. If she were here, she would tell you the same thing. You *will* find a good match. You will find someone that is perfect for you, and who will love you the way you deserve. I am very proud of your sacrifice, but you must promise me one thing. If the King offers you your freedom, you take it without question. We will survive," he said firmly. "We *always* do."

I obeyed because he asked. It's what he needed, and I would always do what I could to help. "You must pick up the rations each week," I replied. "Promise me, you will!"

He kissed my forehead before accepting what had happened. I wiped my eyes and ushered them to the table. I sliced the cheese and bread, giving them each plenty to enjoy, while the stew cooked. My father grabbed my wrist though, forcing me to sit.

"This is for you as well, Kymra," he said before grabbing me an apple. He put it in my hand, giving me a small smile, and then waited for my sister and I to start. I took a bite, and my God it was the best thing I had eaten in awhile! It was juicy and sweet, and I quickly devoured it. I set the seeds aside in attempts to grow anything around here before my father handed me cheese and bread. We sat quietly together, enjoying our wonderful meal, knowing it would be our last one together for some time. I took a peek outside, noticing we had used up most of the time I had left. I stirred the pot to check on their dinner before I turned back to them.

"I must go now," I said quietly, and my father hugged me again.

"You stay safe Kymra, and remember our deal."

I nodded and then hugged my sister.

"This stew will feed you for a few days. Don't burn it, Amarna," I teased, pulling a smile from my big sister. She hugged me once more before I made my way to the door. I know I am doing the right thing, but each step felt like lead. This was harder than I thought it would be, and I turned back one last time.

"I love you," I whispered, and I was out the door before they could respond. I couldn't handle hearing their responses right now as I felt hot tears fill my eyes. I quickly made my feet move further and further away from the small house in the backside of the village. It was nearly dusk now, and I quickly wiped away my tears not wanting to show how hard this was for me. I needed to get a move on though because I did not want to be around when the darkness hit. It didn't take long to reach the gates, and the knights let me in the side.

The cross man was there just like he said he'd be. He grabbed two uniforms from the shelves and handed them to me. I stood there, while he gathered everything I needed before motioning me through the door and across the castle grounds. *The castle was different from what I remembered.* It was darker, more *ominous*, than it ever used to be.

"Hurry, child. It is nearly dark, and we all know what lives in the dark," he said nervously, and I quickened my pace. He led me through a servants entrance, and I couldn't help but search for Thomas. My heart began to race slightly, hoping to see my old friend again, but to my dismay, we saw no one. The cross man led me to a small chamber down a dark corridor and gestured me inside.

"Here is your room for your stay. Report to the kitchen before sunrise to begin your duties. The Head Chef will be in charge of you, so report to her if you need anything. I don't need to remind you to stay out of rooms unless given direction and only speak when spoken too. Goodnight, Miss."

He left me standing in the dark room, and I quickly lit the torch on the wall. Anything to shut out the dark. It illuminated the small room, and I set my things down. *Well this is it. Welcome home.*

I undressed and hung my blue dress on the back of the door before climbing into bed. It was almost too quiet as I lay in bed, watching the fire flicker against the wall. It was a little unsettling, but I somehow managed to drift off to sleep.

Chapter 2

I woke in a frenzy and sticky from sweat. My hair stuck to my face, and my breathing was difficult and labored. *I had a nightmare last night. I must have,* I thought as I rose from bed. My body felt exhausted like I got no sleep at all, but I couldn't remember a thing about the dream. *Whatever happened must have been horrible though if I woke up like this though.*

I ran my hand through my hair, getting my composure when I noticed light peeking through the slots of the shutters. My eyes widened as I flew out of bed, scrambling to get my uniform on. I pulled my sweaty hair back into a braid, unable to do anything about the filth of it now, and raced out the door, trying to remember where the kitchen was located. *I was so late today.* I knew I'd get a lashing if I didn't pick up my pace. A loud commotion led me right to a bustling kitchen in full swing. I walked over to the loud woman barking orders at everyone, assuming she was the head chef.

"Ma'am? I'm...."

"There you are! Paul said I was getting a new worker, but you missed the morning orders," she bellowed loudly. "Nothing to do about it now. Start peeling the potatoes with Sarah and keep busy! Paul tends to check in often and hates idle hands."

She stomped her large frame across the room, and I realized the woman only had one volume. Loud. Just loud.

I turned to find Sarah and looked around the room. There were over a dozen women here, working to prepare the morning meal. No one paid me any mind as I found a tall woman in the back with a large sack of potatoes. I made my way to her.

CHAPTER 2

"Hi, I'm Kymra. The Head Chef told me to assist you," I said as I took the empty seat next to her. I was suddenly nervous with all the commotion going on around us, but the pretty blonde haired girl gave me a soft smile. Like she already knew what was going through my mind.

"Marge is loud but harmless. No one calls her Head Chef here either. It's just Marge. Here's a knife. We're just peeling and dicing this morning, but careful not to cut yourself. Can't have blood in the potatoes, now can we?"

I returned the girl's smile and took the knife from her. We worked away, trying to get through the bag as quickly as we could. *It was a ton of food being prepared for just the royal family,* I thought to myself. *But maybe some of it is going elsewhere?*

"How long have you been here, Sarah?" I asked, picking up another potato.

"About a year now. My family needed help, and I had yet to receive any offers so I ended up here."

I looked at her confused slightly. *She looked to be my age, but I guess I was wrong.* You were not allowed to accept any offers until you turn 18, but she didn't look old enough for that. She smirked at me, guessing my internal thought process.

"I'm 19. I'm just stuck with this baby face, so everyone assumes I'm only 15 or so. It's fine though. The idea of marrying a stranger isn't exactly what I was hoping for. I'm happy for a warm bed, food in my belly, and help for my family. They're proud of me, so I'm content."

I nodded, knowing full well how she felt. "I'm not expecting any offers either. My older sister Amarna just turned 18, so I'm sure my father shall receive a fantastic offer for her hand. I wanted to help since he hasn't been able to work like he used to."

"What does your dad do?" Sarah asked.

"He was the royal physician here at the castle before the great attack, but ever since that dreadful night, he hasn't worked here. There are less and less medicinal herbs to use as well so people have stopped coming to him for help."

"Wow, so you lived here at the castle then?" she asked excitedly. "What was it like? Did you see the Princes?"

I laughed. "Prince Thomas and I were good friends actually. I'm hoping to see him while I work here."

"Oh, he's so dreamy! I nearly swoon every time I see him walking in the gardens or at the royal balls. All the girls love him!"

I straightened. I assumed he would wed at some point, but I guess I didn't expect it so soon. I bit my inner cheek as disappointment rippled through me.

"Is he engaged yet?" I asked coyly, and she shook her head.

"No, and neither is Liam. The King hasn't announced anything along those lines yet, but he's been in intense negotiations with the neighboring Kingdom of Oceanus, so it would not surprise me if Liam is engaged very soon with their Princess," Sarah said before setting her knife aside.

"Girls! Good, you're done. Sarah finish up the potatoes and you... What's your name?" Marge asked, snapping her fingers at me.

"Kymra, ma'am."

"Right, right. Kymra go and set the table before the royal family descends the stairs. Stand with the other help once you are finished. We are to wait on them until every member leaves."

Sarah gave me a small smile whispering, "Say hi to Thomas for me!"

I stuck my tongue out at her before rushing out the door with the rest of the crew. I carried a basket of fresh bread, and it was all I could do not to steal a bite. I had skipped breakfast with the morning announcements.

We made our way into the grand dining hall, quickly setting out the food that was ready, along with the fanciest tableware I had ever seen. Memories of my days here were coming back to me, and while we never ate at *this* table, I vividly remember playing Hide-N-Seek with Thomas and Liam here. Once finished, I joined the rest of the crew off to the side, anxiously waiting to finally see Thomas.

The King made his presence first, and he was decked out in all his typical fancy clothes. He had aged greatly since the last I remembered him and wore white and blue with his sleek sword hanging from his hip. Liam was next to appear, looking handsome as ever. He at least acknowledged the staff, unlike his father, but he did not recognize me. I was a little hurt as he walked on by, but I guess I couldn't blame him. We were very young the last time we saw each other.

I studied Liam carefully. A couple years older, he looked a lot like his father, with his brown hair and bluish-green eyes. He had a kind smile and a confident walk about him. *Liam was going to be a fine match to whatever Princess he was paired with.*

I was anxious to meet my oldest friend though, and I stared at the stairs, waiting for him to appear. My stomach was in knots, and I shifted on my feet. *Would he recognize me?* I wondered. My thoughts ran amuck with endless questions. I couldn't decided which was worse though. Having Thomas not recognize me at all or having him recognize me and not care that I was here?

Thomas finally made his way into the room, and my heart nearly skipped a beat. He was gorgeous, with his sandy blonde hair and brown eyes. His massive shoulders and well defined arms stole my attention. *God, I could see every defined muscle through his shirt from here,* I thought as my heart began to race inside my chest. Thomas stood just a fuzz shorter than his older brother, and I couldn't help but smile wide when he passed by. My eyes lit up, but my face quickly fell when he gave me no more than a passing glance. Thomas sat next to Liam at the table without a word.

He didn't recognize me.

My heart sunk. I was invisible to him, and that freaking hurt. *Was our friendship entirely in the past to him?* All these years, I had *never* forgotten him or Liam, but they didn't even look my way as they conversed with their father. I tried to quickly pushed the feeling aside, focusing on the job at hand, but it took everything to keep my lip from quivering. Ultimately, I was a servant and nothing more, but my heart broke no matter what I tried to tell myself though. I was hoping to reconnect with my friend, but I guess it was just different times now, and that part of my life had passed. I scolded myself for even thinking I was someone worth remembering in the first place. *We weren't children anymore, and I was not royalty.*

The King motioned for us to start, and I realized he expected us to make their plates. I carefully followed the other girl's lead, more afraid I'd do something wrong and offend the King, but no one explained exactly what I should do here. And I hated the not knowing.

Another small girl and I quickly moved, filling the plates of the King and Princes, when Marge came out with the rest of the cooked food. Their plates were mounded by the time we added a little of each item to their plate. I had never seen so much food prepared for only three people before, but I kept my face neutral as I moved around the other side of the table. I set Thomas's plate down in front of him. When our eyes met briefly, my heart couldn't help but flutter again.

"You girl... Where have I seen you before?" Thomas asked as his brows furrowed.

My stomach rolled as I replied, "I am Kymra Fields. Daughter of Uriah Fields, the previous physician to our King. We played as children, Prince."

The King snapped his attention to me. His harsh stare had me wondering if I shouldn't have said anything, but Thomas smacked the table as a grin appeared on his lips.

"Yes! Kymra! We were the best of friends growing up!" Thomas said excitedly. His eyes narrowed then. "You work here now?"

"I recently joined the rations program, your Highness," I responded, and his eyes softened. I couldn't stop my heart from racing inside my chest as he looked to me with such kindness and understanding.

"Please, none of that, Kymra. I'm just Thomas to you," he said softly.

"You are Uriah's youngest?" the King asked, and I gave him a small nod. He motioned to the chair next to Thomas then. "Please, sit and dine with us. For old times sake."

My eyes widened by his request, and Thomas promptly stood and pulled out the chair for me, motioning for the other staff to make me a plate. I felt a little uncomfortable since technically I was supposed to be working, but how could I refuse the King and the royal Prince? I sat down slowly, feeling all eyes upon me now.

"How is your father, child? I take it not too well since you joined the ration program," the King commented, and I tried not to take what he said personally. Marge set a plate down before me, and I tried not to look her in the eye when she stepped away.

"We've been doing alright, my Lord. My father doesn't have as many clients as before since medicinal herbs are difficult to grow around here."

I took a bite of the potatoes and eggs and nearly groaned out loud. *Everything was delicious,* I thought as I shoveled more food into my mouth. Thomas smirked, winking at me when I caught him watching me. I froze before arching my shoulders back and slowing my pace. *I didn't want to look like I haven't eaten in a long time.*

"Ah, yes. Well, once the Lightspark was killed along with my wife, the land has been a wasteland ever since," the King muttered angrily. Both Liam and Thomas looked angry as their father spoke, and my heart went out to them. *I remembered their mother. I hated they lost her.*

"We had always heard rumors of a Lightspark here at the castle, but honestly a part of me wasn't sure if they were a myth, your Highness," I said, taking another bite. I hoped moving the conversation away from their mother would help.

"They are extremely rare, but what our land *needs* to survive. The Nightlocke casts such a vile darkness onto the land, and it kills most things we try to grow. Now, we're forced to outsource our food with deals and treaties. All rather annoying, if you ask me," the King went on, and I gave him a nod of understanding. Even though I didn't really get it.

"I can't begin to image how frustrating it would be, sir. Does anyone know how to even find the Nightlocke?" I asked as I moved on to the fresh cut strawberries and cream. "It would make sense to stop what plagues our land."

Thomas raised one eyebrow at me, and I wondered if I pushed it too far. *Or maybe I had whipped cream on my face?* I thought as I carefully wiped my mouth. All eyes were on me now, and my heart began to race again.

"I meant no disrespect to your Highness," I stammered. "I'm sure you are working very hard at locating him."

"We are actively trying, let me tell you, but no one has ever seen that monster since the night my wife died. We know a few ways to deal with the Nightlocke, but he has never gotten close enough to try, and no one knows where he's hiding," the King answered.

"Isn't he immortal?" I asked, remembering the stories my father told me.

"It is, child. Do you not remember the nursery rhyme? I remember your mother singing it to you and my sons when you were nothing but babes," he said, and I nodded. I had forgotten that song actually.

"I vaguely do, your Highness. I didn't realize there was any truth to it though," I replied, finishing my plate.

Thomas grinned over at me, and my heart skipped another beat. *God, he was adorable. The dimples on his cheeks were quickly becoming my undoing.* I could feel my cheeks already heating under his gaze, and I looked back to the King, trying not to embarrass myself further.

"There is plenty of truth to our old stories, child. It would be wise to learn them all. The more you know, the safer you will be," the King said before standing.

"You are right, sir. Thank you," I said as the rest of us stood.

"Don't keep her too long, sons. She has work to do as do the *both* of you," he said sternly before turning to me. "It was lovely to see you again, Kymra."

Then the King left, leaving me with the Princes. Liam turned, giving me one of his famous smiles. I had forgotten how stunning he looked too. He was just as handsome as Thomas, and honestly they looked very similar to one another now that they were standing together. Liam was just taller of the two.

"It is great to see you again, Kymra," he said as he opened his arms. I smiled wide as he tucked me into his embrace, hugging me fondly. *They did remember me...*

"And you, Liam. It's been too long," I replied, giving the brothers a warm smile.

"I wish we could catch up further, but I have a mountain of paper work ahead of me as do you, Thomas," Liam said, giving his brother a firm look. Thomas just rolled his eyes.

"My work doesn't matter, Liam. I'm not going to be King anyways so nothing I do matters," he replied coldly, and I noticed some tension between the two. I stayed silent, letting them work it out between themselves, and Liam finally sighed before turning to me.

CHAPTER 2

"Please give your family my regards," Liam said as he took my hand and kissed the top. My cheeks reddened again, and I watched the older brother walk out of the room after his father.

"So what mischief shall we get into today, Kymra?" Thomas said, giving me a wink. My knees nearly buckled when he did, and I could not contain the smile that crept up my face.

"Thomas, this is my first day. I cannot skip my work nor should you," I said.

He smiled mischievously back at me, and suddenly I knew I was in trouble. My heart was running away with itself, and there was nothing I could do to stop it.

"Nonsense! I insist you take a walk with me this morning," Thomas said, nudging me. "Will that be alright with you, Margery?"

I turned to find my boss looking upon me somewhat foul. My stomach twisted in knots as she glared, but she smiled to her Prince saying, "That is most fine with me, sir. We shall make do without her."

Thomas smiled, but I knew the point she was making. *I was slacking on my responsibilities, and I did not know what that would mean for my family's rations.*

"Perfect! I'll bring her back by noon, I promise!"

He grabbed my arm, pulling me out of the room before I could protest any further. I scrambled to keep up with his long legs, and soon we were laughing like we did as children, running through the halls away from the Headmistress. We made our way to the outside gardens before he finally slowed his steps. I looked around, remembering so much from when I was a kid. There were not any real plants out here anymore though, and my smile fell. The King had fake plants put in long ago to help with appearances, but it just wasn't the same as the real thing.

"I miss the old gardens Kymra, don't you?" Thomas said, pulling me from my thoughts.

"I do, sir. We used to spend all day out in these gardens, hiding from the Headmistress or our parents," I replied with a giggle.

Thomas laughed, and I realized how much I had missed hearing it. We walked through the archway of ivy before turning to the right. My hand gently floated across the row of tulips, wishing they were the real thing.

"I remember, and please Kymra, no sir or your Highness. We were great friends all those years ago, and I grow tired of all the formalities. Let me just be Thomas, please," he said, nudging me gently. The blush crept up my cheeks again, and I quickly turned away, hoping he didn't see the affect he had on me.

"If that is what you wish, but I must insist on calling you by your title in front of my boss," I insisted. "She seems rather cross with me as it is."

Thomas shrugged. "I'm not afraid of her."

I laughed again. "That is because *you* are her boss. She, however, is very much *my* boss and will tan my hide if I don't follow the rules, Thomas."

He smiled, but it soon fell. Thomas had a sad look in his eyes when he looked at me. I wasn't sure what I said that upset him, and I stayed quiet while he was lost in thought. When he turned to face the gardens again, he finally spoke. "I don't like you on the ration program, Kymra."

Ah, I thought to myself. *That's sweet of him though.* "I know, Thomas," I said softly, "but it is what it is. If I can help my family then I want to."

"It's all the Nightlocke's fault. I wish I could kill the beast myself! Father promised massive rewards to anyone that can kill him, and I can think of a few things I'd want for slaying the beast."

His gaze shifted to me, and I couldn't stop my cheeks from turning red again. *God, I cannot stop blushing around him...*

"How do you know it is a him?" I asked with a sly grin. "What if the Nightlocke is female?"

He gave me a pointed look.

"Because I was in the room with him the day he attacked the castle. He is a tall man with dark features and eyes as black as the night. The left side of his body wore black ink that ran into the side of his neck and head, and he had this dark, heavy cloak, with a large hood on it. I was scared out of my mind when he moved effortlessly through the room, slaying whomever crossed paths with him. Liam and I hid after that, but I still remember the screams."

I dropped my head, remembering my own experience when the Nightlocke attacked. "I was with my sister stuffed inside the pantry. I vividly remember every sound that was made as he cut down the guards in the hall outside the room."

"It was an awful time. I never understood why he attacked the palace in the first place though. He plagued the land for years but never really attacked the castle before. I guess it doesn't matter why, but those who live in the castle have been tormented by the Nightlocke ever since."

My eyes widened. "Tormented how?"

His face fell. "Dad doesn't like us to talk about it, but he plagues our minds most nights. He is a master of nightmares, Kymra, and he uses your worst fears against you. It's like he enjoys watching you become so traumatized with fear that you can't move or breathe. The castle doesn't have a defense against his mind games, so we all just try to deal with it."

I remember how I woke up this morning, feeling sweaty and awful, but I could not remember my nightmare. *Did the Nightlocke plague my mind too?* I wondered. While those in the kingdom were able to sleep in peace at night, we were affected in other ways. *I wondered if the King knew what was happened to his people?*

"Do you remember once you wake up?" I asked Thomas, and he slowly shook his head yes.

"Every single one. When I get my hands on him, I swear..."

"Prince Thomas!"

We turned to see a servant running towards us. He seemed sweaty and exhausted, and I could hear Thomas curse under his breath.

"You are being summoned by your father. The Princess of Oceanus is arriving sooner than expected, so there shall be a ball in her honor tomorrow night. You must come!"

Thomas groaned, putting his hands on his hips. "I'm sure no one needs me, Garrett. I'm not to be King, remember?"

"I must insist, sir," Garrett stammered on, and Thomas turned to me.

"Forgive me, Kymra. I shall see you around, alright?"

My shoulders fell, but I nodded graciously. I didn't want to show my disappointment that Thomas was leaving. He bowed to me before following the servant back inside. There was no reason to stay in the gardens, so I made my way back to the kitchen to find my next job. Maybe it would be enough to get Marge to forgive my absence. *Maybe I could just sneak in and pretend I had returned awhile ago?* But that plan went out the window for the moment I stepped inside, I was flocked by all the young girls working at the castle.

"Girl, spill! Tell us what happened with the Prince?!" Sarah demanded as the others squealed excitedly.

I laughed. "Nothing happened, Sarah. We just caught up a bit is all. Actually, we talked about the Nightlocke more than anything. Thomas told me about his nightmares. Do you all have them too?"

Their cheerful demeanor fell as they looked to their feet, and Sarah rubbed her arm. "We are not allowed to talk about them, Kymra. You would be wise not to ask anymore questions. It never goes well, trust me."

I frowned at her answer, but before I could question her further, Marge came into the room.

"Ah, your back. Didn't expect to see you for the rest of the day."

"He only wanted a walk, Marge. I apologize for the work I missed," I said confidently, but she just shook her head at me.

"That boy takes more *walks* than anyone I have ever met. See a doctor when you are done, if you are smart. Now get to cleaning the mess in here!"

My face fell as Marge shouted orders throughout the room. Sarah nudged me then.

"Thomas has never been short of ladies, Kymra. He's shameless, let me tell you. Feel lucky you caught his attention today!"

She turned, making her way further into the kitchen. My heart felt heavy as their words rattled my mind. It shouldn't surprise me since he is the Prince, but I still hated knowing that was his reputation. *But we were different, weren't we?* I thought as I moved to the pile of dirty dishes. *We've been friends for ages, and I wasn't just another conquest for him... Right?*

I spent the rest of the day scrubbing the pots and pans out and cleaning the kitchen. I ended up getting the majority share, due to my walk with Thomas, and that left me sore and tired by the end of the night. Marge had a never-ending list of things to do for me, it seemed, and I didn't see Thomas again. Even though he was stuck on my mind. I didn't know how to feel about everything. Thomas was a Prince, and I was a servant girl with a crush. Nothing more.

I shouldn't let it affect me the way it did, but it was incredibly difficult not to think about. It just felt easy with Thomas. We were childhood friends. Practically raised together, but I still couldn't shake that awful feeling that I wasn't good enough. That maybe the slight flirtation I saw was all in my head because I *wanted* something.

But I shouldn't let myself think about him or wonder where he was.

One day he'd marry a Princess, and I'll probably still be working here honestly, I thought as I left the kitchen, scowling as I went. I did not like the idea of serving his... *wife.*

I slowly made my way to my room, exhausted from thinking about it all. I didn't want to destroy what I felt like was a good day. I crashed onto my bed the moment I entered my room. I didn't even bother changing out of my uniform.

I was out when my head hit the pillow. Completely forgetting that my mind was vulnerable to the Nightlocke now.

He could do whatever he wanted to me.

And there was nothing I could do about it.

Chapter 3

I awoke in a panic again. My whole bed was soaked with sweat, and I grabbed my chest as I sat forward. I couldn't catch my breath as I struggled to remember what happened. My mind was blank though, but it must have been bad because I felt *exhausted.* Like I did a workout instead of actually sleeping.

I quickly showered in the servant's bathing area and pulled my hair back into a bun, so it would stay out of my face today. *Marge would have a fit if I showed up to work smelling like a sewer rat,* I thought to myself. *And I didn't want Thomas to smell me like that either.* I made sure I was on time for the morning duties and grabbed a bowl of porridge, knowing not to expect another breakfast with the royal family. I looked around for any brown sugar or *something* to add to the bland bowl, but there was nothing set out for us. Frowning, I plopped down in my seat and began to scarf down a very boring bowl of porridge. Marge sauntered into the room with a clipboard in hand.

"Alrighty, so plans have changed drastically today due to the early arrival of Princess Agatha and her royal procession. We will be welcoming her first thing this afternoon. Sarah, you and Kymra shall oversee decorating the ballroom for tonight, where you both will be in attendance. You shall be servers for tonight, unless the Prince has other plans," Marge muttered under her breath, but I just barely caught what she said.

Did Thomas want me to join the ball as a guest? I thought to myself as the corners of my mouth rose. Sarah wiggled her eyebrows at me, and I couldn't help but giggle.

Marge continued, "Lucy, Abigail, and Farrah, you shall start preparing the main courses and grabbing the finest wine in the cellar. The King and Princes are already prepared for her arrival, which will be sometime this afternoon. Now scoot, everyone!"

I quickly shoveled down the last of my bowl before dropping it off at the sink. I followed Sarah out of the kitchen and down the long stone hallway towards the main part of the castle. *It was incredible how big this castle was.* The room was magnificent already, with the entire walls painted white with gorgeous gold trim. Large windows that went from floor to ceiling showed off the gardens in the back, with the biggest chandelier I had ever seen hanging in the center of the room. *The King spared no expense here,* I thought as memories of my early years came to mind. *I wonder if that panel is still loose behind the throne...*

"Gorgeous, isn't it?" Sarah said, pulling me from my thoughts. I smiled and followed her to where all the boxes were set out already. Sarah went on and on about the different balls the King has thrown over the years, and I listened while we worked. My mind was a little preoccupied with the idea that Thomas might ask me to attend the ball tonight, but I felt bad for half paying attention to her. We spent the whole morning setting out glass vases on the table and filling them with real flowers. I had no idea how they managed to get all these gorgeous flowers here without them wilting. Suddenly, the doors opened behind us.

"There you are, Kymra! I've been looking everywhere for you," Thomas said. Liam gave us both a smile as Sarah stared dumbfoundly at the Princes. I gently nudged her, and she shut her gaping mouth before giving them a bow.

"You found me hard at work, Thomas. Hello, Prince Liam," I replied, curtsying myself.

"Ah, Liam is just fine, Kymra. You always were like a little sister to us," he said before kissing my hand. He kissed Sarah's as well, and I wasn't sure if she was going to stay conscious for much longer. She was outright giddy, and her eyes remained as wide as saucers. Liam smirked at me knowingly, and I just shook my head. I couldn't blame her.

I was feeling the same way...

"You work too much, Kymra. Shall we blow off all this work and spend the day in the gardens again?" he asked, winking at me, and my heart did a little flip inside. *What an idea that was.*

Liam laughed. "Dad would kill you if you did not greet our new friends, Thomas."

Thomas rolled his eyes. "They are not *our* friends, Liam. They're only here to see if she is a good match for one of us so they can settle on terms of the new alliance. Kymra is our only true friend, and I'd rather spend my day with her."

I blushed as Thomas slowly looked me up and down, winking at me when our eyes met. *Sarah was right,* I thought. *He was shameless... But what did that make me since it was clearly working.* I was already feeling weak in the knees and thinking about our first kiss. Heat filled my cheeks, and Thomas grinned, seeing my reaction. I only squirmed further under his gaze.

"As much as I would like that too," Liam said, placing his hands on his hips, "we better get a move on. Her carriage was spotted entering town a few minutes ago. I'd rather not die by our own father's hand, Thomas."

"You are the future King, Liam. It doesn't quite matter what I do," Thomas said rather snidely, and I blinked in surprise. *I had never heard this tone from him before,* I thought as I watched the brothers. Liam dropped his head as his face fell.

"Do not start this again, Thomas. Now, let's go," Liam said firmly, dragging his younger brother away from the two of us. Thomas gave me one final wink before they were gone, leaving Sarah and I to finish our task. The second they left the room, Sarah slammed into my side.

"My oh my, he's seriously smitten with you, isn't he? I've been here a year, and he has never once even looked in my direction!"

I giggled, brushing her off. "Nonsense, Sarah. We only knew each other as children, nothing more."

"I don't know, Kymra. I'd wear my nicest dress tonight if I were you," she replied, winking at me.

My stomach twisted violently then. *Surely, Thomas would not ask me to dance in front of all these nobles and lords,* I thought to myself. *Would he?* I am a servant, and while we do not have the rules like other Kingdoms do when it comes to marriage, we still had proper behavior between the classes. Tonight was *not* meant for me, and I had nothing to wear but my simple blue dress anyways. I couldn't keep the disappointment from creeping in as I got back to work decorating the room.

Sarah and I spent the rest of the afternoon getting the room ready before Marge finally dismissed us. She gave us each a new uniform that was fancier than our normal attire before kicking us out to get ready. We still sported the King's insignia on our left chest, but instead of our normal white and blue outfits these dresses were solid white. It was rather low in the chest, and the trim and belt were made of a silky gold material. I had never worn anything as fancy as this before, and I quickly styled my hair the best I could. I had none of the fancy powder the Princesses and Ladies always wore, but that was alright. I was already blushing over being here in the first place, so I didn't think I'd need it anyways.

Marge inspected each and everyone of us before sending us out with trays of food. I followed the others, serving table after table. It was a full house tonight, but everyone and everything looked beautiful. There were so many different colors, and it was a sight to see all the nobles men and their ladies up close like this. I couldn't help but notice Thomas watching me from afar, and he winked at me when our eyes met.

I nearly dropped my tray when he did, earning looks from the table I was serving, and I quickly gained my composure, hoping Marge didn't see. Thomas chuckled from across the room as I scurried back to the main tables. *He was going to be the death of me.*

Thankfully, I made it through dinner service without making a mess, and Sarah and I watched the rest of the ball from afar. Only stepping away from the wall when someone needed a refill. We whispered amongst ourselves, discussing the different outfits we saw tonight and who looked interested in who. As exciting as it was, I wished we'd be able to join in. It just looked like so much fun.

I spotted the visiting Princess sitting at Thomas and Liam's table, and I had to admit she was beautiful. A shameful part of me hoped she looked awful, but she was quite the opposite actually. Her long red hair was styled in tight curls and were a stark contrast to her pale skin. She also had vivid green eyes like mine, but hers were breathtaking compared to my own. Princess Agatha held her head high amongst all the royal Lords, not afraid to speak her mind, and I was mesmerized watching her. I envied her confidence and wondered if I'd get a chance to meet her during her stay.

Soon music filled the room, and I saw Liam take Princess Agatha's hand to the dance floor. It was no surprise that he chose her for the first dance as they seemed rather lost in one another tonight. Most arranged marriages didn't work out that way, but Prince Liam seemed rather fond of Princess Agatha. And I was happy for my friend. Others quickly joined in the dance, and I watched everyone begin to move effortlessly around the room in time with the music. Suddenly, Thomas was at my side, holding out his hand. My heart stopped when he bowed.

"Shall we dance, Kymra?"

I stared at him in disbelief. *He was asking me to dance the first dance?!* I couldn't contain the smile from forming on my face as I accepted his hand and walked to the floor. This was a *big deal* as the first song was always reserved for someone special. I had everyone's eyes on me as Thomas led me to the dance floor. Even the King watched the two of us closely.

He grabbed my waist, pulling me close, and we began the dance. My heart thundered in my chest as Thomas guided me around the dance floor, and for the first time in my life, I didn't think of my station. It felt like I was living a dream, and my heart soared. Thomas's eyes met mine, and I could see desire in them. Then they dropped to my lips, and I wondered if he was going to kiss me. *Was this really happening? Could Thomas really be happy with someone like me?*

"You look beautiful, Kymra," Thomas whispered, and my heart melted again. I didn't care that Marge was glaring at me or that the other servant girls were gawking in the corner or that *every other* nobleman in this room was judging us. In this moment, I was happy and content. I felt safe in Thomas's arms, and I *never* wanted to leave them.

"Thank you, Thomas."

The song came to an end, and he kissed my hand, thanking me for the dance. I gave him a bow before making my way back to where the other ladies stood. Sarah was beaming back at me as I made way to her, and I already knew she wanted to gossip later. My cheeks heated, and I couldn't contain my smile. *I was really grateful to have at least one friend here,* I thought as I passed by a plethora of ladies glaring at me. I held my head high though, refusing to let them ruin my night. Thomas did not ask me to dance again, but that was okay. He asked me to dance the first dance, and that meant the world to me.

I watched as Thomas danced with two other Ladies over the course of the evening. Our eyes met often while he danced, and it was difficult to keep myself from blushing every time they did. His sly smile was adorable, and he made it a point to include me in someway not matter what was going on. Butterflies filled my stomach when Thomas passed by with his friends for the evening, trailing his fingers along my waist before stepping out into the hall. *God, he was gorgeous.* The night was winding down when Marge came up to us.

"You ladies have done very well tonight. You are free to go. The other crew will be assigned to clean up once everyone has gone. The King has given his permission for you to enjoy yourself, *outside* mind you, or retire for the evening."

I grinned wide at Sarah, who was just as excited as I was for the bonus night off. My feet were killing me in these shoes, and I had expected to be stuck cleaning up.

"So shall we take a walk?" Sarah asked, giving me a sly grin. "Maybe gossip a bit before bed?"

"Absolutely!" I giggled, wrapping my arm around her and dragging her into the hall. My eyes roamed the halls for Thomas, wondering where he could be. *I saw him head out with his friends earlier,* I thought to myself. *He must be close. Maybe I'll get that kiss after all.*

Sarah and I walked alongside the grand windows, passing many Nobles and their Ladies leaving for the night. My shoulders fell when I still didn't find Thomas, but when Sarah and I reached the outer doors to the gardens, we heard laughter coming from the other side. My heart fluttered inside when I recognized voice saying my name.

"Kymra is just a servant girl, Benjamin," Thomas said sarcastically.

Sarah and I skidded to a stop just before the door, and my brows furrowed. She looked to me with wide eyes, but I just stood like a freaking idiot. Unable to move or do *anything*.

"Oh, yeah? Then why did you single her out to dance, Thomas? Everyone's talking about it!"

"Shut up, fool! We knew each other as children. It was nothing more than a nice gesture," Thomas replied in frustration.

I took a step backwards, feeling so unbelievably foolish for seeing something that wasn't there. My heart began to break as their footsteps grew louder. Sarah looked at me with such pity then. *They all said he was like this... And I so foolishly thought I was different.*

"Yeah, sure..." another boy said. "We know you, Thomas. I just don't know why you'd stoop so low for someone like her, especially for the first dance."

"Good God, man! What do you want me to say?! She's a beautiful girl with a curvy body, and I can charm her just enough that she can scratch an itch before I toss her aside. It isn't like I'm going to marry her or something," Thomas hollered back.

To my further embarrassment, all three Princes came strolling through the door. Thomas plowed right into me, and his face turned to complete horror when he saw me. My eyes filled with tears as I looked to my feet.

"Busted," one of his friends muttered as they laughed amongst themselves. Shame filled my cheeks, and I pulled away from Thomas.

"I don't think he's getting any now," said the other.

"Kymra..." Thomas muttered quietly, and he slowly raised his hand to mine.

I pulled away from his reach, giving them all a curtsy saying, "Prince Thomas. Excuse me, please."

I ran from my oldest friend. From the man I had been pining after for years. From the one I thought *saw* me.

"Kymra, wait!" Thomas shouted as I ran even faster.

I disappeared in the gardens, running until I could not hear his voice calling my name anymore. I collapsed near the fountain in the back when the tears finally fell. I sobbed, curling in on myself as I wallowed in my complete stupidity. I should have never let my heart run away from me like that. I should have never hoped for more with a man so far above my station. *Now I was about to relive this humiliation day in and day out. Marge wouldn't let me out of my duties because of my own stupidity. She wouldn't make any special favors for someone like me.* I'd be forced to see him for the rest of my life. I wiped my cheek and pulled my knees to my chest.

Suddenly, I heard footsteps to my left, and I stood abruptly as the hair stood on the back of my neck. *Something was wrong.* Something had shifted in the air, and the world had quieted around me. I scanned the gardens, frowning when I could not see anyone.

But I could *hear* footsteps though, and they were getting closer. I looked around the gardens once more, when suddenly a tall man with a black hooded cloak and dark pants appeared from the hedge. His eyes were fixated on the castle, and you could barely see his face under the hood he wore. My eyes drifted to the long black sword at his hip when I recognized who this man was.

I held my breath as fear squeezed my heart.

I knew this man.

This was the Nightlocke.

Chapter 4

I didn't move, didn't breathe as the man walked further into the garden. I felt stuck in a trance watching him as he moved with the shadows towards the castle. *He hadn't even seemed to notice me.* My eyes widened as he lifted his hands towards the castle and black shadows poured from his fingers. *The shadows were real...*

The shadows traveled through the garden like they were *alive* and panic took control of my body as they drew closer towards me. *I had never seen anything like this before,* I thought as I watched the shadows move around objects, inspecting every one before they continued on their path. It was then I realized that these shadows *were* alive. *They were just mere extensions of this demon standing in front of me.* I followed the shadows as they slowly started to disappear behind the hedge towards the castle. *He was going to attack the castle... He was going to hurt everyone all over again.* My chest burned in agony, screaming at me to help those in need, but to my horror my feet moved forward instead of backwards.

My eyes widened as my feet moved towards the Nightlocke before I could stop it, and his head snapped in my direction the second my foot touched the ground. The dark receded from his eyes as he stared coldly at my own. The shadows snapped back towards him as his brows knitted, and my chest heaved as I tried to put air back in my lungs. We stared at one another for a moment, and I didn't know what to do now.

"You... you see me," the Nightlocke spoke. His voice match his dark persona, and the two of us watched one another again.

He and I seemed stuck in this trance together. Like I startled him as much as he did me, but I was too afraid to speak. I was too afraid to even run, but then something unexpected happened. The Nightlocke's face softened, and I could almost see a piercing blue color come through his dark eyes. *They were not black like I thought they were.* I was surprised to see that he had normal looking eyes behind those shadows, and I cocked my head to the side. *What else was I wrong about?*

The Nightlocke stepped closer to me, but then he hesitated. *Did I scare him?* I wondered as he watched me closely. A warm breeze flowed through the trees around us, and I watched the wind die when they neared this dark and dangerous man. It was like everything around him stilled the closer it came to him. He took another step, and my eyes widened. *What would happen if he touched me?*

A layer of darkness followed him everywhere, and his footsteps never left a trail to follow, but I could hear each and every step he took towards me. As he took another small step, the moonlight hit the side of his face, and I realized how beautiful the Nightlocke was. He wasn't a walking corpse like I expect but entirely handsome. *And young. He didn't look much older than I was, but I guess it didn't matter when you were immortal.* My chest burned, pushing me towards this man again. I took a small step, and I saw him blink in surprise. *This drive I had to help people was never wrong, but what could this monster possibly need from me?*

"KYMRA! Please answer me! It's not what you think!" Thomas shouted, and the two of us stopped dead in our tracks. The Nightlocke's eyes darkened again as he turned to the direction of the castle.

My eyes widened as I heard Thomas's step draw closer. I looked back to the Nightlocke then, feeling that burning sensation return. *Maybe this is what I need to do? I just need to warn him before Thomas finds him and brings the Royal guard down upon him.* I took a step forward crying out, "Run!"

The Nightlocke turned back to me, watching me with such scrutiny. Thomas shouted again.

"Did you not hear me?!" I snapped, and his eyes narrowed. "Run now! Before he sees you!"

The Nightlocke didn't run like I warned him to, and my chest burned in agony. I couldn't explain why, but I did not want him to be found. I couldn't bear the idea of him hurt because I was out in the gardens when I shouldn't be.

Thomas suddenly shot into the clearing. His eyes met mine briefly before landing on the Nightlocke standing nearby. He drew his sword immediately saying, "Kymra, you need to move away from that demon!"

The Nightlocke snarled loudly, and I winced at the unholy sound. My eyes widened as fear crept back in, and I staggered backwards. Thomas barely took a step towards me, when the Nightlocke raised his hands and covered the ground in his shadows once more. I screamed when they wrapped around my feet, creating a wall between Thomas and I. The shadows swarmed me entirely, and I lost sight of everything. There was nothing but darkness, and I shot my hands forward as I tried to stumble out. I followed the sound of Thomas's voice, but no matter where my feet moved, I could not find him. I was lost in this dark abyss.

"Kymra!" Thomas shouted.

I opened my mouth to answer him, when suddenly the Nightlocke appeared instantly before me. I screamed as he wrapped his arms around me tightly and pulled me back into the dark. Thomas screamed my name, but the sound grew faint as air rushed past us. It stole the breath from my lungs, and I could do nothing but rest my head against the Nightlocke's chest as we flew through the dark abyss. All of the sudden, we slammed to a stop, and he dropped me.

My hip landed hard on the stone floor, and it took me a second to get my bearings because of how *dark* everything was in here. I blinked as I slowly leaned forward. *I wasn't in the gardens anymore,* I thought as my heart thundered in my chest. There was no light anywhere, and somewhere in this place I heard hear screaming. It was coming from someone or something, and my body shook listening to it. As I forced myself to my knees, my hand touched something warm and wet, and I quickly scurried from it. Rats scurried somewhere nearby around and panic gripped my heart.

What did I just get myself into?

Why didn't I just run?!

CHAPTER 4

Heavy steps sounded to my right, and I slowly looked to the man who stole me.

"Why did you take me?" I asked him quietly.

The Nightlocke removed his cloak, hanging it on the wall, and my eyes widened when I saw his defined shoulders and arms. My eyes roamed the black tattoos running up his left arm and neck. When he turned, I could see rings in his lip and eyebrow. I had no idea that was even possible to have metal sticking out of your skin, but he wore them well, and my cheeks heated at the fact that I *liked* what I saw. The Nightlocke was more than just beautiful. He was *gorgeous*, with his hair jet black and messy. The sides of his hair were so short, you could just barely see the tattoos on the side of his head. I was mesmerized by him. I was utterly foolish though because for a moment I had forgotten *who* he was and *where* I was. I was just lost in him. And I, honest to God, didn't want to be found.

The Nightlocke didn't seem to want to give me an answer as he tossed his sword in its stand. He seemed almost frustrated by my presence now. His eyes stayed black as night whenever he glared at me, and he angrily moved about the room.

Why take me then if you didn't want me here?

"Well?" I asked in a huff. I crossed my arms as I waited for an answer. The Nightlocke paused, cocking his head to the side as he studied me carefully.

"You saw me."

That's it? That's all he was going to tell me? Anger flared within me for some reason, and I stomped my foot in place. "Seriously? You kidnapped me simply because I saw you?! I tried to help you..."

The Nightlocke was suddenly in my face, gripping my throat in his hand, and my eyes went wide as he applied pressure.

"NO ONE SEES ME!" he shouted loudly. His voice *silenced* the screaming in this place. It was entirely silent in here now, and my heart thundered in my chest. *God, I was so stupid. Why did I open my mouth in the first place?!* His dark eyes glared down at me, blurring as my lungs burned. Surprisingly, the Nightlocke let me go, and I collapsed on the floor, gasping for air. His callous hands gripped my arm and hauled me to my feet.

"No one sees me," he growled. "I don't miss *anyone* or anything yet... I missed you."

His brows knitted before his eyes returned to blue once more. They were absolutely striking in color and bright, despite all the dark this man held within.

"I want to go home," I whispered softly.

He snarled angrily again as he stomped away from me. I expected him to lash out again, but instead his shadows swarmed me. I screamed as they engulfed me once more, and the wind soared all around me. I didn't have his massive body to shield me this time either, so the air was ripped from my lungs as I stumbled in the dark. But then the shadows dropped me again, and I was alone inside a cell. My chest heaved as I got my bearings once more, and I scurried as far into the light as I could. The only light came from the moon shining through the small window above me. Even if I tried jumping, it was well above my head, and there were bars on the window. I tried the cell door, but it was locked as well. I looked around the small stone room as my world came crashing down around me. *I was trapped here with the Nightlocke. I was never going home again.*

I slid down the concrete wall, sobbing into my arms. All this happened because of a boy. A stupid, pathetic boy, who didn't deserve my time and attention. *I only ran because Thomas broke my heart,* I thought as the tears continued to fall. *I was only in this mess because of him.*

Anger filled my veins as I scolded myself further. I *knew* better than to be out in the dark at night like that, especially so close to the Forbidden Woods. *And why didn't I run the moment I saw him? Why did I even try to help him?!* My stupid desire to help people has never betrayed me like this before. I don't understand why of all people did it insist I help *him?* I replayed tonight's events over and over again in my mind, trying to make sense of it all. But nothing made sense at all to me. *Why... Why did I have to help him?*

The Nightlocke *was* the scary beast in the dark. Nothing compared to him. Nothing could kill him, and yet I *warned* him of Thomas. I warned him to run from a pathetic human with a sword. I felt like the world's dumbest girl as I wallowed in misery.

CHAPTER 4

My cell was awful. It smelled of rotting flesh and old blood, and it didn't take long before the screaming started again. It sounded closer than before, and their terrifying sounds kept me on edge. The air felt thick despite the window above, and it was nothing but dark and creepy down here. I pulled my knees to my chest as I waited for something to happen. I just wanted to go home to my dad and sister. *The King would surely let me out of the rations deal after this. Wouldn't he?*

Chapter 5

The Nightlocke

    I didn't see her.

    I didn't hear her breathing or hear her soft cries as I stepped into that plastic garden. She surprised me. For the first time since I inherited this dark power, she *surprised* me. I felt something snap between us when our eyes met, and I immediately felt rage over whatever ailed her. This girl was stunning with her white gown and dark long hair, and I felt my eyes clear for the first time in years. The shadows preferred the dark above all else yet with her they wanted my own eyes to shine through. My head felt *clear*, and I was no longer determined to ruin the King's night anymore. I only wanted her... And that *scared* me.

    I remembered the previous Nightlocke's memories. It was fuzzy, but I still remember the anguish and terror coursing through his veins when he accidentally killed his girl. *Did he feel a pull like this with her? What in the world was even happening between us?* I was vile, wicked, and cruel yet she softened me. I should have just killed the Prince that startled us in the gardens, but I left him alive because I was afraid to lose her for some reason. I was afraid to do anything that would put her in danger, and I needed to protect her *instead* of hitting my marks. This wasn't like me.

    I needed to correct this.

    She would always be in danger with a man like me anyways. I kill. I don't *feel* love. Not anymore. Not for a long time. And after everything I had become, I know I didn't deserve any scrap of happiness. I was content in my misery and the dark. I was content to be alone.

CHAPTER 5

I had tossed her in one of the cells below to clear my head, but I could hear her every cry, even from here. We were in tune with one another for some reason, and no matter what I did, I couldn't get her out of my mind. The sobbing broke my heart, and all I wanted to do was fix it, but I shook myself free of those thoughts. I knew better than this... Whatever it was.

No... I thought to myself. *She needs to go.*

I lifted my hand, pulling my shadows to the front to just send her back, when pain rippled through me. The idea of releasing her *repulsed* me. Even my shadows were angry with the idea, and they forcefully pulled themselves back inside my mind, refusing to come out to play.

I rubbed my face as I paced the room back and forth. "What is wrong with me?"

The girl seemed almost concerned for me too, I thought as my mind drifted back to tonight. Back in that garden, she seemed afraid for something to happen to me, and that puzzled me greatly. It was clear she recognized me, yet she wanted me to run to safety? *Why? Why would anyone care for me?*

I shook myself from the never-ending questions I didn't have answers to. One way or another, I was going to find a way to drop her or make her so scared that *she* wanted nothing to do with me ever again. *Yeah... That was it,* I told myself. *It would be easier to dump her if she hated me.* I needed my life to go back to the way things were. I was so close to enacting my revenge on the castle and that arrogant King, and this *girl* wasn't going to ruin it.

I leaned back in my cold chair as my hands drifted behind my head. I forced this girl's gorgeous body from my mind, focusing on the name that prick shouted.

"Kymra," I whispered, and I felt my eyes darken over. It used to frighten me until I learned how to use my power properly. The darkness only added to my sight and improved everything for me, but like the Nightlocke before me, it was taking over a bit too much lately. The more demented and cruel my actions were, the worse I felt. The harder I fell into the darkness my shadows brought, the more I lost the person I was before all this. I needed to remain in control *always*, which was the previous Nightlocke's downfall. He plagued the town viciously, while I took my time. I am careful with how dark I take things so as not to lose control of my mind as quickly as he did. Getting lost in the darkness was easy, but I knew it was only a matter of time before I too was beyond saving.

Did I really want to be saved though? My heavy heart sighed as my past came to mind. I am content watching this awful Kingdom suffer, but that was the opposite of someone worth saving. *But they watched me suffer when...*

I shut that thought down immediately before repeating the girl's name again. I needed to focus on the task at hand.

"Kymra."

I let my shadows find my mark for me, and I could see her in my mind's eye. She was sleeping on the hard floor, half drenched in God knows what was in that cell. I forced myself to ignore it and focused on her mind instead.

"Let's see what you're afraid of," I muttered as my shadows engulfed over her. Inside her mind, I saw all her fears and thoughts happening at once. I recognized this mind from earlier this week. It initially disgusted and infuriated me all at the same time. Her mind had been a difficult one to work through if I remember right, and when I did see anything, it was nothing but the same thing most girls were afraid of. Rejection from some guy, but tonight it was different.

I saw myself or the version she saw me as. I don't know why it bothered me the way it did, but I hated that *this* was how she saw me. A monster... But then again that was what I was.

I snapped myself out of those ridiculous thoughts and forced myself to amplify her fears. *Let her be afraid. Let her hate me so badly, that I can dump her somewhere and never see her again.* I needed to rid myself of whatever *this* was. She was toxic to me, and I couldn't handle what it was doing to me.

I pushed my shadows further into her mind, and her heart slowly begin to race. I smiled when her breathing picked up, and she jolted in her sleep. Despite whatever was going on between us, I gave her the worst nightmare I have ever given before. Her mind was difficult to manipulate when she was at the castle, and I struggled to enter her mind while I was juggling everyone else too. Tonight, she got me all to herself. She began to mutter in her sleep, twisting and turning on the stone floor, so I added more. She needed to be scarred from this dream, and I pushed it further and further than I ever had with one's mind.

Her mind was about to break.

Suddenly, pain rippled through my mind and something forced my shadows out. I was blinded by a bright light, and I clutched my head as she shot forward screaming out. *She woke up,* I thought as my shadows retreated back to me, and I couldn't see her anymore.

"She pushed me out," I said to myself in disbelief. No one has *ever* done that to me before. This just proved I was off my game with this girl, and I stormed towards the cells below.

I stepped into the veil and slammed into the cell bars shouting, "WHAT DID YOU DO?!"

She scurried backwards, clutching her chest as she screamed. Her eyes found mine, and she took a deep breath as she settled herself. "What are you talking about?!"

"You know what! How did you do that?!" I shouted, gripping the bars tightly. Fear filled those beautiful green eyes of her again, and my stomach twisted. *She was scared... Good, she needed to be.*

"I don't understand! I haven't done anything! I just woke up..."

"EXACTLY! You *woke* up, and I want to know what you did to stop your nightmare!"

"What?" she hollered back. Her brows knitted in confusion, and she shook her head wildly. "What are you talking about?! Please, stop screaming at me!"

I glared at the small woman before me. My anger softened slightly when she wrapped her too small arms around her waist. *She really had no idea what I was talking about.*

"Do you remember your dream?" I asked in a calmer tone.

She looked at me baffled by my question.

"What? No, I don't," she cried out, "but will you please explain why you are yelling at me?!"

My eyes widened. *She didn't even remember the nightmare.* That has never happened before. No one has ever been immune to my power, and I know it was affecting her! I saw it! That bright light just forced me out. *What in the world was that even? What was she?*

I darkened my eyes, letting my shadows coat me thoroughly before I let them guide me through the bars. Her eyes widened as I shifted back into her focus and ended up mere inches from her face. She smelled sweet, almost like vanilla in the cakes my mother used to buy me when I was small. My eyes darkened again at the memory. This girl was reminding me of things I didn't want to think about, and that angered me even more.

I snarled at her. "You are my prisoner, got that? You don't get to ask questions!"

Her nose scrunched up angrily before she suddenly pushed me back. "GET OUT!" she shouted.

My shadows fled as I blinked in disbelief again. She shoved me hard again, and my back hit the bars. I didn't expect her sudden aggression. I didn't expect her to put up a fight. Most people just coward when they saw me, but this girl was just mad and determined to make me leave. I watched a tear slide down her face, and I felt guilty for yelling in the first place. My mind and heart were warring with one another over this girl, and it was beginning to make my head spin.

"I SAID GET OUT!" she shouted again.

My eyes widened, and I yielded to her request. I quickly disappeared into my shadows, leaving her in the cell alone. I stood in my bedroom, unsure what had even happened. But one thing was clear.

This girl was going to be the death of me.

Chapter 6

Kymra

I barely slept after that monster left me alone in my cell again. Knowing that creature had been in my mind was unnerving, and I didn't want to give him the chance to attack me again. So I stayed awake, curling up in the corner and waiting the sun slowly wake again. *This place was awful. There was no way I'd ever get used to the constant screaming either.* There was no way I'd *ever* get used to this being my life.

I had nothing to do except wait. Wait to die, I suppose. It felt like the Nightlocke watched me as I sat in this cell, and I tried to keep my face hidden from the shadows that lurked about. I didn't like it, but there was nothing I could do to stop him. There was nothing I could do to hurt him. I stayed alone in my cell for hours. My stomach rumbled with hungry, and my throat burned from thirst, but I didn't say a word to the one watching. I refused to show this man my fear anymore than I already had.

That was easier said than done though. The man was terrifying, but I continued to feel drawn to him. Like he was broken somehow and needed fixed. I tried to ignore it. I told myself that I would not go near that monster voluntarily anymore, but my chest began to ache inside. I knew it would only get worse from here, but I wasn't about to try and fix *the Nightlocke*. He was a monster, and there was no saving someone like him.

My mind drifted back to my only friend back at the castle. My only real friend. Sarah heard everything Thomas said, which only embarrassed me further. My anger returned, remembering the way he spoke to his friends about me. I was stupid to let myself think more than what I should have. I was trash, nothing more than that, and now because I let my fantasies run wild, I was trapped by the monster no one could find and *everyone* feared.

I missed my dad and sister.

I laid my head against my knees as tears filled my eyes once more. I didn't even know I had anymore tears left inside me. I was clearly dehydrated, and if I didn't get some water soon it was going to kill me. *But maybe that was the point. Let me die a slow death just for being a thorn in his side.*

Suddenly, the Nightlocke's dark shadows entered my cell, and I scurried back to the corner again. My eyes widened as they swarmed me again, and soon I was in complete darkness. I held my breath, knowing that the strong wind was coming, and it flooded my system. I knew it was coming, and it still took my breath away. When they finally dropped me, I was back in the first room again, with the dark man staring down at me. I glared at him, and he glared right back.

"Why don't you just let me go? You clearly don't want me here anymore than I want to be here!" I shouted as rage flooded my system, but he didn't respond. He didn't say a word, and that just pissed me off even more.

I opened my mouth to yell when the Nightlocke leaned forward on his knees, his eyes turning solid black as he said, "I don't just let people go."

"Then go ahead and kill me! Because *anything* is better than this!" I snapped back, and his blue eyes returned. He seemed surprised by my request, and I narrowed my eyes. The Nightlocke looked briefly distraught before his eyes darkened once more.

"I thought you might want something to eat. It's been a few days after all," he muttered quietly.

My eyes widened, and we stared at one another. *Has it really been that long already?* My shoulders sunk as I slowly processed what he just said. *Everyone must think I'm dead if it's really been three days.*

Suddenly, my heart stopped. *My Dad! I wasn't there to work for the King so he would no longer receive any rations.* God, they were about to become destitute again, and that killed me inside. *I couldn't help them*, I thought as agony filled my heart. It twisted with the rage I felt, making me sick inside. It bothered me that everyone would just assume I was another victim of the Nightlocke.

CHAPTER 6

But I was though. He just hasn't killed me yet.

"Did you hear me, girl?!"

The Nightlocke's arrogant tone pulled me from my thoughts, and I glared at him. I snarled, "My name is Kymra!"

He cocked his head again as he studied me. He stayed quiet for a few moments before saying, "You really aren't afraid of me, are you?"

"No, I'm livid! You've taken me from my family, which was the only way I could feed them, and I'm sure they all think I'm dead by now! You torture the entire Kingdom, kill whomever you wish just for the fun of it. You are a monster, Nightlocke! I'm not afraid of you. I hate you!"

His eyes darkened again, and he stood abruptly, knocking his chair behind him. I scurried back as he stormed towards me.

"You're right! I *am* a monster, but I've been rather kind to you despite that. Rather than be grateful that I haven't killed you yet, you continue to yell at me. Enough is enough, *Kymra*. You need to understand the situation you are in and where your freaking place is."

The Nightlocke's hands shot forward, and I saw his shadows come alive. His eyes darkened as the shadows covered the floor entirely, and to my horror, bodies stood from those shadows. They were solid black with no face, but you could clearly see their sharp, jagged teeth when they snarled viciously at me. I gasped as terror racked my body, and I tried to run, but something grabbed my foot, and I fell.

His shadow creatures tugged at my hair and clothes, while I screamed on the floor. I bawled, desperate to run away from the terrifying creatures he just conjured on command, but I was stuck. Whenever I stood, his creatures would yanked me down. My clothes tore, and I screamed when the shadow sliced across my arm. My eyes widened, but when I saw him out of the corner of my eye, he was *smiling*. This wicked man was enjoying watching me suffer.

"PLEASE STOP! I'm begging you!" I screamed.

His blue eyes snapped back, and he pulled everything away from me. I fell to the floor, breathing hard as the shadows left me alone. Blood trickled down my face, and my throat burned from screaming. I stared hard at the man in front of me. The Nightlocke's face hardened, and he narrowed his eyes at me.

"I cannot let you go, but I won't kill you unless you provoke me, understand?" he said.

I nodded my head slowly, not trusting myself to speak, and he seemed satisfied with my answer. He walked across the room, grabbing something off the wooden table before dropping it at my feet. I saw recognized the brown paper and could smell the meat from here. My stomach twisted fiercely at the smell, but I hesitated until the Nightlocke moved away. I snatched it the moment he turned his back and took a small piece in my hand. My mouth watered. I desperately shoved the piece in my mouth and nearly groaned out loud. *It was bland as could be, but I don't care,* I thought as I grabbed another chunk. My stomach hurt from hunger, and I quickly became lost in my meal.

The Nightlocke suddenly set down a mug that was filled to the brim with water next to me, and I nearly cried at the sight. I didn't even notice his approaching... The Nightlocke moved away again, and I grabbed the mug, chugging it gone. I shoveled piece after piece of meat into my mouth and licked my fingers along the way.

"Slow down or you'll be sick," he said sternly, picking up his chair again. He sat down, watching me eat my meal like an animal, and my stomach churned a little. I wasn't about to give him the satisfaction of being right though, and I wiped my mouth.

"Why do you care?" I asked, narrowing my eyes. His eyes darkened, and I scolded myself for opening my mouth again. *Just keep your mouth shut, Kymra...*

"I don't," he snarled. No one said a word after that.

As I ate the rest of my meal slowly, I got a better look at the room. There was a table off to the side and three doors total. One behind me to the right that was open and led directly down a flight of stairs. The other was in front of me, and the last was to my left. Those were both closed, and I wondered what lay behind them. The room was cold and full of stone and tapestries that were so dirty and faded, you could not see what the picture used to be.

I pursed my lips together once I had finished eating. *Do I go back to my cell or do I stay here? Where was my cell even?* I thought to myself as I tucked my legs underneath me. *I seriously hoped he didn't move me by those shadows again otherwise I may lose everything in my stomach.* It was already unsteady in my belly as it was.

"Why can't you let me go?" I finally asked as nicely as I could muster. I must be losing my mind though because when I turned to look back at the man, I swore I saw pity in his eyes. I blinked, and it was gone.

The Nightlocke moved his hand away from his mouth asking, "What?"

"You said you could not let me go, so I wanted to know why?"

The Nightlocke studied me a moment more. I realized he took his time before he spoke. It wasn't just because I was a nuisance to him, and he didn't feel like talking. *I don't think he knows what to say to me.*

He finally spoke, "Because you saw me."

"So did Thomas. Unless…" I muttered softly, "you killed him that night."

"So that's his name?" he muttered back to me.

"What does that matter?" I asked, scrunching my nose up. *My father used to tell me as a child that curiosity always killed the cat, but I guess it also killed 17 year old girls as well.*

"Knowing a name makes it easier to locate people."

"Why do you need to find him?" I asked as anxiety rose within me. *Did I just get Thomas killed by giving the Nightlocke his name?* His eyes blackened again as he chuckled, sending goosebumps up my arm.

"It's fun beside he's the one that made you cry," he said as a wicked grin covered his too handsome face. "Right?"

I dropped my head in shame as my cheeks heated, thinking back to that night and the words Thomas said about me. The Nightlocke snorted before crossing his arms.

"I figured you'd *want* me to pay him a visit. I mean most people want revenge," he said, leaning forward in his chair. "What did he do anyways? I've wondered ever since grabbing you."

I remained silent, refusing to speak about this *very* private and embarrassing matter. I didn't owe him anything, and I was not about to entertain him with stories of my own heartache.

"Oh… Did he break your heart, Kymra?" he asked mockingly, and I glared back at him. The Nightlocke's amusement filled the air as his deep laughed echoed in the room.

"Oh, he did! Didn't he?!" he said as he laughed hysterically. "That's pathetic! You're nothing more than a typical immature girl who has *boy problems!* Poor Kymra!"

"Don't be cruel!" I snapped at him, and I watched his eyes return to blue. The Nightlocke quieted down surprisingly, and the two of us stayed silent. But shame had filled my heart because I was immature. I had been foolish, and now I was paying the price.

"Just let me go back to my cell, please," I muttered quickly, dropping my head in shame. I just wanted to be alone.

"As you wish," he said gruffly, hauling me to my feet.

The Nightlocke guided me through the open door and back down the massive staircase to the cells below. I was grateful he didn't send me through the shadows at least. He motioned with his hand towards the cell door, and his shadows shot out passed us, opening it. He tossed me inside and stormed away.

I slid down the wall, and the second I could not hear his footsteps, I cried myself to sleep.

Chapter 7

The Nightlocke

I stormed away from her feeling utterly ridiculous. I was angry discovering that prick did something to hurt Kymra, and I covered up my frustrations by making fun of her. She was completely broken up over whatever happened, and I was nothing more than a jerk to her because I was *uncomfortable* with the way she made me feel. *Like a freaking idiot.*

I stormed back up to my room and chucked my hood off. It was exhausting stressing over this girl. It was exhausting keeping myself in the dark when I was around her. Her presence seemed to give me more control over the darkness within me, and that both intrigued and alarmed me. It was like the darkness was able to stay in its proper place, instead of taking over like it always tried to do. I felt the old me start to come back, and that scared the living daylights out of me. *I need to figure her out because I'm way too freaking exposed over here.*

And I didn't like it.

I laid back on my bed, shutting my eyes to try and sleep, but it evaded me. Again. Every time I closed my eyes, Kymra appeared. I couldn't get her out of my head. Like she was *my* nightmare sent to weaken me. Exasperated, I sat up and leaned against the wall instead. *Might as well have some fun if I'm staying up. Maybe this would be enough to tire me out?* My eyes darkened, and I released my shadows. I followed them as they left my castle in the Forbidden Woods and moved towards the Kingdom of Odemark. It didn't take long to reach the border, and they shot out just past the castle grounds.

"Let's find this *Thomas*," I whispered.

My shadows heard their mark and moved effortlessly through the castle. It was late so most were already in bed and getting past the guards was a breeze. It didn't take long to find the prick asleep in his large, fancy bed. My rage grew, knowing he saw her disappear with me, yet he had no problem falling asleep. *This Prince wasn't looking for her or anything...* I let my shadows engulf him before piercing his mind harshly.

"Let's see what we're working with," I muttered to myself, and I saw Kymra's face *everywhere* in this guy's mind. Anger rose within me then. This bothered me more than it should, and I decided to look into his memories. *Let's see exactly what happened between them anyways.* It didn't take long to find as it was forefront in the prick's mind, and what I saw *disgusted* me.

I heard every word.

And then I saw her face.

Kymra was crushed, and I was livid.

"How dare he?!" I shouted as I shot off my bed.

This was no longer fun and games.

He had officially become a mark, and I plagued his mind. I twisted his memories, toying on his affection for Kymra. I had him picture her with me instead. She insulted him for being a weak man, unable to care for her as a man *should,* and then I had her kiss me. I watched him begin to sweat as I tormented his mind, amplifying his biggest fear... Failure. I felt his heart begin to race, and I slowly smiled.

"Let's make this worse," I muttered softly. I slowly turned the tides, letting him now fail at saving her. Over and over he had to watch her die because of his inadequacy. He wasn't strong enough or he wasn't brave enough. It was all his fault.

Thomas tossed and turned on his bed, and I kept him locked inside, unable to wake until I said so. He didn't have control over his mind like Kymra did, and I plagued him until he screamed. His screams echoed the halls, and a low chuckle escaped my lips. It felt good watching him suffer just like he made *her* suffer.

Kymra's face suddenly appeared in my head, and I blinked. My rage *softened.* I tried to focus on my mark again, but it was difficult to keep the connection now. I had messed with him for the last few hours, but I had planned to for the rest of the night. It's what he deserved, but seeing Kymra's face softened my anger somehow, and I didn't feel like. I pulled my shadows out, shutting off my connection to him entirely. I dropped my mark, which was a first for me. My mind was stuck on Kymra though, especially after watching all the imagines I just created in Thomas's mind. *Why did I use me? I should have just chose the other Prince or something...* The second I thought that, my shadows seized inside me angrily. They did not like that one bit. I sighed, rubbing my face again. I needed help.

Serious help.

Watching her eat today sparked something inside me too. She was rather thin and clearly malnourished, and that bothered me. Kymra looked so weak and frail, and I knew I was only making it worse by keeping her down there. I haven't cared about the people starving in the Kingdom before, so why should I care if *this* girl goes hungry? The last person I cared about feeding was... Momma.

Frustrated, I covered myself in my shadows and drifted through the veil, landing just outside to the far off hill. I wasn't getting any sleep tonight, and I needed air.

The night was nice out despite the coldness of my castle. I could improve the place, but I never had any desire to. I liked it dark, menacing, and invisible to anyone who stumbled upon it. It looked abandoned from the outside, and I preferred it that way. Looking on it now though, I realized it just looked run down. It shouldn't bother me, but it does for some reason. Annoyed, I turned away from my castle, forcing it out of my mind.

"Hey, Momma," I said quietly, sitting down in the soft grass against the massive oak tree. I had a small headstone put in the ground the day I buried her here. I had just found the castle and wanted her close by. It was unmarked as I had stole it from a man in the kingdom, but it didn't matter. I knew who lay here, and no one else would need to visit her grave anyways.

I liked to sit out here every so often just to feel close to her again, but she's gone, and she's never coming back. My anger returned, and I was desperate to cling to it again. It was all I had left, and I didn't know how to let it go. I didn't know how to be *anything* other than the Nightlocke. I leaned my head against the tree, listening to the forest move about in the dark. There was a great deal awake right now, but it didn't matter. Nothing dared to come close to me, especially at night.

Kymra's face reappeared, and I thought about her and what was going on with me. I sighed, knowing I wasn't going to find any answers here. I rested my hand on Momma's tombstone, hoping to get some insight as to what I should do, but as usual Momma was quiet.

I was on my own here.

And for the first time since Momma died, I wasn't okay being alone.

Chapter 8

Kymra

I awoke in my cell like I had been doing for quite some time now. It was hard to know how many days had truly passed because I haven't seen outside since I came here. The only light I got each day was from a tiny slot in the window, but even then a dark shadow seemed to cover it during the day now. The only indication a day had passed was the moonlight that the Nightlocke allowed through. I don't know why I bothered trying to count my days. All I did was sleep anyways.

Food would appear everyday at some point, but the plain boiled beef was starting to get to me. If I never ate beef again, it would be too soon. I had yet to see the Nightlocke since my outburst, where he showed me what we could do and how terrifying he could truly be. I was grateful. I never wanted to see those shadow creatures again.

What I really needed though was a shower and new clothes, but I doubt I was going to get that anytime soon. If *ever. Prisoners don't exactly get cared for, now do they?* I thought bitterly as I played with the ends of my servants dress. You could barely see the white anymore. I was becoming frail and weak just sitting on the hard ground and not going to lie... I was bored out of my mind.

He suddenly appeared in front of my cell one day. No shadows or anything with him. Just him, and his eyes were his normal piercing blue. *It's funny how that was becoming my way of knowing what his mood was lately. It's funny that I was even getting to know him in the first place.*

"I thought you might like a change of scenery," he said quietly, and I slowly stood to my feet. My eyes narrowed. *Was he serious? He was letting me out of* here?

The Nightlocke opened the cell door and gestured towards the hall. When I refused to move, he cocked his head to the left. I wasn't sure if I was irritating him or confusing him by the look he was giving me, but this felt like some sick joke. *Why just let me out all of the sudden like this?*

The Nightlocke snarled at me, causing me to jump slightly. "Look, this isn't a kind gesture. You are stuck with me as I am with you, so you might as well earn your keep. If I am to feed you, then the least you can do is work for it."

My eyes widened. *And there's the punchline...* Rage burned through my veins as I glared at him. *He's the one who kidnapped me in the first place, and yet I'm required to cook and clean because he's stuck with me? Why continue to keep me here?!*

The corners of his mouth rose as if this was nothing more than fun and games for him.

"What is the matter now?" he asked in a clipped tone, crossing his arms as he leaned against the door.

"You took me in the first place, and now you want me to work? I didn't ask to come here, nor do I want to be a slave," I replied snidely.

He laughed loudly. "I'm sorry, but were you not already a slave to the King?"

My mouth dropped, but I quickly snapped it shut. His smirking only infuriated me more.

"The way I see it," he replied as he took a step closer, "not much has changed for you, so let's be a good girl and get to work."

I snapped.

"I *volunteered* for the rations program to feed my family. You stole me away, which means the King more than likely won't continue to send my father any food because I'm not there to physically do the work! Are you planning to feed my family then? Otherwise, everything's changed for me, Nightlocke!"

He frowned, watching me with such scrutiny that I was starting to get a little nervous. *At least they haven't darkened yet.* I should have kept my mouth shut, but here I was digging another hole for my grave.

CHAPTER 8

The longer I looked at him the more I realized how handsome the Nightlocke really was. *He couldn't have been much older than I was,* I thought before I remembered he was immortal. His age seemed frozen at a low 20 if I gad to guess, and he was definitely well built by the way his arms looked. *I could only imagine how good he looked under that shirt...* Suddenly my cheeks turned multiple shades of red. The Nightlocke was a *murderer. A person who took pleasure in other's pain and suffering, and I was checking him out?* This wasn't a man capable of even reciprocating those feelings. He stole me away and hurt me.

"I have no desire to feed anyone, let alone you. I chose not to kill you, and I missed my marks that night, so you will work for me at my castle in exchange for your life and the marks you ruined. This is not up for debate. Now move your feet or I'll make you start in the ruins instead."

"The ruins?"

"Do you not hear their screams, Kymra?" he replied, and my eyes widened. He continued stepping closer to me. The shadows swirling between the two of us as he said, "My army needs fed. They are basically animals now, and you are nothing but a weak girl. How long do you think you'll last down there? Think carefully, Kymra. I am being nice now."

Disbelief filled my face, and another scream echoed in the room. I forced myself to move towards the door. I didn't want to get close enough for him to touch me, and I didn't want to travel through the shadows ever again. I was afraid he'd yank me close and disappear to another part of the castle before I could object.

I had no way to trust this man other than to go ahead blindly. He could simply change his mind and toss me below, and there would be nothing I could do to stop it. I just prayed he wouldn't. Their screams and wailing were terrifying enough as it was, and maybe just obeying would be enough to keep myself from doom. I stepped out of the cell and scooted to the other side, waiting to follow the monster of the dark. His smirk irritated me, but I kept my mouth shut. The closer we got to the main floor, the less screaming I could hear from below, and I had never felt more grateful in my life for that.

I shuddered imagining his army down there, and I prayed they remained trapped below. My cell's iron gate door suddenly became my new best friend as it would keep the army at bay if they ever got out.

As I followed him up the stone stairs, I noticed the tattoos on his arm and neck. They were very detailed and *very* dark in nature. The lines twisted and curved, following his each and every muscle on his arm and traveling all the way down to his hand. As we walked, I could see the tattoo spread onto his fingers even. No one ever wore ink on their skin, I thought as we went up the last flight of stairs.

He guided me back through the first room, and I couldn't help but hesitate, remembering when his shadow creatures attacked me. They way they tore my clothes, slicing my skin as their sharp nails slashed the air. My hand drifted to the scab now on my arm.

"You coming?" he snapped, and I jumped at the sound of his voice.

I scurried after him, refusing to open my mouth and say something to piss him off. He grunted annoyingly as I stepped through the open door, and we continued down the hall, giving me a better look at this place. *The castle was falling apart,* I thought to myself as I looked around. *It needed some desperate repairs in some spots but most of the place looked like it just needed a good cleaning.* We passed by an empty throne room, and I wondered if this was his place. *Or did he just find it abandoned and moved in?* A sickening thought occurred to me then. *What if he slaughtered everyone before taking the castle for himself?* I shuttered, trying not to think about it further.

At the very end of the hall was a kitchen of sorts. It was old but surprisingly clean in here. *It must be one of the few places he frequented often,* I thought to myself. The Nightlocke walked around the island and pulled a slab of raw meat from the cabinet.

He grabbed a knife, and I watched him slice the meat with ease, but *all* I could think about was how easily it would be to slice someone open with that knife. *Had he use that knife on someone before?* My eyes widened as a thousand different questions ran through my head. He noticed me watching him, and he set the knife down slowly.

"I promise, I won't hurt you, Kymra," he said quietly.

"You already have so forgive me for not trusting you, Nightlocke," I snapped before slamming my mouth shut. His eyes narrowed in frustration, and I waited for the lashing to come.

"Arthur."

I blinked.

"What?"

"My *name* isn't Nightlocke. It's Arthur," he answered before picking up the knife again. He started chopping the meat more forcefully this time, while I processed what he just said. *He had a name. A normal sounding name, and he told me. Why would he tell me? Why would he care that I knew his name?*

That pull towards him came back then. It burned inside my chest, and I couldn't understand why I felt this way about *him*. He was cruel, so why should I care to help him? Why would he *need* saving? That drawl began to ache in my chest, and I forced myself to speak. I had to do something to distract myself.

"Would do you want me to do then?" I asked.

The Nightlocke stopped moving as his eyes slowly dragged to mine. He studied me a moment before dropping the knife and gestured for me to step forward.

"Start with the meal," he grunted, stepping away from the counter.

"Do you have anything else than meat?" I asked, making a face at the giant slab sitting on the counter. He just grunted instead of answering me, and I nearly rolled my eyes. *He seemed to communicate a lot like that,* I thought as I looked around the kitchen. The Nightlocke pointed to another cabinet, and I slowly made my way over and opened it. Inside were *plenty* of vegetables, fresh herbs, and even freshly baked bread.

I was in awe.

Where did he get all this? And why is he just now bringing it out? I thought annoyed that I had been eating nothing but boiled meat for what seemed like forever. I bit my lower lip to keep myself from lashing out. He must have seen the questions written on my face because he smirked at me and crossed his arms.

"It's not that hard to steal from *your* King," he replied quietly.

My mouth dropped open before I quickly shut it. *So he's a thief too?* I thought, rolling my eyes when my back was towards him. *How original...*

I ignored that piece of information and went back to making dinner. I grabbed carrots, potatoes, and an onion and started chopping everything on an old block of wood. I started a fire, throwing everything in a large pot and doing my best to ignore the brooding man behind me. It didn't take long for the pot to get hot, and I chopped garlic, while the rest cooked. It felt good to be doing something instead of sitting it that awful cell, and before long I started to hum to myself. It was just a silly song my mother used to sing, but it was comforting humming the melody. It wasn't until I noticed the Nightlocke, or *Arthur*, staring at me so intensely that I realized I never asked him what I was supposed to make in the first place. I had just started working on a pot roast and fear gripped my heart that I made a mistake.

"I'm sorry," I stammered. "I should have asked what you wanted instead of..."

"It's fine," he said, interrupting me. Suddenly, he stormed out of the room abruptly, leaving me alone in the kitchen.

I waited a moment to see if was coming back to scold me or something, but he never did. Sighing, I focused on preparing the meal instead of that dark man. *This man had everything though,* I thought to myself as I added salt to the food. Salt was a luxury that I certainly couldn't afford, and pretty soon the whole room smelled amazing. My mouth watered watching everything cook in the pot. I toasted the bread and found bowls in the cabinet. I jumped when I turned around to find the broody man just staring at me from the doorway.

"I made a pot roast," I said, breaking the silence. "I hope it's acceptable to you."

"It's fine," he said quietly back.

I cocked my head to the side as I watched him. He seemed unsure as to what to even do now, and I stood there waiting because I was *not* about to make the first move. The Nightlocke just stared at the plate in front of him, and I wondered when the last time he ate a home cooked meal like this. *I just assumed the boiled meat was another form of punishment for me, but maybe it was all he knew how to do?* Pity filled my heart before I shook myself from those thoughts. *I didn't need to understand the Nightlocke nor did I need to help him. I needed to find a way to go home.* I rubbed my hands together as my nerves rattled me. My stomach rumbled, and I stared at my bowl. *God, I was hungry… I just wanted to eat.*

"Do you want me to eat in my cell?" I asked quietly.

He glared, snatching one of the bowls from the counter. "I don't care where you go at the moment. Just make sure this place is cleaned spotless, and stay out of my way."

The Nightlocke grabbed a pile of bread before storming out with his bowl, and I stood there in shock. My hands clenched into tight fists. *I don't know why I felt the need to help him. I understood when I was pushed to help those less fortunate, but this monster?*

I hated that this always happened to me. I hated this *gift,* if you could call it that. *It's been like this for as long as I could remember.* Just a pull towards someone suffering or in need, and if I tried to ignore the pull then it became painful in my chest. Like my heart was *physically* breaking if I didn't help them. It didn't stop until I finally caved and helped the person out the best I could. *But why him?* The Nightlocke left a trail of blood and misery wherever he went. For the first time in my life, I was genuinely angry I wanted to help him. But even now as I stared at the empty doorway, I couldn't help but think he just seemed like a very lonely and damaged individual, and for some reason that *bothered* me.

At least for now I could eat in peace.

I pulled a chair up to the counter, deciding to just eat here. I groaned when I took that first bite. *My God, it was the best thing I had eaten in a long time,* I thought to myself as I licked my spoon. *Even better than that breakfast with the royal family.* I frowned, shoving those memories away as I dipped my bread in the juice, not leaving anything behind. I didn't want to think about Thomas or the Nightlocke. I just wanted peace…

After cleaning the kitchen from dinner, I waited in my seat for the Nightlocke to return me to my cell. After an hour I began to wonder if he was ever coming back. I slowly looked to the open door. *Might as well explore the castle. The Nightlocke never said I couldn't.* Grinning, I left the room and stepped out to the empty hallway.

I followed the long hall back the way we came but instead of returning to that first room, where he showed his true colors, I turned left. *I already know what lies that way,* I thought as I rounded the corner. I made my way down to the very end and decided to brave opening a door. On the left was a large wooden door, and I grunted as I pushed it open. *God, it was so freaking heavy...*

But then my jaw dropped.

The Nightlocke had a magnificent library, with tall ceilings and shelves full of books from top to bottom. A large fireplace sat along the back wall, with large cushioned chairs scattered throughout the room. Everything was covered in a thick layer of dust, and the curtains were drawn closed, making it extremely dark in here, but I was in heaven nonetheless. *Books were everywhere. I had never seen so many books in my life.* I loved reading, but I sold all my books a long time ago when we needed food, and the village didn't have *anything* like this available. In fact, they really didn't have anything at all.

I took a step towards the luxury, when I froze. *Would he be mad I was in here?* A small smile curved on my lips. *He did say I needed to clean this place, and I finished the kitchen already.* He never told me *where* I was supposed to go next so technically I wasn't really disobeying anything by being in this room. Although, I knew there was no way I'd be walking away from all these books. No matter what lie I told myself.

I took advantage of the quiet and closed the door behind me. I went straight for the windows. *We needed light in here if I were to read... I mean clean.* It took all my strength to move the massive curtains, but I managed to pull them back, letting in a tremendous amount of light. I smiled wide.

I opened every curtain in this room, taking in how beautiful this library truly was, and started wiping away all the dust I found. I was quickly becoming covered in a thick layer of grim that came off of everything, but I didn't care. My fingers scanned every shelf, finding books on every subject imaginable. I was in my own world, when suddenly darkness filled the room, and I jumped.

Shadows moved throughout the room, covering everything in a thick layer of black before heading straight towards the windows. They blocked every inch of light that came through, leaving me in utter darkness again. My mouth dropped, and I turned to find the Nightlocke standing in the door frame with his arm raised.

"I don't believe I gave you permission to enter this room nor did I allow you to let in the light," he gruffly said, stomping over to me. My anger flared as I stared at the shadows blocking the light. I turned, gritting my teeth as he towered over me.

"You never said I wasn't allowed to!" I shouted. "You told me to clean, and that's what I'm doing!"

The Nightlocke snapped his mouth shut, *knowing* I was right. He narrowed his dark eyes on me, and I watched the wheels turn in his mind as he tried to figure out how to get the upper hand here. I just glared. I was so angry being here with him. I was *so* angry for being scolded for no reason at all.

"I don't like the light!" he finally bellowed angrily.

I scoffed. "Well, I do! I need to be able to see what I am doing anyways!"

His ragged breaths were the only sound in the room, and suddenly I just snapped.

"What is your deal with the light anyways? Does it hurt you or something?" I asked him, and he rolled his eyes.

"Nothing hurts me, little one," he snarled back.

"Then why does it matter if I let the light in this *one* room? If you don't like it, then you can leave!"

Shadows flooded the room, swarming the two of us, and I held my breath. My heart thundered in my chest as he stepped closer, towering over me until my back hit the wall.

"Do not forget to whom you speak!" he snarled. His voice sounded different mixed with the dark, and my lip quivered. "This is my castle, and what *I* say goes. I never gave permission to allow the light inside, and you dare speak to your Master like this?! Maybe I should have just killed you in that garden like I should have done?! I would have saved myself the headache that is *your existence* and still got the marks I needed to get that night!"

Tears filled my eyes, and my bottom lip quivered hard. His words felt as cruel and as painful as if he pierced my chest with that knife. *I didn't do anything wrong... I don't deserve this.*

His blue eyes suddenly returned as a tear rolled down my cheek. I tried with all my might to hold them back, and I watched as confliction swept across his face. The Nightlocke rubbed his face roughly and opened his mouth, but no words came out. Instead, he snapped it shut, clenching his jaw and shaking his head angrily.

Suddenly, he disappeared into his shadows, leaving me alone in the library. I collapsed in the chair as tears finally fell down my face. *This isn't fair,* I thought as my heart broke in two. *I was a good person. I did everything for everyone. Why is this my life? Why does everyone seem to hate me?* Suddenly, I just couldn't stay here any longer, and I got to my feet and ran.

I was leaving, and I didn't care if he caught me. I fumbled through that first room and managed to find the grand entrance just past it.

I refuse to stay here any longer, and into the woods I went.

Chapter 9

The Nightlocke

I had never eaten anything as amazing as the meal she made for us. Watching Kymra cook was too much. She moved around the room like she owned the place, and I hadn't seen anything like this since Momma. I bolted out of that room as fast as I could. Anger coursed through my veins, burning the shadows within because I told her my *real name.* No one *knew* my name. The last time I heard someone say my name was my momma, and it was right before she slipped into a coma and never woke up again. Yet here I was telling *Kymra.*

I knew better.

She was becoming a weakness for me, and I didn't know how to handle it.

I stayed away from her, trying to clear my head to no avail. Even my shadows were itching to find her again, and they got the better of me and pushed me to finally go. Guilt ate at me for just leaving her alone in the kitchen, and I'm sure she was probably lost. This castle was massive, and this was her first real time out of her cell. My guilt turned to shame just thinking about putting her back down there, and I growled, darkening my eyes as I stepped through the veil. *I shouldn't feel bad for keeping her there.* That's where prisoners *belong.*

The kitchen was emaculate as I stepped through the veil, but it was empty. I walked around the room slowly. My hand running along the spotless counter towards the heavy outer door. I frowned. The bolts my shadows held in place were still there. *So where was she?*

My shadows pushed to be released, and I let them go. They seemed to be in tuned with the girl for some reason, so I followed them to the opposite end of the castle and in the library of all places. My eyes widened when I stepped through the doorway. The whole room was lit up with tremendous light, and my blood boiled. I wasn't used to this much light being in my home. I wasn't used to all *this*, and I let my temper flare.

This was too much.

The light was too *much*.

She was *too* much.

And it needed to stop.

My shadows shot out from my hand, startling her as they covered the windows once more. I exhaled deeply when the dark returned, and then I rolled my shoulder and stormed towards her.

"I don't believe I gave you permission to enter here nor did I allow you to let in the light," I bellowed.

"You never said I wasn't allowed to!" she shouted right back. Her nose scrunched in fury, and suddenly I was all too distracted by her full lips and rosy cheeks. "You told me to clean, and that's what I'm doing!"

My mouth dropped. *God, she was right,* I thought angrily as I snapped my jaw shut, clattering my teeth as I did. I knew I was being a jerk, but I clung to my anger and the dark fiercely. It was all I had left. I shook my head, trying to figure out how to get the upper hand again, but I didn't know what I was doing. I wasn't *treating* her like a normal prisoner even. I had never kept one alive long enough to know what I'm doing! My temper flared again, and I settled the panic rising within me. She was screwing with my head, and I needed to *fix* that.

"I don't like the light!"

"Well, I do!" she hollered again. That adorable nose scrunched even further, and my heart *responded*. My eyes widened slightly as my heart fluttered inside my chest and panic surged even more. *I shouldn't think she's being adorable. I shouldn't be attracted to her...* But I was.

"I need to be able to see what I am doing anyways!"

She seemed as angry as I was, but I was slowly losing steam. I didn't know what I was even doing here. *What was the harm in letting in the light? I never*

CHAPTER 9

told her she couldn't do these things. I'm only being a jerk because she's *freaking* me out. But she hadn't had enough. She stepped closer and started shouting back at me.

"What is your deal with the light anyways?! Does it hurt you or something?"

"Nothing hurts me, little one," I snapped back, but she pushed forward, forcing me to step back. I had *never* had someone even dare to approach me, and it scared me half to death when she pushed again. *A tiny girl was scaring me half to death.*

"Then why does it matter if I let the light in this *one* room? If you don't like it, then you can leave!"

I snarled then, and my shadows reacted. They poured out around us, rising with my uncontrollable temper, and she finally seemed frightened with me. *But she needed more to learn her place here.* I needed to learn where she belonged. I advanced towards her until her back hit the wall and terror had filled her eyes.

"Do not forget to whom you speak to! This is my castle, and what *I* say goes. I never gave permission to allow the light inside, and you dare speak to your Master like this?! Maybe I should have just killed you in that garden like I should have done?! I would have saved myself the headache that is *your existence* and still got the marks I needed to get that night!"

She flinched worse than if I had physically struck her. All the fight left me in that moment. When her beautiful eyes filled with tears, and her lip quivered, I remembered finding her that first night looking so broken. I was ready to destroy anyone and anything that did that to her in that moment, yet here I was the one inflicting pain. My guilt tore me up inside, and my shadows suddenly left me. I felt vulnerable as I stood here watching the fallout from losing my temper. I was exposed, alone, and afraid. *Like before...*

I was not the Nightlocke in this moment.

I was just Arthur.

And he was never good enough.

I stepped through the veil, disappearing to the safety of my room. My chest constricted under all this guilt and shame, and I couldn't keep my feet still. I immediately started pacing back and forth because this was *way* too much to handle.

She was too much!

I needed to just cut her loose. I couldn't handle her being here after all. I lifted my hand to command my shadows but froze. The thought of returning her to that life at the castle killed me. I wouldn't be able to protect her there. I wouldn't be able to keep that prick from touching her again, and that possessive, dominating feeling I'd been experiencing these past few days rose to new heights and I dropped my hand. *I can't do it...* Groaning, I rubbed my face and started pacing again. *What was I going to do?*

I stopped dead in my tracks when I realized that I haven't tormented anyone other than that Prince since she arrived. I froze. *I hadn't thought about any marks, nor have I collected another vessel for my army,* I thought as my eyes widened. *I've done nothing but leave the kingdom in peace for weeks because of her.*

All because of her.

I haven't thought about my rage or anger with them. I've not even cared about it once, being too consumed by her and her presence alone. She was changing everything in me, and I didn't know how I felt about it. *Could I really let go of my anger just like that? Could I honestly be okay with just being Arthur instead of the Nightlocke?*

I abruptly stepped through the veil, leaving my room and the castle entirely. I let my shadows take me to a place I *never* wanted to visit again. In a far off part of the forest, where I watched my mother die, sat what was left of the first Nightlocke's home.

I stared at the broken remains of this haunted place and tried not to let myself shake. Down below the earth was the Nightlocke's private room full of his personal effects. It was fully preserved in the dark, and I only found his room when I let my shadows out to explore the woods. I had only ever stepped foot in here once before, and I didn't stay for very long. The evil in this room was thick, and I hated being in here. You could just feel his anguish and pain the moment you stepped inside, and that was nothing compared to the memories I had of this place. He took *everything* from me before, but now he may be able to assist me.

CHAPTER 9

I stepped through the veil and into the underground room. Goosebumps covered my arms as I went through the small room, trying to find anything that was of any use. I moved to the trunk first, finding nothing but extremely dusty cloaks that he once wore. I covered my nose because they honest to God still reeked of blood. I carefully tossed them aside, wiping my hands on my pants before moving on. There was nothing left in the trunk, so I stomped over to the bookshelf. *This place made my skin crawl...*

I quickly discovered the man liked to write. Like *a lot*. Most of the books here were just old journals. I tossed the guide book on different plants and herbs and the one concerning mythical beasts of old. *Neither of those would help me.* I groaned when I realized I'd have to just read the coot's old journals to get anywhere. Flipping through the first book, I grimaced when I realized he had let himself go completely to the darkness. *He began to lose his mind rather quickly.*

"Nightlockes need balance..."

Ya-da, ya-da, ya, I thought as I chucked that book. *I'm as balanced as I can be.* I paused at I opened the next book.

"There's a way for us not to lose our minds. We don't have to lose who we are."

It would be nice if you said what we needed, I thought as I flipped to the next page.

"I am the heart of the forest, and I belong to a grand race of powerful men and women. Even if I am alone."

I rolled my eyes. *That's a load of crap.* I'm simply the only person who can safely navigate these woods, but I guess it did make sense as to why I felt more at home here than I did anywhere else.

"You need to have a heart before you can be the heart of something," I muttered to myself. I flipped to the next page.

"The darkness connects everything here with the Nightlocke being it's center. We were made to protect the dark."

Yeah... Because that was super clear and made perfect sense, I thought to myself.

God, all I wanted to know was why I was obsessed with this girl... I winced the second that thought left my head. *It had gotten to that point, hadn't it?* I sighed and grabbed another book. I wasn't going to comment on that thought anymore. I flipped through the pages, sighing as I went. *All this man seemed to do was kill, torture his victims, and write.*

I grabbed another book after turning slightly green by his last torture method of liquefying his victims from the inside out, when I found something that made me freeze. Deadly Nightshade. I was immortal and nothing could kill me because of the shadows I possessed. *That much I already knew.* My shadows would simply stitch me back together if I was gravely injured, and I did not get sick like most people did, but his next passage made me pale.

"*It's the only way possible to kill a Nightlocke. Deadly Nightshade would always kill our kind. There was no cure, and Nightshade was once highly sought after by the kingdom. Because a person could steal the shadows from another.*"

My eyes widened reading that.

Someone could steal my shadows? I thought as my stomach dropped. *They'd become a new Nightlocke entirely.* My mind drifted back to that horrid day when I inherited the shadows. I was 15, and I had stabbed the Nightlocke in the chest with one of his daggers. I always wondered how I was able to kill that man when nothing would kill me, but now I knew. He had covered every weapon in that room with Nightshade so no matter what I chose, it would kill him.

Bile rose to the back of my throat as the memories of that day split my head in two. I couldn't go down that road again, so I forced those thoughts from my mind and quickly went back to the book. I needed to know *everything* about my one apparent weakness.

"*It is poisonous to our skin, and it would kill us slowly if ingested. According to the scrolls I found near Agnimeru, it will eat away at a Nightlocke from the inside out just like acid. The fastest death would always be with a blade through the heart.*"

I slumped to the floor. My stomach twisted inside as I stared at the passage. *All this time I thought nothing could touch me...* This whole time knowledge about something this *important* just sat here for the taking. I felt stupid and arrogant for leaving it to chance for so long, and I shoved that book in my pocket, deciding to keep it close to me instead. *I wasn't going to make that mistake again.*

I went back to the journals with a new sense of purpose. *What else did the crazy old coot know?* I still needed to know why I was so drawn to Kymra too. But I was running out of journals. Only a few were left on the shelf, and I tried not to let myself worry that I wouldn't be able to find the answers I need. Not yet at least. I opened the next journal, and my eyes widened. *Something drew him in.* I quickly scanned the passage. He got a glimpse of perfection, and it pulled his shadows in. The pen marks were deep now. Like he had pushed the quill down in anger, splattering ink across the page.

"I have found happiness, but it's locked away. Out of reach."

My eyes narrowed. *I could go anywhere I wanted with my shadows.* There was no place that could keep me out if I had a line of sight or a memory to pull from. *Either he didn't know the full extent of his power or something else was blocking him from it. What could stop us though?* It wasn't like Nightshade was common knowledge otherwise I'm sure the King would have raided my castle long ago, sacrificing whomever to kill me. *Right?*

I was missing something.

I thought back to the day the first Nightlocke tricked me into killing him. He said he could not bear what he had done and chose me to take the burden instead. I could not remember the details anymore though and that angered me greatly. *I only saw his memories once, and even then they didn't stick in my head!* I threw the journal at the wall, sending a plum of dust throughout the room. I rubbed my face, knowing the answer was right in front of me. *What was I missing?!* I looked back to the shelf, finding one *last* journal. I sighed and reached for the book.

My eyes widened.

Written on every page of this book was one word. Just one word over and over again.

Julianna.

It was like everything clicked then. The tiny bit that I could remember from his memories flashed before my eyes. I watched him slaughter *everyone* in the castle. He cut them down like it was nothing, and I had nearly forgotten about it till now. I've been lost in my own revenge all these years, but he killed Julianna. He *loved* her, yet he killed her.

I searched my own mind, trying to see her face, but everything was so hazy. The shadows seemed to let go of the memory entirely once they bonded me, and I groaned as I went over everything from that night. *His journal said he needed balance, and that she was his happiness,* I thought as I picked up the previous book, scanning the words again. His emotions were clear in my memory despite the memory being fuzzy. He loved her, and then went to all the trouble of tricking me into killing him with Nightshade when she died. He used Momma and I because he *lost* her and couldn't live with that. My mind ran amuck until suddenly a fragment of that night came to mind. He burnt his hand when he touched Julianna's fallen body. Her wide, lifeless eyes staring back at him. The searing pain from touching her...

I sunk to the floor as the rest of his story fell into place. The King's land went dead after that night. I never once paid any attention to it but...

This was a problem.

Julianna was the Lightspark.

She was the reason everything grew for the King, and she was the Nightlocke's love. He burned when he touched her, and I slowly pulled the book back out of my pocket. I turned back to the page about the Deadly Nightshade.

It burns our skin.

It kills us, and somehow Julianna was coated in the stuff. The King knew about the Nightshade and kept her locked away, where his shadows could not reach, and the Nightlocke went mad because he could not save her without killing himself. My eyes went wide. It's why he was so unstable that night.

I'm drawn to Kymra like he was drawn to Julianna.

Julianna was the Nightlocke's balance with the darkness.

Julianna was the Lightspark.

Does this mean Kymra is the new Lightspark?

I couldn't stop the endless questions that flooded my mind. Everything made sense now, and I was foolish for not knowing sooner. My anger ignited my shadows as I thought how reckless I had been acting because I thought I was untouchable. And Kymra lived and worked in that castle! *If the King had known...*

CHAPTER 9

I shook myself from those thoughts as I paced the room. *She can never go back.* I don't care that she's never showed any signs of being a Lightspark. Kymra can *never* leave the Forbidden Woods.

Suddenly, my shadows were on high alert. *Something was wrong,* I thought as I listened to the woods around me. The shadows of the land echoed in my mind, and I waited, listening for the danger that had my shadows agitated. But then I heard a scream pierce the air, and my heart stopped because I recognized that scream.

It was Kymra!

Chapter 10

Kymra

The forest was unusually dark, and I struggled to make heads or tails of where I was. We moved with his shadows when we first came here, but now I was completely lost and had no idea where his castle even was. I had gone far enough that I couldn't even get back there, and my heart thundered in my chest with every sound the forest made.

This was not good.

The Forbidden Woods was banned to the villagers from entering. It was lost years before my parents were even born to the foul beasts that lay within. Only the strongest ever dared to enter, but when they stopped coming back, the King placed a ban from *anyone* traveling that way. It was the King's favorite way to execute the ones he deemed unfit to live, and now I know why. *This place is horrible.* Absolutely *wretched.*

Another snarl sounded behind me, and my made my feet move faster. Something very large was on my trail, and I was struggling to stay far enough ahead of him. *If I didn't have this God forsaken dress on I might be able to run faster!*

God, I was foolish.

I left one evil only to be found by another.

The Nightlocke at least hadn't killed me, while this beast surely would. I should have just dealt with *His Royal Grumpiness* and at least stayed alive.

I barely stole a glimpse behind me, and I screamed at the sight. My heart raced at the beast behind me, and I could not tell if this was a man or a *beast.* It stood well over 9 feet tall, with a massive fangs sticking past it's upper lip and dark fur covering its body. It snarled and howled like a wolf but ran upright on two legs like a human. It roared again, and my body shook with fear. *It was most definitely not a human!* I had never heard of a beast like this before, and I tried to make my feet move faster, but I was running out of steam. And this God forsaken dress was slowing me down! The corset made it hard to take a deep breath, and I was already gasping for air as it was.

I looked behind me again and stumbled forward. I screamed as the bark of a fallen log sliced open my hands, and the earth shook behind me. The scent of blood seemed to send the beast into a frenzy, and I forced myself back to my feet. He was *right* behind me as I shot past the thick foliage. *I wasn't going to make it out of here.*

The forest opened up to a sunny spot, and I skidded to a stop to keep from tumbling off the cliff side, but I was running too fast. I dug my nails into the dirt as my feet dangled over the edge. The scream died in my throat as gravity tugged my legs down, but I managed to stop myself from going all the way over. I let out the breath I had been holding, pulling myself back over, when the beast flew into the clearing. He's hollered loudly, blocking the sun from his eyes before settling back on me.

I looked over the edge to the massive drop below, which was most definitely not an option. *The only way back was passing right by the beast,* I thought to myself as my chest heaved. *There was no way I'd make it.* My shoulders fell, and in a last ditch effort to save myself, I searched the ground for anything I could use. I grabbed a rock barely bigger than my hand and threw it shouting, "GO AWAY!"

The beast snarled, unphased by the rock hitting his chest, and then he lunged for me. My eyes widened, and I screamed again as his sharp nails dug into my ankle. He began dragging me towards him. Saliva dripped from his mouth, and I nearly gagged at the rotten stench coming from him. His nails dug in deeper. Warm blood trickled from the wound, and my ankle burned in agony. A sob escaped my lips as his large paw hovered over my face.

Suddenly, he took a swipe, and I screamed as his claws shredded my skin. Three large gashes appeared across my chest and shoulder. *Everything* hurt, and I panicked at the sight of blood trickling from the wound. The creature roared in my face, and I shut my eyes tight, waiting for the final blow.

Except it didn't come.

A sickening crunch sounded, and my eyes opened to find a long black sword piercing through the creature's chest. The sword was *inches* from my face, and the creature slumped as it took its final breath. Blood dripped from the sword as my body shook. I couldn't stop shaking from the terror currently coursing through my veins. The creature's body was abruptly hauled off me and thrown across the yard. In front of me stood my savior.

The Nightlocke.

He came for me, I thought as we stared at one another. I didn't even know what to even say to the man. *He was the villain in our story... But he saved me.* Why?

I was enthralled watching the Nightlocke before me. His shadows shifted with the wind, and I held my breath when they came to me. They inspected every wound, hissing as they looked me over before returning to their master.

The Nightlocke didn't look happy under that heavy hood, and he took a step towards me. Suddenly multiple howls rattled the woods behind us, and he stilled. He turned as my heart thundered in my chest. Nearly a dozen more of those creatures shot through the brush, snarling when they looked upon the body of the creature Arthur threw to the side. He casually twirled his sword, waiting for them to make the first move, and his shadows swarmed around his feet. My eyes widened when they came to me then.

The pack howled, running towards Arthur, but he was ready for them. Arthur moved so fast that I couldn't track him with my eyes. He'd disappear in the dark, and then suddenly appear in an entirely different place. *He was traveling by his shadows,* I realized as I watched him take on the pack. *Just like when we moved across the forest when he took me.* Arthur sliced limbs from their bodies with ease. He dove out of reach of their sharp claws, and all I could do was watch. Watch him risk his life to *save* me. He was flawless, and I began to question everything I knew about this man.

One of the creatures got past him, and I screamed. It lunged for me, when Arthur abruptly turned, launching his sword through the air and striking the creature in its heart. I dove to the side, narrowly missing the sword as the creature fell over me. It's weight had my legs pinned down, and I tried to tug them free. My eyes widened as I turned to Arthur again. Without his sword the shadows came out to play. *He was memorizing.* I realized how badly I wanted to be like that. *I didn't want to be some damsel in distress.*

My heart stopped when those shadows creatures he had made before stood tall. They were just as awful as I remember, and I watched in horror as they lunged, shredding the beasts around their Master. *What he did to me was child's play compared to this right now.* They were dismembering the creatures left and right. Skinning them alive, and I watched completely terrified at the gory sight before me. All while Arthur *smiled*. But then Arthur turned, and a creature rushed him from behind.

"ARTHUR LOOK OUT!" I screamed, but it was too late. Arthur's eyes went wide as the creature's claws pierced his shoulder and chest. He yelled, pulling his shadows back towards him. They wrapped around the creatures head, and with one quick motion, they snapped it's neck. The forest finally fell into silence again. My eyes were glued to Arthur. He staggered a bit in his stance, and my heart began to race. My chest burned to run to him. To help *him*.

"No, no, no!" I shouted as he dropped to his knees. I heaved the creature off my legs, breaking my back in the process of getting free. I hobbled over to Arthur, who was knelt over and breathing hard.

"Arthur! Please let me help you!" I shouted, kneeling down to him. His eyes were bright blue when they looked to me.

"Kymra..." he said with a raspy voice, but I quickly shushed him.

"Tell me where to go, *please*. You need help," I said, putting pressure on his wound. His blood covered my hands, and my lip began to tremble. *I could not be the reason for his death!* I thought as I stifled a sob. I don't know why I felt so strongly, but I *had* to save him. *He saved me after all.*

Arthur seemed nervous with me being so close, but then his eyes dropped to the wound on my chest.

"You're hurt," he said softly.

"You are hurt far worse," I stammered, unable to keep my voice from shaking. "Please tell me what to do to help you. You should not die because of my stupidity."

"Hold on," he whispered.

Arthur wrapped his hands around my waist, and my breath caught in my chest. He covered us in his shadows, and I buried my face in his neck as he moved us. The wind was nearly unbearable, but I was starting to get used to it. We slammed to a stop back in his castle, and I never thought I'd be relieved to be back here. I rushed to the kitchen for supplies. I had helped my father many times before, and Arthur had everything I'd need to help him now.

I filled a bucket of water and shredded rags into strips before grabbing the herbs and supplies I'd need to make the healing concoction. I barreled into the room, with him watching my every movement. He had moved to his chair and never said a word as I worked as quickly as I could. I mashed the herbs together, adding water to the bowl before setting everything in front of him.

"I need to remove your shirt," I said softly.

Arthur sat forward, removing it with one hand, and my eyes widened. All I could think as I stared at his perfectly sculpted torso was that this man was *gorgeous*. I could finally see his full tattoo, and I couldn't stop my eyes from roaming over every inch of it. Down his arm was a tribal tattoo, with jagged sharp lines that ran all the way to his fingers, but on his shoulder was a dragon. I had heard the legends and stories about those creatures that once roamed our land, but they had been extinct for years. It's tail followed down his arm slightly, while it's wings and head spread over his chest and back. As if *protecting* Arthur. Black swirls that looked like shadows surrounded it, and everything blended perfectly together.

I wanted to reach out and touch the work of art because that is what it was. *Beautiful* art, but my eyes met Arthur's, and I realized I'd just been staring at him. I jolted into action, willing my cheeks not to turn red as I dipped a rag in the water.

"This might hurt some," I whispered, and Arthur nodded.

He had five deep puncture wounds on the right side of his chest, and I quickly wiped away the blood. Thankfully they were not bleeding anymore, but I wondered why. *Arthur should be pouring out blood from a wound like this, but he wasn't.*

"You are hurt, Kymra," he said, pulling me from my thoughts. He grabbed my wrist, stopping me from continuing.

"I am fine, Arthur. Just let me help you," I replied quietly. My chest burned again.

"Why?"

Our eyes met, and my breath caught in my chest as I got lost in those beautifully blue eyes of his. But then guilt reared its ugly head again, and I dropped my gaze. "Because this is my fault, and I *need* to help you. I can't explain it anymore than that, Arthur. Please... Just let me."

I felt his intense gaze linger on me for a moment before finally letting me go, and I quickly dipped my hand in the healing mixture. I covered each wound carefully before wrapping his chest. The pain in my chest eased the moment I finished, and I went to stand, forgetting about my ankle. The adrenaline must have masked my pain earlier because I stumbled the moment I put weight on it. I gasped as my body crumbled, when two solid arms caught me. Arthur looked distraught, and I blinked in surprise. *I thought he hated my presence...* Worry lined his brow, and he effortlessly picked me up and gently set me down in his chair. Arthur knelt down to my eye level, and I was surprised by how gentle he could be.

"Kymra please... Tell me what I need to do to help you," he whispered, handing me the empty herb bowl.

"You want to heal me?" I asked quietly. My brows knitted as I could not believe what I was hearing. I had to ask. "Why save me today, Arthur? I've been nothing more than a headache to you, and you would have gotten your wish if you had simply left me out there with those monsters."

His face hardened, darkening ever so slightly, and I waited for the lashing to come. Except he dropped his head instead, as if in *shame.*

"I was harsh with you earlier, Kymra. You are *not* a problem to me," he said quietly, grabbing my supplies. He grabbed the herbs around us, mashing them together in the bowl rather roughly. "You are actually the first person I haven't wanted to kill."

My eyes widened. *Why... Why did that one slightly morbid sentence make me feel so special?* I sat forward, putting my hands on his and halting him entirely.

"Allow me," I whispered, and he slowly handed me the mortal and pestle.

I slowed my pace this time, letting him see how I pulled the herbs apart and which parts I used in the mixture. He watched my hands work closely and handed me water when I asked for it. Once it was done, I asked for a rag to clean the wound.

"Just let me," he said so quietly that I almost missed it. Arthur started with my foot and carefully cleaned the wound. It stung, but at least it shouldn't get infected now. Once it was free from dirt, grime, and whatever awfulness that came from that beast, he applied the mixture before wrapping it.

"I... Um... I should cleaned your arm now," he said, motioning to my chest. My face turned multiple shades of red then.

"I can do it, Arthur," I stammered. I would have to remove my dress in order to clean it entirely. To my dismay, he shook his head.

"You need new clothes anyways, and I only need to cut the sleeve off. I just don't want it to fall when I do. Can you... umm... Just hold it here?"

My face flushed with heat again as he pointed to the spot he wanted me to hold. Nerves rattled my body as this absolute gorgeous man removed a small knife from his boot and sliced my dress with ease. He tossed the knife aside as I lifted my arm up, and he carefully removed the sleeve. My arm was stiff and sore, but nowhere near as painful as I thought it would be. I looked down, and my eyes widened.

"Whoa..." I muttered softly. The wound was a lot smaller than I realized. *I could have sworn it was wider than it was though,* I thought to myself before noticing a worried expression on Arthur's face.

"You okay?" I asked quietly, and he shook himself from his thoughts.

"Yeah."

That was all I got as he quickly cleaned the blood and grime away and applied what was left of the mixture before wrapping it like I did for him.

"Hang tight," he commanded before stepping into the shadows and disappearing. I sat back in his chair in disbelief.

"He saved me," I whispered to myself. The corners of my mouth rose before he suddenly shot back into the room, and I jumped hard. He froze, scratching the back of his head as his lips pursed together.

"Sorry, I forget you aren't used to that. It's just only ever me here so..."

CHAPTER 10

Arthur quickly shut his mouth, but I could help but smile. *I liked seeing him babble like that. He was more like me than I realized.* I narrowed my eyes watching him. He seemed almost nervous around me when his shadows weren't out to play. My smile fell as I began to wonder just how long he's been alone. *I* was lonely here after the short time of being here, and I couldn't imagine how he must feel.

"I don't have women's clothing, but I can get you some. For now, you can wear this," he said as he held out one of his shirts.

"It's one of mine..." he muttered. "It's all I had."

I blinked again. Slowly, I took the shirt from him saying, "Thank you, Arthur."

He nodded once and waited. My eyes widened slightly and another blush crept up my cheeks.

"Arthur?"

"Yeah?"

"Can I have some privacy to change?" I asked nervously.

Arthur's face flushed, and he took a step away from me. I couldn't contain the grin from forming on my face as he stammered, "Of course."

Shadows filled the room, and he disappeared in them. I chuckled to myself as I began to discard my ruined clothes. *I had flustered the Nightlocke,* I thought as I tossed the dress to the floor. This scary man was *embarrassed*, and I would have never expected to see this side to him.

I wished more than anything for a shower, but the clean shirt was a huge improvement. His hooded shirt was surprisingly soft, and it came to about mid-thigh on me. I smiled, knowing how ridiculous I probably looked right now. But I didn't care. It was clean, and that was more than enough for me. I hobbled over to the table covered in supplies and found a thin piece of rope. I tied it around my waist, hoping I wouldn't look like I was swimming in his shirt and stepped towards the mirror to inspect my handy work. The corners of my mouth rose. I actually liked the way I looked wearing the dark shirt, and I slowly put the hood up. You couldn't see my face at all, and I grinned. *I get why he always wears this.*

Sighing, I stepped away from the mirror and looked around the room. I wasn't sure where to go from here. *He may have saved me today but that doesn't mean I'm free.* I wasn't sure what to make of the Nightlocke now.

No... Arthur.

Nightlocke no longer felt right for some reason.

I sat down in the large chair to get off my aching foot and pulled the hood forward a bit more. I shouldn't do anything without his permission. I already learned my lesson with that.

Exhaustion took over, and soon I had fallen asleep.

Chapter 11

Arthur

I paced back and forth in my room, unsure when I should go back to Kymra. Even though she was healing herself just like my body did, she was still hurt, and I *needed* to make sure she was okay. Seeing her get struck like that just about broke me today. Kymra came way too close to death, and I was not happy about it.

I changed my own shirt and tossed the bandages aside. My chest had completely healed, and I wiped the herb mixture off. Whatever she did with those herbs, she did it well because it felt amazing the second she put it on my skin. Little did she know she did not need to help me heal, but I needed to see if she was drawn to me like I was with her. I *wanted* to know if she would choose me, even if she hated me. I heard the Bloodhound behind me, and I let him strike, but I did not anticipate the scream of pure terror that came out of her. Then I was just mesmerized by how attentive she was despite *everything* I put her through. No one has ever cared for me like that before.

No one.

It was a selfish thing to do, but I couldn't stop myself watching her rush around the castle, trying to *help me.* I paced more in my room, struggling with the dark shadows pushing to be let out. To find *her* again.

She was a Lightspark.

I confirmed it on my way to save her. I discovered her blood on a fallen log, and everywhere in a 5 foot radius had flourished. The grass was bright green and was covered in beautiful flowers. Then when I saw her arm downstairs, and it was already halfway healed… It only proved it more.

She was my balance. My other half, and I nearly *lost* her today.

That was unacceptable, and I would not fail her again. I needed to keep her safe. Far away from everyone that would drain her dry to save themselves like the King did with Julianna. I paced the room, clenching my hands at my sides remembering all the King had done. *He would need to be dealt with at some point.*

First things first, I needed to take care of Kymra. Her powers were coming to light, and there would be no hiding it from her soon. I groaned as I rubbed my face in frustration. *How was I supposed to tell her about this? How was I supposed to tell her that she belonged to me just like I belonged to her?*

My behavior these past few weeks came to mind, and I cringed. The fear and hate in her eyes every time I stepped in the room. When she saw my shadows... She had seen my ways and felt my power first hand. *How was I supposed to convince her to stay now? How could I convince her I wasn't lost to the darkness entirely and that I wouldn't harm her again?* I groaned again. Already knowing the answers to those questions. I had made it my mission to scare her half to death and simply telling her I changed wasn't going to work. *This is utterly ridiculous.* Yet somehow we belonged together, and I wasn't letting her go.

Yup... I was selfish. Now that understood this pull between us, I *couldn't* let her go. But if she didn't stay with me... If she didn't *accept* me on her own accord then I would lose what little humanity I had left forever. I'd lose my mind to the dark and anxiety rippled through me as I thought about how dangerous I would truly then. My mind drifted to my army down in the ruins below, twisting my stomach as guilt ate me up inside. I had taken control of people, killing who they were in the process of turning them into the beasts I needed. They became like feral animals to do my bidding, and my bidding *alone*. It was an accident when I got revenge on the bar owner that turned on me long ago, and ever since I discovered what to do, I had been slowly building an army over the years, waiting for the perfect time to strike. I had planned to rid this world of the kingdom and it's pompous King, but it took a tremendous amount of power to change someone like that. The dark took over for a long time afterwards so I could not do it often. The feral creatures simply sat waiting for my command. *What would she think when she sees them?* I thought in agony. *Would she hate me further for it?*

I collapsed on my bed, tossing an arm over my face. She was a Lightspark, which meant she could heal the land and the people in it. The *opposite* of what I had been planning for them. Frankly, they all saw my mother and I suffering and never once tried to help us. I had seen it happen to countless people on the streets too. *Do I want even want her to save them?*

She would though. Once she knows what she is, Kymra would do whatever was needed to help them, even to her own detriment. *I mean she willingly volunteered to go into slavery to save her family...*

I shot forward suddenly.

Her family.

They were probably starving without those rations, I thought as guilt tore into me again. Without hesitation, I stepped into my shadows, appearing in my kitchen. I gathered all the supplies I could fit in a bag before stepping into the veil again. This time I appeared in a dark alley in the kingdom. It was dark outside, and thankfully everyone was shut in for the night. I let my shadows guide me, looking for her home.

As I stepped silently through the old alleys that used to be my home, I started to really take notice of the kingdom. Like my mind had cleared enough to really notice how broken and rundown everything was. *Far more than when I lived here,* I thought to myself, frowning as I turned the corner.

My shadows finally stopped at a small door, and I carefully tried the handle but something blocked the door from opening. Sighing, I placed my hand on the wooden door, and my shadows poured under the door and into the house. It was easy to see inside her home, and I moved the piece of wood blocking my path. The door opened with ease.

There was nothing fancy about this place, but it was clean, and I remembered how well Kymra took care of my home. I hated that I even demanded that of her and stepped further into the room. Soft snores sounded from one of the back rooms, and I carefully set the food on the table before sneaking back out. I closed the door, using my shadows to secure it again before disappearing back to my castle.

There. That should last them quite some time, I thought to myself, but I would need to pay a visit to the dear King again. Suddenly stealing from the King just became all the more dangerous. All these years, and I never knew he could have killed me if he ever found me. He somehow kept Julianna hidden against her will, and I nearly snarled picturing Kymra captured too. *To think, she was living there right under his nose, and he had no idea what she was.*

My shadows hissed at me, but I knew how they felt. We both *needed* to see Kymra. *It had been long enough,* I thought as I strolled down the hallway. I shoved the door open and stopped dead in my tracks when I found her. Kymra was curled up on my chair asleep. She didn't once stir, and that broke my heart. *She was spent.*

A smile curved on my lips as I drank in the sight of her. She looked *absolutely* adorable in my shirt, and I loved how she put the hood up just like I did. I didn't expect to feel so amused by that, but it made me feel good that she decided to wear it up like she matched me in some way now. I carefully knelt down beside her, moving a piece of fallen hair from her face, and she didn't bat an eye. Sighing, I scooped her up into my arms, and I looked briefly to the door that led to the cells below.

"Never again," I whispered, turning to the opposite door instead. I held her close, hoping not to wake her, but she only snuggle further into me. *God, she was perfect. Why did I fight this for so long?* My mind and body felt clear now that I understood who she was to me. I still felt powerful and strong but far more in control, and I could feel emotions I had never felt since gaining my power. Things like empathy, happiness, and one I never thought I would feel again... Love. Once I finally stopped fighting against the changes within me, it was like everything fell into place, and I could breathe. I had fallen hard for this girl, and I was determined in that moment to win her over.

I'd make her see the real me.

Someone worth saving.

I was nearly at my bedroom, when I halted. Despite wanting nothing more than to take her to my room and hold her all night while she slept, I didn't want to scare the girl when she woke. It felt like pulling teeth, but I forced my feet to enter the room across from mine. It was dusty and awful inside, and my heart sunk. *Well, now what do I do? She couldn't stay here either.* Shifting nervously on my feet, I decided to just take her to my room and let her take the bed. Kymra immediately rolled over to her side when I laid her down, and I covered her with my favorite fur blanket. I smiled, watching as she got cozy before making my way to the chair I kept in here. I grabbed another blanket, getting comfortable myself before leaning back and closing my eyes. *At least she was safe now,* I thought to myself. For the first time in my life, I slept sound.

Chapter 12

Kymra

I awoke in a mess of soft bedding and fur, feeling completely well rested for the first time in a *long* while. I stretched out my arms, my eyes fluttering open, when I realized I was no longer in the chair. *I was in a bed.* My eyes widened, and I shot forward, seeing a room I had never been in before. The window on my left had been boarded up, leaving the room as dark as can be, and I squinted my eyes, trying to make out the rest of the room. It was simple in here, with only a table and a chair on the other side, but then my gaze settled on the dark figure sitting on that chair.

Arthur.

Did he bring me here? He was sleeping in the chair, and I was surprised when he didn't stir. *I didn't even know the Nightlocke needed to sleep...* My mind ran amuck as I quickly scurried off the bed. *His* bed. I wasn't sure what to do now or where to go. *Do I leave before he wakes? Am I supposed to wait here for him to tell me what to do?*

Clearly running away wasn't an option, but yesterday was just weird. Arthur wasn't the same since he saved me. *Would he return to his normal brooding ways or was this a turning point for us?* My lips pursed together as I watched the man before me. My gaze settled on his exposed chest, when I suddenly remembered his wound.

It would need a new bandage today, I thought to myself, feeling my chest burn again. I just needed to make sure it was responding to the herb mixture I put on it. I took a step towards him but hesitated, feeling guilty about waking him up. *Maybe I could just take a quick peek without startling him awake?* Arthur never moved as I stepped quietly towards him. Carefully, I pushed his shirt to the side, trying to find the bandage, but it wasn't there. *Strange.* I frowned, pulling his shirt further to the side. *I know I wrapped the whole shoulder...*

Suddenly, he moved. His hand shot forward, grabbing my wrist and yanking me towards him. I sucked in a breath, when I felt cold steel pressed hard against my neck. The familiar sting of my skin getting sliced open happened, and my eyes widened. Arthur opened his dark eyes, which returned to his normal blue when he recognized me.

"Kymra..."

He immediately released me, and I stumbled backwards, clutching my neck. There was blood on my fingers when I pulled my hand away and horror rippled through me. *Arthur cut me.* He jumped to his feet, and I quickly scurried back from him.

"I'm sorry! I was only trying to check your wound!" I cried out, raising my hands to block his advance. My heart thundered in my chest, but Arthur surprised me yet again, when he tossed the knife aside, putting his hands up slowly.

"Forgive me, Kymra. I didn't know it was you," he said quietly as shame filled his face.

My eyes narrowed, but I didn't know what to say. *How do I even respond to this man now? Was this just a game to him? Get me to trust him just for the other shoe to drop?*

Arthur's eyes drifted to the blood on my neck. "Can I see?"

I bit my lower lip as I watched him. *No shadows were out now, and his eyes were still his breathtaking blue.* Reluctantly, I nodded my head. My eyes were glued to him as he slowly approached me, but he seemed almost *nervous* with me too. I carefully moved my head to let him see the cut and heard him sigh. He grabbed a rag from the table, putting it carefully against the wound.

"It's just a small cut, so it will heal quickly," he said softly. "Please forgive me, Kymra. I was startled, and my first reaction is..."

"Violence," I answered for him. I replaced his hand with mine and took a step back. "It was my fault anyways. I should have waited until you woke up. I just wasn't sure if you would let me check your wound and..."

My voice trailed off then. I wasn't sure if I should tell him about the way I felt. The drive to help those in need. I had tried telling my father about it once, but he just told me it was because I had a big heart. *He didn't understand what I was talking about, and could I honestly expect Arthur to understand if my own father, the doctor, didn't get it?*

Arthur studied me as I shifted on my feet.

"I am still sorry. I'm not used to... people."

My eyes met his when I heard the word *sorry* leave his mouth. *He apologized*, I thought to myself, narrowing my eyes as I watched him. *I didn't think the Nightlocke was capable of feeling sorry...*

"Can I change your dressing?" I asked, and his eyes widened. He ran his hand through his messy hair nervously, and I wondered if I crossed a line again.

"It's..." Arthur stammered, shaking his head, "it's fine. I will change it when I clean up for the day, but would you mind following me though?"

I nodded slowly, wondering which room he wanted me to clean today. I knew I was in for it after running away and putting my new *master* in danger like that. I followed Arthur out of his room, and we went straight across the hall to the door directly before us. He opened it and gestured for me to follow. It was a grand bedroom, with a large bed in the center and two large windows on either side. The room was decorate in elegant gold and white colors and must have belonged to a Prince or Princess before. It even had it's own bathing room attached to it, and my hand gently roamed over the ornate bed frame.

"I thought you might like this instead of the cell below," Arthur quietly said, and my eyes widened. *He wanted me to have this room?* My heart fluttered in my chest as I took another look around the room. I couldn't contain the smile that spread across my face.

"Thank you, Arthur," I replied, and he tensed when his name left my lips.

"I like when you call me by my name," he said, so quietly I nearly missed it. I blushed, turning away from him again. *What was wrong with me?*

"I'm sorry it's so filthy, but I thought with the work you did in the kitchen the other day, you'd have it cleaned in no time," he said as he cleared his throat. Arthur raised his hands, releasing his dark shadows, but for the first time, I wasn't afraid of them. I couldn't help but watch as they encircled me. They felt wispy, almost like a cloud, and I lifted my hand to touch them. *They were surprisingly soft and gentle,* I thought as they wrapped around me playfully. Suddenly, they raced towards the windows, pulling on the boards and heavy curtains and light filled the room.

"Really? You don't mind?!" I asked as I spun around to face him. My smile grew wide as I noticed the light covered every inch of the room before me. He squinted hard, giving himself a second to adjust to the bright light before giving me a small smile in return.

"This is your room, Kymra. Do with it as you wish. However, I do ask that you give me time with the rest of the castle. Please."

With that, Arthur left me standing there with my jaw dropped.

"What just happened?" I whispered in disbelief. The corners of my mouth rose. *This was mine. All mine.*

I went straight to the windows, looking out at the forest that surrounded the castle. For being filled to the brim of horrible creatures and vile darkness, the Forbidden Woods was actually beautiful. Everywhere the eye could see were tall, dark trees, and I noticed an overgrown garden down on the left. *Maybe Arthur wouldn't mind taking me there sometime.* I would love to get my hands dirty and... My smile fell when my family came to mind. They were starving without me working, and here I was planning my life like I planned to stay here forever. *How was I going to help them? And shouldn't I be trying to go back to them?*

Sadness swept over me, and I left the window sill. *I couldn't even leave the castle grounds without getting myself killed,* I thought as I made my way to the kitchen once more. *How in the world was I going to help them?*

I gathered supplies to clean the bedroom and started towards the stairs. I grunted, shifting the heavy bucket in my hand as I struggled to juggle everything. Black shadows suddenly appeared next to me, and one of Arthur's creatures stood tall. I froze. My heart began to race inside my chest, waiting for it to attack me again, but it didn't move. I frowned. *Could this thing even see me?* It had no eyes or even a face. I wasn't sure what to do and was about to call Arthur's name, when the creature abruptly bowed to me and then extended his hand.

I blinked. Slowly, I handed him the bucket, making sure not to touch the shadow creature. He took the bucket, and I flinched when it raised it's other hand. Stealing a peek, I found the creature standing there, entirely frozen as he waited for me. I looked down in my arms and gave him the broom and mop that I was holding. It seemed to be what it wanted, and the dark shadow creature meandered up the stairs, leaving me dumbfounded.

It was helping me.

The shadow creature stopped at the top of the stairs and waited for me to join him. I slowly took step after step until I reached the top too, and he continued on to my room. The creature stepped inside the bedroom, set down my items, and drifted away from sight. I looked behind me, wondering if Arthur was somehow nearby, but I was all alone. I didn't even know he could do that without being present. I closed my door, feeling my nerves come undone a little. It was easier when it was just his shadows, but those creatures were a whole new nightmare I never wanted to experience *ever* again.

The room was caked in dust, and it didn't take long for that heavy fear to subside. I felt lighter as the day went by. I always liked working. It was something mom and I did together before she died and watching this room slowly turn back into its former glory was exciting. I gathered all the bedding up, setting it by the door to wash later. Opening the walk-in closet, I found a plethora of old dresses and clothing. *I wonder who's clothes these were...*

I laid them all out to get some air, when I found something incredible tucked away in the back. Pants. Men's pants, I think, but they were much smaller than I expected. *Either a tiny male wore these dark pants or a woman did.* The memory of me tripping because of that awful dress came to mind. *But it would be scandalous to wear anything other than a dress,* I thought before frowning. I blinked. *I lived here with the Nightlocke away from High Society now. Who cares what I wear?* A small smile curved on my lips, and I stepped into the pants.

I pulled them over my hips and was surprised to find that they fit rather well. I pulled the strings, tightening them to my waist, before tying them into a knot. I felt... *free*. I was completely covered yet I could move. I could run... The possibilities were endless because I wasn't cage in some corset and gown. My fingers played with the end of Arthur's shirt. *I wonder if Arthur would care if I hemmed his shirt? I'd look just like him then.*

I snorted out a laugh at the thought. Like it would make a difference. Looking intimidating and actually acting intimidating were two totally different things. *If only I had a fraction of his confidence though,* I thought as I admired my look in the standing mirror. I could have stood up for myself with Thomas instead of running away like a injured puppy.

"I see you've found some clothes," Arthur said, and I jumped hard. I turned, bumping into the mirror and found the Nightlocke standing in the doorway.

My face flustered, and I nervously twiddle my fingers together. "I did in the closet here," I replied. "I didn't think you'd mind."

Arthur smiled softly. *He looked really good today,* I thought as my eyes drifted up and down his body. He had gotten cleaned up, and his hair was somewhat messy still because it was still wet. Arthur wore his typical hood, with a bow and arrow tossed over a shoulder. He was excellent with a sword and knives, but I didn't know he used a bow as well.

"No, I'm glad. I didn't know there was any. I never came in here before," he said, and we stayed silent for a moment.

"So this wasn't your home originally?" I asked, putting my hands behind my back, and he shook his head no.

"I found this place shortly after..." Arthur's voice trailed off, and I wondered what memory he was stuck in. He quickly composed himself though, moving away from whatever ailed him. "Anyways, the castle was abandoned when I found it. I simply moved in."

Silence fell between us again. It was hard to process his new behavior though. He just seemed kinder than before and patient. It was easy to forget the dark power he held within, especially when his beautiful blue eyes were looking at me the way they were right now. My cheeks flushed.

"Are you hungry?" he asked.

"Oh," I answered somewhat startled. My lips pushed together in a tight line as I looked back at the Nightlocke. "Yes, actually."

Arthur smiled softly and motioned for me to follow him. Anxiety rippled through me, and before I could talk myself out of asking, I blurted, "Umm... Arthur?"

He turned back to face me again, and my heart thundered in my chest. I played with the frayed ends of the rope that wrapped around my waist, knowing I looked like an utter fool just standing there. *Just ask you fool...*

"Can I keep this shirt? I was... ah... wondering if I could cut it down to size for me, if you didn't mind? Or if you have any material left over I could make my own."

My cheeks heated, and I forced myself to shut up. Arthur just stared at me, and I felt so silly for even asking but then something unexpected happened. He *smiled*.

"You want to keep my shirt?"

I stammered again, "It's rather comfortable, and I like the hood. I understand why you wear it always, but if you don't want..."

"No, it's fine," he interrupted. "I have many more. Go ahead, and do with it as you please. I can get you whatever you need to make more, Kymra. Just let me know."

He gestured to the door again, and I gave him a genuine smile.

"Thank you, Arthur."

I stepped past him into the hall and followed him down the stairs. For weeks, the Nightlocke has been nothing but moody and temperamental, but now he was so different. I didn't understand what caused this change in him, but I was starting to enjoy his company. That thought made me shake my head. I was *enjoying* the Nightlocke's company. *If only everyone else got to see this side of him.*

"I like the pants," he said quietly, pulling me from my thoughts.

Another blush crept up my cheeks. "I fell because of that stupid dress. I don't like being unable to defend myself. Although, who am I kidding? I wasn't going to win against that beast."

"Bloodhound," Arthur said with a smirk.

"What?"

"It was a Bloodhound that found you," he explained. "You summoned the others when you bled on that log."

I cocked my head to the side. "Interesting. I had never heard of them before."

He gave me an odd look. "Did no one in the kingdom teach you about the monsters that lived in these woods?"

I shook my head. "No. There are only laws about entering the Forbidden Woods."

Arthur grunted at that. "I was taught by my father at a very young age. You should know the monsters you live so close to."

"Well, the only one we needed to know about was you. You have plagued this land for decades," I replied, and he abruptly turned to me.

His eyes darkened, and I suddenly felt so stupid. *I should have never said a thing,* I thought to myself, wondering if I just ruined his newfound good mood. He stormed into the kitchen, and I hesitated at the door. Two dead chickens lay on the counter, and I watched him start to pull the feathers off aggressively. My chest burned again, and I sighed as I stepped towards him.

"Arthur, I'm sorry. That was rude..."

"It's true though. Everything, but one simple detail," he said as he worked on cleaning the bird. He never once looked at me and guilt ate at me.

"What are you talking about?"

Arthur stopped now and slowly turned to me. His eyes were a blend of color, and I held my breath, waiting for him to continue.

"I have plagued this land, but *not* for decades. I only became the Nightlocke seven years ago."

My eyes widened. "But I thought you were immortal..."

"I am," he replied, turning back to the bird. "The rest you don't need to know about, but I am telling you the truth. I have only been your monster for the last seven years. The man before me passed the torch, so to speak."

Guilt rippled through me. I felt horrible for hurting him like this. He deserves the blame for a lot of things, but he seemed almost mad that I thought he did everything. Suddenly, it dawned on me.

"The attack on the Castle. That was seven years ago," I said quietly, and his whole body stiffened. I had struck a nerve, it seemed, but he quickly went back to work, trying to play it off.

"That wasn't me. That was the last work of the previous Nightlocke. Now are you going to help me with this or not?" he snapped at me.

I scurried to the other bird, and we worked in silence after that. I didn't mean to upset him, and my chest continued to burn like I had not completed my job. But more than that, I just wanted to fix what pain I had caused. *I had hurt him, and I hated myself for it.*

"I'm sorry," I finally whispered.

Arthur slowly stopped, looking at me with narrowed eyes before turning back to the bird.

I sighed and went back to my own work. Despite the pain in my chest, I let him be. *If he needed space, then I'd give it to him.*

Chapter 13

Arthur

We worked in silence for some time, and I felt awful for snapping at her. It shouldn't surprise me that she thought everything was my fault, but I hated the man before me. I wanted nothing to do with him, but that was impossible when I was basically a carbon copy of the guy. I followed in his footsteps, and no matter how badly I wanted to insist we were not the same, the truth was that we were. I was changing though. For her, I was trying at least. I have not done anything to the kingdom since she arrived. *That had to count for something, right?*

Kymra felt bad, which only made me feel worse. I quietly watched her prepare some sort of chicken dish, trying to stay out of her way and cleaned up the feathers and blood left behind for her instead. I could not make anything like she could, and I did not want to ruin this dish by attempting to help.

Kymra worked quietly behind me now, and I couldn't help but watch her. Seeing her in pants, which was a complete *no no* for the women in this kingdom, did something to me. I could see her every curve, from her slender legs to her tiny waist. Every time she bent down to grab something from the cabinets below I noticed how much those pants hugged her waist and backside. She was doing me in, and I struggled to stay a gentleman. Because I wanted her. I wanted her like I've never wanted anything in this life before.

I liked seeing her rebel somewhat. *I could only imagine what people would say if they saw her. Can't be worse than seeing her with me, I suppose.* The silence was becoming awkward though, and I felt compelled to fix it. I wanted her to be happy here, but I was so clearly bad at this.

And it was pissing me off.

"What are you making?" I finally asked, and she slowed her steps, turning towards me. Those big, green eyes of hers melted me inside, and I held my breath, trying to keep my composure.

"It's just a garlic chicken dish. I was going to make rice with it, but I couldn't find it," she replied, thankfully missing the way my entire body shook when she got close. But then my eyes widened. *I had forgotten I gave it all to her father.*

"I'll get more," I said finally.

"It's okay. It still works with potatoes as a side instead."

We stayed silent for awhile, when her tiny voice spoke up, "Are you going to steal from the King again?"

I leaned against the far wall, studying her. She was trying hard not to look in my direction. *I didn't like that.* I didn't want her to be afraid of me anymore, but it was hard when she always asked questions that I didn't want to answer.

"Probably," I finally said, and I watched her slowly process that. She seemed bothered with it, and it was hard not to think it was because of that boy back at the castle. I suddenly felt possessive and jealous, and I crossed my arms. "You have an issue with this?"

"I don't think you should steal is all, especially from the King," she said, with more confidence than I expected. A sly grin crept up my face.

"The King ought to give food to his subjects, don't you think?"

The look she gave me made me laugh out loud. I think I surprised the girl because she looked at me like I had three heads, which only made me laugh harder.

"I didn't know you could laugh," she muttered, and I slowed my roll.

"I haven't had the best of company until I met you. You amuse me, Kymra," I replied, winking at her. Her face went an entirely new shade of red, and she quickly turned away from me. I smiled, knowing I got to her.

"I don't think the King considers you one of his subjects, and the Lightspark was killed during that attack so food is scarce as it is. You shouldn't steal anyways."

My eyes blackened, hearing her talk of the King like this. *The way she views him was wrong,* I thought before stomping over to her. Her body froze as I pinned her against the table. I put my arms on both sides of her, commanding her full attention. *She needed corrected on this.*

"Your *King* is not a nice man, Kymra. I know *exactly* how the Lightspark was killed because I have the previous Nightlocke's memories, but I am telling you, her death was an accident. He was trying to rescue her from the King, not kill her. You need to be very careful around that man *and* his family."

Kymra stood frozen mere inches from my face, and I felt like I got my point across. *The King was a dangerous man and so were his spawns. I may be a bad man, but so were they.* I backed away, giving her space again, when her nose suddenly got all scrunched up. I almost laughed again at the sight. *She was cross with me now,* I realized.

"You may not have been the one to do the deed, but that Nightlocke killed the Queen that night as well. The King's a good man, and he would never…"

Now, I laughed. "I saw everything, Kymra. The King is not a nice man nor are his children. Did you already forget what Thomas said about you?

Her eyes went wide, and I cursed myself for the slip up.

"How do you know what Thomas said?"

I stared long and hard at her, debating to tell her the truth. *I had really stepped in it now.*

"I saw his memories. I see everything when I enter a mind, Kymra. I know exactly what that prick said about you," I finally answered, and I couldn't help the rage coming through in my voice nor could I stop my eyes from turning black. There was only so much control I had, and she looked frightened again. Her fear quickly turned to embarrassment, and the shadows receded from my eyes. I wasn't trying to throw it in her face or anything, but I also couldn't stand the way she talked about the royal family. The King sat in his castle with plenty of food, even without a Lightspark, and *none* of it went to his kingdom. *I don't see him sharing any of his wealth.*

"Let's just talk about something else, Kymra," I said quietly, but she chose to cook in silence instead. I stayed quiet against the wall, waiting until she was ready to speak again, but she never said a word until the food was done. She handed me my plate before excusing herself.

"If you don't mind, I'd rather eat in my room. I'm rather exhausted from working today," she said to me, all while refusing to meet my eyes.

I hurt her.

Again.

"Sure," I responded, and she bolted from my presence. I groaned when I was alone, frustrated with myself. I shouldn't have opened my mouth in the first place. *She must have really cared for the Prince for his words to affect her the way they did, and here I go throwing it back in her face,* I thought angrily. I pulled the chair over, choosing to eat here instead of my own room.

I stabbed the chicken with my fork, stuffing it into my mouth and nearly groaned again. *Good Lord, Kymra was a fantastic cook!* The symphony of flavors burst in my mouth, and I wiped the oil that dripped off my chin. *I could not believe I had grown content with plain meat and bread all these years.* I licked the plate clean, my belly completely full, before I sat back trying to think about how to smooth things over with Kymra.

My mind immediately went to the library.

I rarely spend time in there honestly, but I didn't have the heart to get rid of the books either. They mostly just sat there collecting dust, but maybe I could do something for her.

Yeah... She'd like that.

I shot to my feet, making my way down there as quick as I could. I pushed the heavy door open with ease and stared at the massive room. It looked better, but was still a long ways off from being perfect. I sighed, knowing the first thing I needed to do.

The light didn't hurt me per say, but it just made my skin crawl. I've always preferred the dark, but ever since Kymra arrived here, I've been tolerating the light more and more. With a wave of my hand, my shadows dove for the long curtains, shaking them about and pulling them aside. When the dust settled, the room was bright and sunny.

Giving myself a second to adjust to everything, I got to work.

Chapter 14

Kymra

I was humiliated.

I didn't know Arthur knew what Thomas said about me. *I was hoping that would be something I could have kept private, but I guess not.* Somehow, he saw everything, which means he even saw the way I reacted. I groaned, utterly frustrated with the situation and the way he spoke of the King. He acted like King Alexander was a very bad man, but I wasn't sure if I should believe him with that. The King never seemed bad, and I thought long and hard about what Arthur said. He had the previous Nightlocke's memories, so he saw first hand what happened that night, *if* he was telling the truth. *Did the King really keep the Lightspark hostage? He wasn't capable of that. Was he?*

It was only his land that was flourished back then though, and I've always wondered why. *Shouldn't she be allowed to do more for everyone? Isn't that the Lightspark responsibility? To help and protect her people?*

But who protected her?

There must have been a reason though. I mean the King never seemed cruel when I was a child, but there was a tremendous amount of food made for just the three of them, and I remembered the amount in the ration bag they gave me. In comparison, it wasn't even close, but I mean there must be a reason it was done this way.

Right?

I rubbed my head, frustrated by the lack of answers. I was sweaty and gross from cooking and cleaning all day, and I was desperate to wear a shirt that fit me well, instead of swimming in one. I looked throughout my room for a knife or something to cut the shirt with, but I didn't see anything in here, and I did *not* want to go back downstairs. I quickly snuck a peek out the hall for Arthur, but he was nowhere in sight. Taking a deep breath, I bolted across the hall and into his room, closing the door behind me. *Now to find that knife.*

I went straight to the corner of the room and sighed in relief. *It was still there.* I picked it up, careful not to touch the sharp blade, when something caught my eye. Under his chair was a worn out book. I grabbed it, realizing that it was rather old and worn out looking, and I started to skim through it. My eyes went wide when I realized what I had discovered. *This was the journal of the first Nightlocke,* I thought as my finger gently touched the page. I held my breath as my eyes skimmed the passage below. *He only wrote about one thing in particular. Deadly Nightshade.*

Oh my, you could kill a Nightlocke... It was actually possible, I realized as I read as quickly as I could. My eyes widened further. *You wouldn't just kill him. You could actually steal the shadows from him.* It was the only way to take the power from another, and I slumped on the floor. That meant Arthur used Nightshade when he killed the first monster that plagued our lands. *Did he know or was it an accident?*

My mind raced with this newfound knowledge that I knew he would *not* want me to know. Panic filled my chest as I stared at the book. *He can't catch me with this.* My body shook slightly as images of those shadow creatures attacking me filled my mind. *God knows what he'd do if he ever knew...* I started to put the book back, when my chest suddenly burned. I hesitated, not knowing what I should do now. Whatever was going on inside me didn't want me to put the book back. I scooted from the shadows and stood tall.

"It was too dangerous to be left out," I muttered quietly. Arthur may be a complicated person, but I didn't *want* anything to happen to him. A sickening thought came to mind then. *Did he want to die? Was the reason this book was just lying around because he hoped someone would kill him and take his powers?*

My heart shattered at the thought of him dying. I hated wondering if he was so sad that he might feel that way. Arthur may have done horrible things, but I was beginning to see a whole different side to him. He just seemed so lonely, and I couldn't imagine spending years with only dark shadows to keep

CHAPTER 14

me company. *Something tragic happened to him, and it wasn't just gaining the Nightlocke powers.* There was something more, and I felt like I needed to try and help him. *Starting with this book.*

I opened the book quickly and tore the pages mentioning Nightshade out. My chest calmed, and I put the book back, shoving the pages in my pocket. I grabbed the knife and ran back to my room, feeling good about what I had done. My thundering heart was the only sound in the room as I searched for a place to hide these pages before I could get a chance to burn them. *That was the only way to make sure no one would ever find them.* I would keep the Nightlocke's secret, and *no one* would ever find a way to harm him.

I felt the burning need to help Arthur completely subside, and I took it as confirmation that I did the right thing. *This must be why I felt the need to help him when we first met,* I thought to myself as I shoved the mattress up and hid the papers underneath. *It all led up to this.* It really wasn't the best place to hide them, but hopefully I could just destroy them soon. Then he'd be safe.

Now that *that* was done, I untied the rope around my waist and took off Arthur's shirt. I didn't ruin his shirt needlessly so I took my time figuring out the best way to go about this. With the sewing kit I found in one of the drawers, I carefully cut the shirt. It took some time, but soon it was adjusted to my size, fitting perfectly snug against my body. I even added a ribbon I found to the front to cover some of the excess cleavage, but I didn't touch the hood as it was magnificent already.

I smiled softly. *I actually did a halfway decent job.* I gathered the shirt up and made my way to the bathing room. I stripped out of the rest of my clothes and removed the bandages on my arm. I blinked in surprise. My wounds were gone. Like *entirely* gone. I twisted and turned, trying to figure out how this was even possible, but not even a scar appeared. *Those healing herbs must seriously work magic.* A slight frown appeared on my face, doubting the truth then. *But what else could it be?*

I enjoyed my bath, despite this heaviness sitting on my chest, and Arthur never came for me. I wasn't sure why it saddened me, but it did. *I mean I was mad at him in the first place. Yet, I still wanted to see him.* Sighing, I pulled the plug and stepped out of the water. I quickly changed and was drying my hair when I heard a knock on my door. I opened to find a shadow creature standing there. He motioned for me to follow, and I looked nervously out the door. I didn't see Arthur *anywhere*. The creature was not barring his teeth or snarling viciously. *Maybe Arthur truly didn't know I stole those pages?*

He motioned towards the stairs again, and I forced myself to follow. I assumed we'd be heading back to the kitchen. I had yet to clean up from our meal, but he surprised me when he went the other direction instead. My brows furrowed when we stopped at the library of all places. *Did Arthur want me to clean here instead?* I wondered as the shadow creature pushed the door open for me. My jaw dropped.

Light. Light filled every nook and cranny in this room. I slowly stepped through the door, turning slightly as I tried to take in the whole room at once. Everything looked brand new again. From the sparkling crystal pieces on the fireplace mantle to the breathtaking stained glass artwork framed along the back wall. I covered my mouth with my hand, feeling silly and absolutely emotional over it all.

"Do you like it?" Arthur asked, and I turned, finding the Nightlocke's gaze fixated on me. I blushed under his intense stare.

"Did you do this for me?" I asked with a smile.

He gave me a small nod before taking a step closer. My heart began to race with every step he took. He kept moving until he was so close that I could feel his breath against my skin. My heart *thundered* in my chest.

"I wanted to apologize, Kymra. I did not mean to insult or embarrass you. We don't have to discuss the King. I was hoping we could start anew actually, and I thought you needed a special places to call your own," he said seductively.

My knees *wobbled*. I had never felt like this before, not even with Thomas. With the Prince, I was just giddy and nervous like a child was with their crush, but with Arthur... He swept me off my feet. He made me feel *alive*, and this wasn't just attraction I was feeling. No, he took my breath away. Arthur always noticed when I entered a room. I felt seen with him, even when he behaved more like the Nightlocke than the man standing before me, Arthur always noticed me. And then there was this gesture. No one had ever done anything like this for me before. No one had gone against their own desires and wishes just to do something *nice* for me.

"You're giving me the library?" I asked, trying to understand why he would offer something as grand as this.

He nodded. I blinked when his gaze dropped to my lips. *Does he want to kiss me?* My stomach did a little flip. I couldn't help but drop my gaze too and heat crept up my face as I looked at his perfectly full lips. *I cannot believe I'm feeling this way about the Nightlocke of all people.*

"It's my gift to you. Please forgive me for earlier," he said gently, and my heart swelled. Tears filled my eyes, and I lunged, hugging him so tightly that I felt him flinch. *It was this or kiss the man, and I wasn't bold enough for something like that.* To my surprise, Arthur relaxed and wrapped his arms around me.

"Thank you, Arthur! Oh, this is wonderful! I absolutely love books, but I haven't read anything in such a long time!"

Oh, I was happy, I thought as I let the Nightlocke go and fluttered around the room. I never thought I'd feel this way when I came here, but I felt more at home here than I ever thought I would. *Whoever owned this castle before had everything,* I thought as I scanned the shelves. From fantasy and horror fiction books to cookbooks and educational books. I was in awe, and I settle on a fantasy book about wolves called Shifter. There were nearly 11 books in the series, so it would keep me busy for some time.

I plopped onto one of the chairs, and Arthur came to stand behind me. He leaned over the chair, looking at the book with me, and I frowned when I saw the look on his face. *He seemed I don't know... puzzled, maybe?* I thought as he narrowed his eyes on the first page. But then it dawned on me. He can't read. *That must be why he left that journal out in the open in his room!* God, I felt so dumb as I tried to think back over my time spent here. I never saw him read anything, and my shoulders fell. *Everyone should know how to read. How long had he been alone for?*

"Arthur?" I said, looking up at him.

"Hmm?"

I looked into his gorgeous blue eyes, trying to find a way to help him without offending him. My mouth opened, but the words wouldn't come out. His brows furrowed then.

"What do you need, Kymra?" he asked softly.

I closed my book and whispered, "Do you know how to read?"

His eyes flashed with amusement briefly, but he didn't say a word in response. Embarrassment washed over me, and I began to stammer.

"It's okay if you weren't taught! I wasn't taught a great deal of things, it seems, but I'd be happy to help you learn if you'd like..."

Arthur put his finger over my lips, shushing the slew of words pouring out of my mouth.

"You want to teach me to read?" he asked, his eyes softening as he looked at me, and my heart broke a little. *He really was just alone here.*

"I would love to Arthur. Come sit here with me," I replied with a smile, dragging him to the couch instead. *Here we would both fit together.* To my surprise, he followed.

"Okay, so do you know your letters at all?" I asked, and he nodded. "Good! That's a great start, so we just need to work on their sounds and then putting them all together."

We spent hours in the library reading the fantasy book about wolves and bears. He was slowly starting to pick it up and was even helping me read the smaller words towards the end. He seemed to have a basic knowledge of the skill, which made it much easier to build upon. Towards the end, he asked if he could take a break and if I would continue reading to him instead, which I was happy to oblige. Soon, it was too dark to see the words on the page, and I left Shanely and Bastian in peace, closing the book for the night.

"Thank you for today, Arthur," I said, and he smiled back at me.

"Thank you as well, Kymra. I like spending my days with you," he replied. I smiled wide.

"Arthur?"

"Hmm?"

"Can I ask a personal question?" I asked quietly. The last time I mentioned anything about his past he became extremely upset. I didn't want to ruin our day, but I was really curious about this man. I wanted to know more about him. He gave me a slow nod, and I took a deep breath.

"I don't mean to pry…" I stammered, my heart beginning to race again, "but how old were you when you became the Nightlocke?"

He stiffened at my question and fear filled my heart. I held my breath, watching the Nightlocke mull over my question, noticing his eyes stayed crystal blue. *He wasn't upset with me,* I thought as the corners of my mouth rose. For some reason, that meant the world to me.

"I was 15," he finally replied, and my smile fell. I abruptly turned to him, placing my hand on his arm.

"15?! Oh, Arthur. Have you been alone ever since?" I asked, and he just lowered his head.

Arthur didn't say another word, and I pursed my lips together, feeling awful for him. I decided to leave him be and gave his hand a gentle squeeze.

"Thank you for answering, Arthur," I said softly. "You didn't have to, but I'm glad you trusted me enough to. My mom died when I was three, and my older sister was always the favorite to everyone. I often felt very alone myself, but it was definitely not the same as what you went through. I'm so sorry that you did."

Arthur looked to me now, narrowing his eyes as he studied me carefully. Heat filled my cheeks again, and I quickly stood and put the book back on the shelf. I made my way to the door, when he finally spoke.

"Sometimes the worst kind of loneliest comes when you are surrounded by people, Kymra. Don't short change yourself or how you feel," he said, his voice dropping lower as he stared at me intensely.

I shook my head and stepped out the door. *He was becoming the death of me.* And I was beginning to love it.

Chapter 15

Arthur

I rattled her. My voice was firm, but she didn't seem frightened by it. In fact, she seemed *smitten* almost, and I couldn't contain my grin when she fled out of the room. I could not believe how our day went. Today was honestly the best day in my entire life, and I didn't want it to end. I was ready to chase after her. To scoop her up and finally find out what those thick full lips of hers felt like.

But I stayed put.

The whole day passed by, and my mind was clear. I felt like the old Arthur again. I was still strong and powerful, but my shadows weren't clouding everything like normal. They seemed calm, content almost, and I liked it. I *liked* how I felt when I was with her.

I'm sure she will be mad at me later for lying, but when she offered to teach me to read, I couldn't pass it up. I was simply reading alongside her, trying to understand what drew her to this book in particular, when she took it as a struggle to read altogether. The way she looked at me was just adorable, and I let her teach away, pretending I had no idea. I just wanted to be close to her, and this seemed like the perfect opportunity to get my wish. She honestly was a great instructor, but it was rather difficult to keep up the facade, so I just asked her to read instead. I loved hearing her voice, and surprisingly the book was rather decent. *Please, let this be a daily thing between us.*

But then she started talking to me, asking questions I was too afraid to answer. She didn't get mad when it took me awhile to figure out what to say. She didn't push when she saw how uncomfortable I was. She was giving me space with my past, which meant the world to me. She just understood how I felt and backed way off. One of these days, I planned on telling her everything. I wanted her to know about momma, and what happened seven years ago. I'd tell her the truth about who she was, and then I'd confess everything I thought and felt about the girl. It wasn't the time though.

Soon, but not yet.

My mind drifted back to her beauty, and the smile crept up my face. *God, this girl was beautiful.* She had fixed my shirt during our time apart, and when she walked in today, my jaw nearly dropped. Without the bulky dress or oversized shirt, you could see every curve on her body, and she was just perfect. The curves on her hips captivated me, and I couldn't keep my eyes off her when she walked. She wore her hood up too, and I don't know why it affected me so much, but I *loved* it. I loved that she was beginning to look so similar to me. I don't know why, but it just felt like acceptance. Like I wasn't some horrible monster no one wanted around. I was just... me.

I sighed, shaking my head from my thoughts as I stood. I needed to get my head in the game before I left for work. It had been long enough, and I couldn't put it off any further. I made my way to the door before slamming into Kymra on the other side.

I grabbed her waist, yanking her towards me until she righted herself on her feet. "Kymra! I thought you left."

She blushed again. "I did, but I came back. I thought about what you said earlier. About feeling alone while surrounded around a lot of people."

My eyes narrowed, and I took a step back, getting some space from the girl. I was going to kiss her if I didn't.

"And?" I asked quietly.

She shifted nervously on her feet. "You just seemed so sure of what you said earlier. You've been alone since gaining this power yet..." her voice trailed off as she looked at me. I nearly melted with that one look. That one look nearly brought me to my knees, and I held my breath as she sighed.

"You seem fully convinced that the sort of loneliness I've felt was worse than the way you've felt. It's not sitting with me right, and I..."

"Kymra," I said, cutting her off. I smiled softly. "I'm convinced because

I've experienced both kinds of loneliness. Trust me when I say, it is better to be alone than surrounded by people who refuse to care or even see you."

Her eyes widened then. "You've been invisible too..."

I blinked, stepping towards her as I crossed my arms. "What now?"

She quickly shook her head and gave me a tight lipped smile. "Nothing," she muttered, "but that is very true, Arthur. It's not easy finding your place or people that genuinely care about you."

I heard her correctly the first time. *How deep did her wounds go?* I knew things were rocky with her and that prince, and I understood the pain of losing a loved one, but how lonely did Kymra feel? I wanted to heal her wounds, even the invisible ones, but I frowned, having no idea how. *I destroy everything I touch*, I thought angrily. *I wasn't good at mending or healing. I wasn't a Lightspark.*

"Thomas was wrong about you, Kymra," I blurted, and her eyes widened. "You deserve better than that."

Silence filled the empty space between us, and I felt like an utter fool just standing there. *What else do I say? Do I give her another hug? Would a different present help maybe?* My mind ran amuck, thinking of anything I could possibly do to bring that gorgeous smile back to her lips.

"Thank you, Arthur," she said, startling me. "Honestly, it was foolish of me to have a crush on a Prince anyways. He was a childhood friend, and I thought... Well it doesn't matter what I thought."

I frowned.

"Why did you join the rations program, Kymra? You could have received a hefty dowry for your family instead of becoming the King's slave," I finally asked, needing to know the answer to that question more than I wanted to admit. Her face suddenly fell, looking somewhat defeated, and I didn't like where her mind went. My shadows burned inside, but I waited for her to tell me. I didn't want to search her mind to find out what I wanted to know. I wanted her to confide in me instead, and that was going to take patience on my part.

"My sister will receive a dowry, Arthur, not me. I have this..." her voice trailed off again, and my eyes narrowed. She finally sighed. "I have strong desires to help people anyway I can. The rations program was the only thing available for me to do to help them, so I joined."

My eyes widened. *How couldn't she believe she wouldn't receive an offer for marriage?* I thought as that new piece of information rattled me. This girl became a slave because she didn't think anyone would like her. That killed me. *She has no idea how special she is. I mean, I didn't just like this girl. I freaking loved her, and if I wasn't the shadow of death then there would be nothing stopping me from running to her father and asking for her hand...*

My heart stopped. I just admitted that I loved this girl. That I loved someone *period.* That piece of truth rattled me a moment. My eyes drifted back to her then, and I quickly shook my head, shoving my fears aside. *I loved Kymra, and I wouldn't be afraid to say it.*

"I think you're wrong, Kymra," I said softly, taking her by surprise some.

Suddenly, a loud chime went off, startling her. I smirked as she jumped hard by the sound, but my eyes widened when she pushed herself against me. My heart nearly stopped at the contact. *She moved closer to me, not away from me.*

"It's alright, Kymra. I fixed the clock in the library is all, but I do apologize because I must take my leave. Can I escort you back to your room?" I said, extending my hand out. To my utter delight, she accepted.

"Where are you off to tonight?" she asked casually, and I gave her a sideways look. She seemed troubled by my silence now, but I felt like admitting what I was about to do would only ruin our day. I didn't want to take a step backwards. Not after everything that's happened.

"Are you going to hurt people?" she whispered, and I stilled. I didn't know how to respond to that question, but my silence must have been enough of an answer for her because she pulled away slightly. My heart sunk.

We ascended the stairs, and I wasn't sure what I should tell her. I *am* the Nightlocke. This is what I do, but tonight I just needed information really. I need to see what the King is up to and to make sure he has no plans against me or Kymra by extension. I stopped at her door before turning towards her. *I can tell her the truth.*

"Not tonight, Kymra. I promise," I said and relief washed over her.

"Can I come with you then sometime?" she asked, and I blinked in surprise.

"You want to come with me. In the shadow veil?"

She nodded. "I'm getting used to your shadows, and I don't like knowing how defenseless I am. I thought maybe I could go with you the next time you go hunting or something."

This girl surprised me constantly. I gave her a sly grin, and she rolled her eyes. "Not when you're hunting people, Nightlocke, but if you hunt food for us, I'd like to learn. I saw the chickens, Arthur. I know you didn't steal them."

I laughed unexpectedly. "Alright, Kymra. I'll teach you how to use a bow tomorrow. How does that sound?"

She beamed back at me. "It sounds perfect! Thank you!"

Kymra started to walk inside, when she stopped suddenly. Her face twisted in concern as she leaned against the door frame and asked, "If you are leaving the castle, what if something decides to attack? What should I do?"

She was afraid, I realized. *She was afraid to be alone and afraid of what would happen when I left.* If that didn't make me feel good, I don't know what else will. I stepped closer towards her, never wanting her to feel fear ever again. I was *always* going to be here to protect her, and she needed to understand that.

She held her ground, holding her breath as I invaded her personal space. I gave her a wicked smile before grabbing her hand and placing it gently on the shadows that were cast against the wall in her room. "Touch the dark, and say my name. I will hear you always, Kymra. Always."

I was mere inches from her now and dying to kiss her goodnight. It was literally killing me inside, but I didn't want to ruin today. She seemed to be so much better with me, and since she was stuck here in this castle with me, I just couldn't push her before she was ready. I gently rubbed her hand, giving it a final squeeze before I let her go.

"Goodnight, Kymra," I said, before stepping into the shadows and leaving her for the night.

I smiled, feeling content and almost happy for the first time in my life. I had never felt quite this free before, but I rolled my shoulders, getting mentally prepared for the night to come. This would require the work of the Nightlocke and not Arthur. It was going to be way more dangerous now that I knew the King knew my secret. He would need to be disposed of soon, but tonight I needed to steal food and information. Nothing more, sadly.

I was back in the King's garden within seconds, and I took a deep breath of the warm air outside. *I haven't been here since I found Kymra a couple months ago,* I thought to myself. My shadows and I moved without sound, and soon we were outside the castle's wall. I watched and listened, but it was quiet tonight. The guards were on rotation, but no one liked to get too close to my land. *I'd be safe for the moment.* Slipping into the shadows again, I stepped into the hall outside their grand ballroom. I moved quickly and carefully through the castle, making sure to not be seen. Before I never cared if I scared the help, but tonight I wanted to be alone.

I made it to the kitchen and filled up my bag entirely. I also filled a smaller bag for Kymra's father again, and once they were loaded, I moved them back to the gardens with the help of my shadows. The amount of food this King had while the rest of the kingdom starved baffled me. He was still looked upon as a good King too, like the people had no idea what was really going on or they were too scared to do anything about it. I shook my head, slipping out of the kitchen and focused on my surroundings. I still had a job to do, and I stepped further down the hall.

"Find me, Thomas," I whispered, letting my shadows out. I followed them deeper in the castle, and soon I began to hear voices. I followed them, pulling back my shadows slightly when I recognized one voice in particular.

"We need to find her, father!" Thomas shouted.

I stole a peek inside the room that was barely lit by candles. Plenty of shadows lay above in the high ceiling, and I moved into them with ease, grinning at the fact that their greatest enemy was in the room with them right now, and they were none the wiser. I hung from the rafters and watched from above. *This was too easy.*

"Son, I will do no such thing. We are spread thin as it is, and we need to prepare for Liam and Agatha's wedding," the King replied, and I snorted. It didn't surprise me to find out that he has no desire to look for Kymra. *That man was selfish...*

"Kymra is important, Dad. The Nightlocke took her..."

"Yes, he did!" the King shouted. "He stole her right out from under your nose, and you didn't kill him!"

"I know what this beast looks like now, and I can right my wrong! I am begging you to let me pursue this!" Thomas shouted back to his father.

"You know nothing of this beast, Thomas, and it would be foolish to go out alone. Do you not remember your mother and how she and half the castle fell that night seven years ago? And you want to take him on alone?! All you discovered Thomas is that this is a new Nightlocke and nothing more. We are no closer to knowing who this man is nor do we know how to find him!"

"What I want to know is *how* do we have a new one? This creature is immortal, is he not? Did you actually manage to kill him all those years ago father?" Liam asked, and the King grunted.

"Nightshade is it's weakness, we know that much, but I didn't think we did enough damage to actually bring him down that night. We don't really know how much Nightshade is required to kill the beast for good. He merely burned his hand from what I remember, but I don't know. He wanted the Lightspark for some reason though, and he only took damage when he grabbed her fallen body. We had her coated in Nightshade to keep him from stealing her in the shadows and ruining the Kingdom for good. Although little good it did in the end. We kept her locked up tight away from everyone and everything, so our Kingdom would flourish, yet she still died."

"And now he has Kymra! He specifically went right for her that night in the garden instead of engaging me! She's in danger, and we need to find her!"

Suddenly, the King stood abruptly. "Wait, he saw you and still chose to go to her instead?"

Thomas rolled his eyes. "I've told you all this before, father, don't you listen to me? I drew my sword, but he moved so fast *towards* her. They were gone before I could reach her."

I straightened. The King was lost in thought now, sending my nerves through the roof. He was so focused that even his son's noticed.

"Father... What is it?" Liam asked.

"You are *my* son, yet he chose to spare you and take her instead. Why? Why go after a servant girl?" the King asked as his voice trailed.

"He wanted her," Liam chimed in, making my whole body tense up.

"Yes, I was there! What does that have to do with anything?" Thomas bellowed, and the King smacked the table forcefully.

"QUIET! This is just another reason why you are not the chosen heir, Thomas. You are too rash and cannot see the full picture."

Thomas gritted his teeth angrily but said nothing in return. Liam finally sat forward, his eyes wide.

"My God, do you think Kymra is a Lightspark?"

My heart stopped as Thomas jerked towards his brother in shock.

"You can't be serious! She shows no signs, brother!"

No, no, no, this cannot be happening! I thought as my shadows hissed in panic. *They are figuring things out too quickly.* I needed to dispose of the King sooner that I thought.

"I do. The previous Nightlocke had a fixation with the Lightspark for some reason, and for him to pass on a chance to inflict pain to the royal family after everything... It has to mean something! We need that Lightspark for our Kingdom. Thomas, I give you full permission to find Kymra and bring her back here. In exchange for your sacrifice, I will allow marriage between the two of you."

Thomas slumped back in chair, shaking his head in disbelief. He gave his father a sharp nod in response, and rage filled me to my core. My eyes darkened. *This was a problem,* I thought to myself. *A very serious problem.*

"Where are you even going to start?! No one ever finds this monster! Chances are she's dead somewhere, and her body is lost to the gruesome monsters of the Forbidden Woods or wherever he's dumped her," Liam said, throwing his hands up angrily.

"Actually, that is exactly where I plan to start looking," Thomas said casually, and my eyes widened. *God, I've been too arrogant and careless for too long!* I needed to correct this.

"You can't be serious, Thomas. You'll only die out there!"

"Really Liam? As future King, you shouldn't be such a coward," Thomas replied coldly, and Liam glared at him. There was no brotherly love here as the two stared one another down.

"I agree," the King said.

"I am *not* afraid, but we all know what lives in those woods. Why do you think the Nightlocke lives there as well?"

"I've been thinking long and hard ever since he took what was mine. It would make perfect sense that his home is there. We have laws forbidding anyone from entering. It's filled to the brim with Bloodhounds, Wraiths, and the Deadly Mist, not to mention wolves and poisonous snakes. It's easy to get lost, and that's not even mentioning how dark everything is. It makes sense he'd fit right in."

This was getting way too close to home now, I thought as panic rose within me. No one had dared stepped foot in my woods *willingly*, and I had no defenses set up for the castle. I never needed any before, and I was paying the price for it now. My army wasn't ready to take over the Kingdom here, and I didn't want to waste them unless I was sure I could overthrow everything. It was difficult enough converting people in the first place.

"Do we really think it is wise to provoke him like this?" Liam asked, and I cocked my head to the side. *Someone seemed to have some sense.* The destruction I'd bring down on this kingdom for harming Kymra...

"You can't be serious!? You want to just leave Kymra with her?" Thomas shouted.

"No! I don't mean that. I do want to help the girl, *if* she's still alive, but if you are right and he wanted her for whatever reason, do you really think it's wise to take her from him? Who knows what we will unleash on this kingdom!" Liam shouted.

"If I am right, and she is a Lightspark, then she belongs to the people, to us! The Nightlocke is a dangerous man, Liam. Have a backbone or I might have to reconsider who ought to lead," the King scolded.

Liam's eyes went wide as he gritted his teeth. "All I meant was that we have no idea *why* he wanted her. We could be unleashing something we have never encountered by taking her back. I don't think this is a wise decision. My marriage with Agatha is bringing in a tremendous amount of wealth and food. Enough to restore the Kingdom back to it's..."

CHAPTER 15

Thomas scoffed. "You want to *give* the money and food away?"

"Son, while a noble thought, it's better to keep it close at hand. The kingdom has survived long enough the way it is, and it will continue too. Plus, having the kingdom destitute brings in more volunteers to the rations program, and we will need all the hands we can get for the expansion."

"Expansion?" Liam asked, confusion furrowing his brow. I leaned forward, trying to make sure I didn't miss anything. *This was news to me too.*

"We need a better line of defense against the Nightlocke. I told you I will not lose the Lightspark again, Liam. I've been in the works about making new additions to the castle and the walls, but first things first, we need to find Kymra. Thomas, you will bring that girl back to me, do you understand?"

"Yes, however when I do, I want to choose when and where the wedding will take place," Thomas replied smugly, and it was all I could do not to rip that smile off his face.

"Whatever, Thomas. All I care about is finding that girl and seeing if she is the Lightspark. We desperately need her," the King replied as Liam slumped back in his chair, looking defeated.

Rage coursed through my veins, darkening the corner of the room I was hidden in. *They will never find Kymra. I don't care what I have to do, but I will never let them hurt her.*

A servant came in, interrupting the men talking. I watched the King get pulled away to deal with God knows what, but I had heard enough. It was clear they *all* needed to die, but I needed to be careful how I handled this. I started to leave, when Thomas leaned forward on the table, smirking arrogantly at his brother.

"You know Liam... Father has offered up a massive reward to anyone who can kill the Nightlocke," he said as Liam glared.

"What of it, Thomas?"

Thomas grinned wickedly. "I wouldn't get too comfortable on that throne, Liam. You won't be staying on it for very long."

He stood now, giving a small salute to his older brother, who glared back at him. Liam was fuming mad but said nothing back. *And they were supposed to be brothers?*

"Yeah, I'm not too worried about you killing the Nightlocke, *brother*," Liam said to himself before walking out as well.

At least this one had a lick of sense, I thought before I drifted into the shadows again, feeling rather exhausted from it all. I needed to prepare for war, but nothing was going to happen tonight. I grabbed the food bags I had taken and made my way to Kymra's house. It didn't take long moving in the veil, and I unlocked the door once more. I put the smaller bag down on the table and quickly unloaded everything like I had done multiple times since taking Kymra, when the door to the bedroom suddenly opened. I froze as a rather tall man stood in the door frame. He eyed me, and I stared right back.

I had no intention of him ever knowing it was me delivering the food, and I swore under my breath. *I was making mistakes left and right, it seemed.*

Kymra's father didn't make a move, and I wasn't sure what to do. *Kymra looked just like the man other than his eyes,* I realized as I stepped away from the bag with my hands raised. I meant no harm, and I put my hand to my lips, warning him to stay quiet. With a wave of my fingers, shadows pulled at my feet, and I dropped into the veil.

I exhaled the breath I'd been holding the moment I stepped into my woods. The reality of my situation weighed on my chest as the night's events flooded my brain. *This was getting to be rather difficult,* I thought as my body ached. I needed to sleep before I made anymore mistakes. I jumped to my castle, dumping the bag of food on my bedroom floor and collapsed in my bed.

I'd figure it all out in the morning.

Chapter 16

Kymra

My eyes fluttered open as the morning sun gently touched my face. A small grin appeared on my lips before I bolted out of bed. I quickly dressed and braided my hair down my left shoulder, completely ecstatic to be learning how to hunt and defend myself this morning. *Arthur promised to take me today,* I thought as I bolted out my bedroom door and across the hall.

I knocked on Arthur's door, rocking back and forth on my heels, but there was no answer. I frowned. *I thought he'd be back by now. Did he leave without me again?*

I knocked again, waiting another minute more, when I decided to just check. I quietly opened the door, only to find him passed out in his bed still. *He didn't leave me...* I thought when my gaze drifted to the mess on the floor. A large bag of food lay scattered about like he came home and just dropped it. I knew he stole it all and chances were it was from the King. My shoulders fell as I stared at the food that should rightfully go to the people. *I thought maybe he was changing... What could I honestly expect though? I was falling for the villain here, not the hero.*

I carefully began to pick the bag up, when he shot forward out of bed. He had me by the throat in seconds, and my eyes widened. I dropped the bag, spilling apples all over the floor, knowing this was the second time I made this mistake. He softened when he saw me and let my neck go.

"Kymra," he said as he collapsed against me, pushing me against the door. "You have got to *stop sneaking up* on me like this."

I chuckled softly, rubbing my neck. *At least this time he didn't have a knife.*

"I'm sorry. I did try knocking, Arthur. I really didn't mean to startle you."

Arthur lifted his head, smirking down at me. He gently moved a stray piece of hair out of my eyes, and for a moment, I thought he was going to kiss me. My heart began to race when his gaze fell to my lips, but to my dismay, he stepped back some. My face fell, and I quickly dropped to the floor to hide my embarrassment. I grabbed the apples that had fallen from the bag, and he reached down to help, rubbing the back of his head sheepishly.

"I had meant to put this all away..."

"Before I saw?" I asked calmly, and he sighed.

"Kymra..."

"Arthur, you and I do not agree when it comes to stealing or the royal family, but I cannot control your choices. I understand that. I don't agree, but I don't want to fight about it either. Let's just put this away, so you can teach me how to shoot."

Arthur cocked his head to the side, studying me before slowly nodding.

"Alright. Let's go then," he said, standing up and grabbing his bow off the wall where it hung.

"What about this?" I said, gesturing to the mess.

"It's not going anywhere, and right now I want to teach you how to shoot. You coming, Kymra?"

I gave him a sly grin before chasing after him. He led me outside to the Forbidden Woods, stalking into the dark with ease, but I ground to a halt at the edge of the shadows. Fear trickled in as I remembered the Bloodhounds. I looked around to the area around the castle that was full of sun and light.

"Can't we shoot here?" I asked, and Arthur turned.

His eyes narrowed, and I couldn't keep my cheeks from turning red as I stood there like a chicken. The Nightlocke moved, gliding through the shadows until he towered over me.

"The Forbidden Woods isn't as bad as one may think, *if* you know what you are doing. Come," he said, dragging me into the woods abruptly. He stopped and pointed just ahead.

"The trees will be your guide," he said firmly. "If you are afraid then you will miss the subtleties the forest gives to guide you. The darker the path, the more dangerous the ground you tread."

My eyes widened. The forest before us *was* darker on the left than the right. *How had I missed this before?* I wondered as Arthur took my hand and pulled me along the path that went to the right.

"Bloodhounds have a distinct smell," he went on. "Make sure you are upwind if at all possible and run if you smell blood. If one gets your scent, then the whole pack gets it. You will hear Wraiths coming long before you see them. They screech loudly to scare their prey into bolting. They are wicked fast so best thing to do is hide as quick as you can. They hunt more with their sight than smell, so just be smart and pay attention to your surroundings, Kymra. The only real thing you need to worry about is the Mist."

"What's the Mist?" I asked cautiously, noticing he still held my hand. My heart began to flutter in my chest, but it wasn't fear that was making it race. It was *him*.

"The Mist is a thick greenish fog that rolls through here every so often. It is alive though, Kymra, and it hunts *anything* with a heartbeat."

My eyes went wide. "How do you survive it?"

"I disappear in my shadows, but no one else in existence wields the same power I do. You won't stand a chance if it overtakes you. Should you ever find yourself near the mist, *run*. Shout my name, touch the dark wherever you can find it, and I *will* come for you. You keep running, and I promise I will come."

Arthur turned to look at me, and his stare was so intense that I knew he meant every word. *And by God did that make me feel good.* I was standing here in the middle of the Forbidden Woods with the Nightlocke himself, and the only thing I was truly afraid of was how hard I was falling for him.

"Now," he said, pulling me from my thoughts as he put the bow in my hand, "you hold the bow like this, and the arrow sits here. You pull back until you feel the string give, and you look right down the arrow like this."

Arthur walked behind me, helping me get into my stance before raising my arms. He motioned for me to draw the bow, which I struggled to do, but after a moment I finally managed to get it. Keeping it pulled back was rather difficult, especially when his hands went to my waist. My stomach did a little flip as he lifted his left arm to help me hold the bow, guiding my face to where

I needed to look.

"Now just breathe," he whispered in my ear. Shivers ran down my spine as I stood there rigid against him. Arthur raised his right hand and shadows poured out from his fingertips. My eyes widened as I watched his shadow figures stand before me.

I gave him a sideways look, but he nudged my head back towards the creatures.

"Focus, Kymra. This is target practice," he commanded.

I tried. I *really* tried my best, but the arrow shot off to the side, missing the three creatures entirely. I groaned as he grinned at me. His shadows brought back the arrow, which he handed back.

"Not bad for your first time. Try again, little one," he told me.

"I completely missed!" I protested, but he just smacked my hips back into place. My heart skittered inside and heat traveled up my cheeks.

"You can do this, Kymra. I'd feel better knowing you can protect yourself too. I will get you a smaller bow later tonight, but for now you can practice with mine. It has a heavier draw. Now again."

"Bossy..." I muttered under my breath, and his eyes darkened playfully. I giggled before getting back in my stance. "Alright, alright."

I drew the bow back myself this time and tried to aim at the middle creature. I let the arrow fly, and it shot over his head.

"Dang it!" I shouted, and Arthur laughed.

"Try again. That was a bit high, so make sure to make corrections on your next shot," he said, handing me the arrow back. I pursed my lips together, glaring at those shadow creatures. *Now, I was getting frustrated.* I drew the bow back once more, determined to hit one freaking shadow creature at least and let the arrow fly. To my surprise, it did! It blasted right through the creature's neck, and it disappeared from sight. A sense of calm washed over me as I stared the bow in my hands. *I did it... I freaking did it!*

"Well done!"

I turned, grinning ear to ear as I jumped up and down excitedly.

"I hit him! I got it!"

Arthur laughed, handing the arrow back to me. "Do it again, Kymra."

CHAPTER 16

The smile stayed on my lips as I got back into my stance. *This was something I wanted to perfect,* I thought, feeling *empowered*. I took aim, exhaling slowly as I let the arrow fly once more and hit a shadow creature in the chest.

"You're a natural, Kymra! You just need your own bow now and some practice, but I'm sure you will be better than me in no time!"

"Oh, nonsense! No one could be better than the Nightlocke, but you do seem to be improving little ole me," I said, with a grin.

Our eyes met, and I stilled. Arthur's eyes were black for some reason, and he stalked towards me slowly. Nerves rattled my core, but I didn't run. I watched him come right for me. We were so different in so many ways, but the longer I stayed with him, the more I realized that it didn't matter. He wasn't the monster everyone thought him to be. Arthur was a good man deep down. He had qualities and skills I've always wanted, and I liked the way I was when I was around him. I felt stronger, bolder, and way more confident than I had ever felt before. I liked who I was with him, and I wanted to show him I wasn't afraid of him. *Not anymore. Not ever.*

Arthur towered over me again, and I held my breath. "Don't you see, Kymra?" he whispered softly. "*You* are far better than anyone in this life. I'm not improving you, little one. Oh no, it's quite the opposite. You are making *me* a better person, and I cannot thank you enough."

Suddenly, his lips were on mine, and I dropped the bow. He deepened the kiss, pushing me until my back was against a tree. For the first time, I felt whole, like I was *exactly* where I was supposed to be. His hands drifted to my waist, pulling me closer until our bodies were lined with one another. I stood on my tip-toes and wrapped my arms around his neck. I couldn't get enough of this man. I needed him like I needed air, and I kissed him even harder.

Arthur groaned slightly, and my heart fluttered again. To my surprise, he pulled away, resting his head against my own. I jutted out my bottom lip pouting.

"Forgive me," he chuckled softly. "I have been wanting to do that for quite some time."

I blushed. "And here I thought you just tolerated me."

Arthur smiled wide, shaking his head at me. "Come. I want to show you something."

His shadows engulfed the two of us, and he pulled me through the shadow veil. It wasn't as harsh as the first time, and I held on to him tightly as he took me to a secluded spot near the castle. We stopped on the massive hill that overlooked the back part of his castle, and I smiled, taking in the beauty of this world. The Forbidden Woods went on for miles, and way off in the distance was the Kingdom of Odemark. I could see the spot where the dark clashed with the light. *Sort of like me and Arthur*, I thought to myself as I grinned wide. I turned around to say something, when my eyes fell upon the big oak tree and a small grave beside it.

"Arthur..." I said, my voice trailing as he took my hand and pulled me close.

"This was the last person I ever cared about before I met you. This is where my mother is buried," he said, and my heart shattered. I looked up at him, seeing pain in his eyes once more. He just looked so sad. *He wasn't the Nightlocke right now. He was just Arthur. The man who was broken and lonely. The man who needed me.*

"Arthur, what happened to you mother?" I asked quietly, and he slowly sat down next to her grave. He reached for me, and I let him pull me in close. My chest burned in agreement now. I needed to help him with this somehow.

"She was killed by the Nightlocke," he finally answered, and my eyes widened. A thousand questions ran through my mind as I slumped against him.

"Oh Arthur..."

"We were starving along with the rest of the kingdom, and Momma was weak. No one in the village would heal us nor would the King. My father had passed away years prior, and with my age, there was nothing I could do for her. I watched the castle under attack that night, and when the Nightlocke screams filled the air, his shadows hit the two of us, marking me on the wrist."

Arthur lifted his arm, and I saw a hooded mark on the inside of his wrist. My eyes soften as I gently touched the ink on his skin. He let me.

"I didn't know what it meant, but everyone else in town seemed to understand, and they chased Momma and I into these woods. I met the

CHAPTER 16

Nightlocke then, but he seemed like any normal man. He offered his assistance, and with no other options, I followed him. Little did I realize it was all just a ruse to get me to kill him. I watched my mother die right in front of me. I lost it when he laughed, calling me a fool for trusting him. I *hated* him. I hated him so much that I killed him, Kymra."

My heart was so still as I listened to him get everything off his chest. The pain he endured, the loss he dealt with every day... I couldn't imagine going through what he had. *And to become the thing you hated...*

"He passed the burden of the Nightlocke to me because he couldn't handle what he had done. I took my anger and grief out on the only ones left. Those in the kingdom shunned us, denied us even the most basic human needs, and refused to show us any kindness or decency. It cost me the only person who ever cared about me. I brought you here because I wanted you to know that I wasn't always a bad person. I know I have done bad things, but deep down... I'm still Arthur."

Tears filled my eyes as he looked so broken before me. *He was a victim of the Nightlocke, just like everyone else, and had gone through so much pain.* I leaned into him, trying to give him comfort somehow.

"I am so sorry, Arthur. *No one* should have ever gone through what you did. If I had met you all those years ago, I would have helped you," I whispered, and he hugged me tighter.

"I know you would have. You are too good for this world, Kymra. I love that about you," he said, and the corners of my mouth rose.

"My momma used to say that about me. Sometimes I wish I had more of a backbone though. I feel like I am too caring sometimes," I whispered, getting close to admitting the truth. Arthur made me *want* to tell the truth though.

"Nah, you are perfect, Kymra. Don't ever change that about you, please. I also wanted to apologize for how I treated you when you first came here and for taking you in the first place. It was wrong, and I'm sorry."

I waved him away. "Honestly, after everything Arthur, I am happy we met. I feel better when I am with you. Like I'm finally becoming this strong, independent women that can say no for a change."

He cocked his head to the side. "What do you mean, Kymra?"

I sighed. "You'll think I'm crazy."

Arthur shook his head. "Never."

"Something in my chest burns deep within me whenever someone is in trouble or needs help. It's been like that for as long as I can remember, and I've let people walk all over me because of it. It gets painful when I don't so I've just let it decide for me. Don't get me wrong, I love helping others and being useful, but when I always give everything up or take every slight without saying anything, it begins to take it's toll. It's why I joined the rations program, why I didn't say anything to Thomas when he insulted me, and why I walked towards you the night we met."

He blinked in surprise, and I held my breath. Fear trickled in that I said too much, when he sighed heavily, turning me to face him better.

"Kymra... I need to tell you something," he said, when the forest suddenly came alive.

The trees seemed to shudder as if *warning* all those who lived here that something was wrong. Massive ravens took off from the forest's entrance, and Arthur hauled us to our feet. His eyes blackened as he listened to the forest, and I knew he was searching for the source of the problem.

"Arthur, what's wrong?" I asked, taking his hand and squeezing tightly. Anxiety rolled in my stomach as I scanned the treetops for any sign of what was in these woods, when Arthur turned to me.

"Kymra, I need you to listen to me. Okay? I need you to lock yourself in your room and do not come out until I come for you. Can you do that for me?"

My eyes widened. *Something was very wrong.*

"Arthur, tell me what's wrong."

"Everything."

Chapter 17

Arthur

Kymra looked alarmed as she turned back to the forest. She couldn't see what I could, but I couldn't tell her what was wrong. I can't risk her, I won't risk her. Thomas had entered my forest with a small army, and I needed to drive him out *by any means necessary.* She'd try to come with. I just knew she'd want to get involved, but I couldn't have that. I couldn't have them knowing exactly where Kymra was.

"Arthur, I don't understand," she said, her voice shaking, when I grabbed her hand.

"Do you trust me?" I asked.

Kymra looked up at me with those big green eyes of hers, melting my heart with that one look before nodding her head. I sighed in relief.

"I do, Arthur. I trust you."

"Then *please* hide in your room. If anything comes for you, reach for the shadows. I will do everything I can to protect you, Kymra."

She gave me a small nod, and I kissed her hands.

"Come."

I pulled her through the veil, setting her safely inside her room in a matter of seconds.

"Lock this door," I commanded. "Barricade it, and do not open it no matter who's voice you hear, alright? Trust me!"

I didn't give her a chance to ask anymore questions, and I shut it behind me. I hated to leave her, but I needed to make sure Thomas didn't get close to the castle or *to her.* I heard her lock the door and pride filled my chest. I took off then, reaching the front door to the castle, when I suddenly heard her voice.

"Be safe, Arthur."

My heart soared hearing her voice come through the shadows. It gave me the extra push I needed to rid the forest of those who did not belong.

"Let's see where you are, Thomas," I said, darkening my eyes. I sent my shadows out to find their mark, and they bolted through the trees, finding the group quickly. They hadn't made it very far, but then again one step inside my forest was too close for comfort. They stayed in a tight formation, with Thomas the dead center of everything. I rolled my eyes.

"Coward," I whispered to myself. I debated releasing the creatures in my dungeon to annihilate them. *They hadn't been fed in awhile,* I thought, smiling at the gruesome image that came to mind, but then another thought occurred. If I killed them all the King would only continue to send more troops, especially if I slaughtered the Prince. *No... Killing them was not the way. I needed to scare them so badly that they never wanted to return.* They would spread the word that this is *my home,* and Kymra belongs to *me.*

I had to get closer for this to work. Saving my energy, I started running through the woods, adrenaline pumping through my veins. The forest brightened on the path before me as if wanted me to clear them out too. Suddenly, I could hear them whispering, and I slowed my pace, kneeling down by a tree.

"Stay alert, boys! Kymra *has* to be here!" Thomas shouted in a hushed tone, and I darkened my eyes again.

"You won't touch her, prick," I whispered, raising my hands.

My shadows rushed forward, surrounding *His Royal Highness* and his soldiers. They all drew their swords, cursing as the shadows covered them entirely. It would take a whole lot of concentration to enter this many minds at once. They were never awake when I attempted this before either, so this was a new thing for me. My shadows entered each and every mind, seeing their fears come straight to the forefront, and then I amplified them. It was tricky staying locked onto every fear, but I managed. *This. Was. Fun.*

Their guttural screams rattled the woods, and then came the clashing of swords. The scent of blood filled the air, and I smiled wickedly. I held them a moment longer before the familiar stomping of a Bloodhound sounded behind me. I withdrew my shadows and half of the Prince's security force lay on the ground, either dead or wishing for death's embrace. They had killed one another fighting their hallucinations. *This was too easy*, I thought as I rolled my shoulders, ready for the next attack.

Thomas cowered beneath his men, rising slowly to his feet, his sword shaking. *He deserved more...* I turned to look behind me then. Three Bloodhounds sniffed the air not far from me. *It would be entertaining to use them*, I thought to myself, when another brilliant idea came to me. *I don't even know if it is possible, but if I could pull this off...*

"It better work," I muttered as I stepped into the veil. The Bloodhounds snarled when I stepped into their path and then roared before charging. I raised my hands quickly, and shut my eyes, trying to focus. Their thunderous footsteps pounded the ground before me, but I stayed still, waiting for the right time to strike. *Bloodhounds were strong. I had one shot to get this right...* My shadows hissed in warning, and I released them towards the Bloodhounds, hitting them square in the chest and forcing them down their throats. My shadows spread across their body, halting them in their tracks. My eyes opened, and my chest heaved as we stared at one another. *I had learned a new skill, it seemed. Shadow Bending.*

I clenched my fists together, forcing them to move their feet. They couldn't make a sound, couldn't *move* unless I told them too. They were now at *my* bidding. My head began to throb as they struggled against me though, and I frowned. *This would take some practice.* The Bloodhounds stood tall over me, drool dripping from their snout as they snarled. I grinned wickedly.

"Let's go, boys."

I drew my hood over my head, covering most of my face, and we walked towards the group of invaders. It took nothing to reach what was left of Thomas's men. They all shook with fear as I stepped into their line of sight with three monstrous Bloodhounds behind me.

"I don't believe I invited you into my home, Thomas," I snarled. My head throbbed again as they pushed against my shadows.

Thomas's eyes widened. "You know my name, Nightlocke?"

"I do. You have done horrible things to the one that belongs to me," I bellowed, outright claiming what was mine. He gritted his teeth in anger, the *foolish* boy.

"Kymra is not yours, and if you were smart you'd let her go!"

"So you could lock her away to torture her for being a Lightspark? I don't think so," I replied, losing my grip on the Bloodhounds slightly. It roared loudly, and the guards stepped backwards. Thomas simply glared.

"You seem to know everything, Nightlocke," Thomas finally said, and I laughed, scaring his men even more as my shadows swirled around them.

"And yet, you all seem to know nothing at all. These woods are *my home*, and you are not welcome here! Kymra belongs to me! If you continue to pursue her then a fate far worse than death awaits you. There will be no place in the world for you to run, Thomas! I will *always* find you."

I raised my arms, shooting the last of my shadows towards the invaders, marking them all. It was a simple locator mark in the shape of a black circle, and it etched itself onto their wrists. Now, we were forever bound together until I removed it.

"This is your only warning! Step into my woods again, and I will know! Step towards my girl, and I'll release the Hounds! Step across from me..." my voice trailed off as I took a step towards Thomas, "and find out *exactly* why everyone fears me."

Thomas's eyes widened before drifting to the mark. Fear rippled across his face before a calm rage appeared. *He's too arrogant.* Suddenly, a sharp pain pierced my skull, and I sucked in a harsh breath. The Bloodhounds were gaining control again. My mind was too exhausted to hold them like this for *this* long. They snarled, and the stench of piss filled the air.

"I won't leave without Kymra!" Thomas shouted.

"She's happy, Thomas. I can love her the way she deserves, whereas *you* are just a pathetic boy stuck in his brother's shadow. You are nothing more than a disappointment to everyone, Thomas. And you are seriously starting to piss me off. Now, *get out!*" I shouted as my head throbbed. I let the Bloodhounds go and stepped backwards into the veil. Their snarls were the last thing I heard as I traveled far enough behind to watch the carnage unfold. Thomas shoved one of his men into the arms of the Bloodhound before taking off towards the edge of the woods.

"Prick," I said, swaying on my feet. My chest heaved as I struggled to catch my breath. *I had overdone it,* I thought as I gave myself a moment to rest. I was weaker than I thought, and that *alarmed* me. *I had to get better at this.*

The Bloodhounds tore the guards limb from limb. Their sickening screams filled the air as they met their end. The few survivors ran to safety after Thomas, who was leaps and bounds ahead of everyone else. I shook my head. *Some man he was...*

A screeching wail sounded through the air, and I froze. I dove into a thicken bush as a Wraith flew overhead, racing to the bodies before the Bloodhounds ate them entirely. I slumped against the ground. *At least it was not the Mist.* My body pulsed from overexertion, and I didn't have the strength for another jump. I stole a peek from where I hid.

Wraiths were a lot like Nightlockes, looking nothing more than a large shadowy figure with a hooded cloak. These creatures flew around the land, opening themselves up when they found their victim. They'd swallow them whole, and once they passed through, they simply left a pile of bones behind wherever they went. They were vicious creatures but thankfully solitary. The Forbidden Woods did not have many in abundance, but still enough you needed to be careful. They were hard to kill, and the only way to do it was with fire. You had to time it perfectly though as their only weak spot was internal, so you had to get the flames on the inside, if you even wanted a chance to live. And I didn't bring my bow.

I watched the Wraith screech again, scaring the Bloodhounds off before stealing their kill. *They were hungry little things. It was now or never.* Exhaustion weighed me down as I made the slow walk back home. My head was at a dull throb, but my shadows felt the same. *Maybe it was more so an issue with me than not having enough shadows.* I couldn't help but wonder. I had never really pushed myself like that before for fear of losing my mind faster like the Nightlocke before me had. My feet were heavy by the time my castle came into view. It was all I could do to put one foot in front of the other at this point.

I immediately went to Kymra, needing to see that she was still safe and alright.

"Kymra!" I shouted, hitting her door. It flung open, and there she stood, safe and sound. I relaxed, feeling utter relief even though she wasn't even near the danger. My shadows sung, but I swayed hard on my feet. And then my body was falling. I didn't have the strength to stand upright anymore, and I fell when my legs gave out.

"Arthur!" she cried out, but that's all I heard before everything went black.

Chapter 18

Kymra

Arthur crumbled, hitting the ground in a loud thump, and my heart stopped. *This was bad! This was really, really bad!* I thought to myself as I rushed to his side. I grabbed an arm, tossing it over my shoulder as I tried to stand and grunted. *Good Lord, he was heavy!* I shimmed his body to my back and pushed with my feet. Dragging him across the room was the hardest thing I had *ever* done. But I *had* to help him.

I shoved Arthur up on my bed and collapsed against him as my chest heaved. My body rose with his, and I sighed in relief. *He was at least breathing.* I sprung into action and began checking his vitals. I searched his body for any visible wounds, but he looked fine, other than being unconscious. *Maybe he was okay then?* I got him as comfortable as I could and waited.

I needed to make sure he was okay.

I waited for hours with nothing but the sound of Bloodhounds in the woods to keep me company. Arthur never once moved a muscle, but his breathing was steady, and I was grateful for that. The idea of something happening to him struck a nerve in me, and I couldn't begin to imagine being in this dark castle all by myself. I couldn't begin to imagine being in this world without him, and I gently ran my fingers through his wild hair while he slept. My feelings for this man didn't frighten me like before. I just wanted him *safe*. My eyes began to droop, but I forced them to stay open.

Another hour went by, and I leaned my head against my hand, trying to rest my neck. I was exhausted, but Arthur took up a large portion of the bed, and my face heated at the idea of me sharing a bed with him. I stayed on the chair and waited some more. Time seemed to drag on so slowly, and I honestly wasn't sure how much longer I'd last. I pulled the blanket up a little further and got comfortable.

Suddenly, Arthur groaned, and I shot up out of the chair frantically. I rubbed my eyes, realizing my room was no longer dark and gloomy, but rather bright and sunny. *I fell asleep!* Panic swelled inside as I rushed to Arthur's side.

"Arthur! You're alright!" I shouted as he finally opened his eyes.

He looked confused for a moment, but he smiled when his eyes finally settled on me. "Hey, Kymra."

"What happened?! You just collapsed in my room!"

Arthur sat up, noticing that he was sprawled out on my bed before turning to my makeshift bed on the chair.

"Did you stay with me all night, Kymra?"

Heat crept into my cheeks then, and I straightened. "I had to. You just collapsed, and I wasn't going to leave you like that. Now *please,* tell me what happened!"

His smile remained, and he sat forwards, stretching out his arms above his head. "Nothing, Kymra. There was a threat, but I took care of it, and now there's not. We're safe, I promise."

I blinked. "That's it?" I asked, my eyes narrowing. "You won't tell me anything else?!"

Arthur gave me a pointed look. "Do you really want to know, Kymra?"

My face fell, knowing it was probably violent. I understood he was the Nightlocke, but it still was unsettling thinking about the things he probably did. "I suppose not. Why did you collapse though?"

"I just used a little too much power yesterday. I was weak and needed to rest. Nothing even came close to touching me though."

My face softened. "I didn't even know that was possible with you."

He grinned mischievously. "I like you believing I'm all powerful, love. You can keep thinking that if you'd like."

I playfully slapped his arm. "Arthur..."

Arthur yanked me forward, slamming his lips on mine before I could question him more. I yipped at his abruptness but quickly melted further into him. *I had missed him.* He pulled away, grinning like a mad man.

"Arthur, you can't just kiss me when you don't want to answer my questions," I said, putting my hands on my hips.

He chuckled before wrapping his arms around my waist. "But it's more fun this way, don't you think?"

My heart stopped as his husky voice deepened. I shook my head and gently slid out from his embrace. *He wasn't going to play fair,* I thought to myself, letting my hips sway with every step. I grinned when I turned, finding him staring at me with those onyx eyes of him and his shadows. *I liked that I could mess with him too.*

"Where are you off to, Kymra?" he demanded, narrowing his eyes on me.

"You need to eat. If you won't tell me what happened then at least let me care for you. I need you healthy because I want to practice with the bow again today," I said, sauntering out the door and down the hall. Heavy footsteps pounded the floor after me, and I couldn't contain my laughter.

"Wait for me!" he hollered, and I ran faster. Suddenly, dark shadows filled the ground beneath me, and Arthur swiftly came through the veil.

"Cheater," I muttered quietly, and he laughed loudly before falling in step with me. Soon, we were in the kitchen, and I began rummaging throughout the cabinet. The corners of my mouth rose when I realized how cozy I was becoming in this castle now. I moved around the room without needing help from Arthur. The Nightlocke collapsed on one of the chairs while I made a giant pot of porridge. I laughed when I set a bowl down before him, and his face fell.

"What's wrong with breakfast?" I asked, and he gave me sly grin.

"Nothing. I just thought you were going to make something fancy is all," he said quietly, and I laughed even harder.

"You're getting spoiled, Arthur," I replied, and he grinned.

"I only tease," he said before taking a bite. *It was nice to see his playful side.*

"Hold on there. I wasn't going to leave you hanging," I said, grabbing the cinnamon and brown sugar. I sprinkled both in before adding milk. He mixed it around, and I grinned wide when he actually groaned after his next bite. *God, he was freaking adorable.*

"You're amazing, Kymra," he said, taking bite after bite. I made my own bowl, and I had to admit, it was pretty good.

"This was my momma's recipe, so thank her," I said as he cleaned his bowl.

"Well then, thank you Mrs... What's your last name?"

I laughed again. "Fields. Pleasure to meet you, Arthur Nightlocke." I gave him a mocking bow, and he shook his head at me.

"That's not my last name," he replied, scooping the last bite from his bowl.

I cocked my head to the side. "Really? I just assumed..."

"Nightlocke is *what* I am, not who I am. My last name is Drakos."

I took another bite. "Interesting. Well, nice to meet you, Arthur Drakos."

He grinned and gave me a small nod in return. "And you, Kymra Fields. Alright, you ready to go?"

"Yes!" I said, tossing my bowl aside to clean later.

He grinned as he stood from his seat. But then he hesitated and turned to me. "Before we go, just make sure you stay close to me, alright?"

"Why?" I asked, my smile falling. *Was it even safe to go out?*

"There were Bloodhounds and a Wraith near the castle yesterday, but they should be cleared out by now. Just in case though, stay close," he said, grabbing his bow and another one off the hook. He handed me the smaller one, and my eyes widened.

"Try this one today. It might be better for you," he said, and the corners of my mouth rose. The bow was beautiful. Made of dark wood with a perfectly white string. The etching of a rose on the handle, it was breathtaking. *When did he even grab another bow?* I wondered to myself as I looked back to him. *Arthur just gave me another gift and has no idea how much it means to me.*

Arthur took off outside, and I scurried to catch up with my new bow and quiver in hand. We went back to the same spot as the day before, and he conjured his shadow creatures again. This time, he joined me. We went over the basics again, and the first thing I noticed was that *this* bow was so much easier to work with. It wasn't such a difficult pull as the one before, and I was actually able to aim with this one. I wasn't struggling so badly to keep the line pulled tight, and I started hitting the targets with this new bow. We spent the morning practicing, and I let my last arrow fly, hitting the shadow

CHAPTER 18

creature in the head.

"You are a natural, Kymra. I think bows were meant to be your thing," Arthur said, and I grinned wide.

"Well, I have an amazing teacher," I replied, and he abruptly dropped his head. The tint of pink showed on his cheeks before he turned around, grabbing his quiver. Pity filled my heart. I truly meant the compliment because he was an incredible teacher, but seeing how he reacted made me remember how alone he's been.

"How about we test these new skills?" he suggested, pulling me from my thoughts. "Let's see how many you can get before the creatures reach you."

My eyes widened. "Do you think I'm ready for that?"

"No one is ever ready, Kymra. You just start and work your way from there. It's entirely different than shooting stationary targets, but a necessary skill to learn. More often than not, your target will be in motion. Come, we can try it together."

"Can I watch you first? I might have a better idea of what I'm supposed to do," I asked, and he nodded.

"Sure. Just know it's a little like cheating because I know where they will be, but I'll try to get close to what you should be doing," he said, drawing his first arrow. Arthur took in a deep breath as his shadows went out into the woods again. He drew up ten creatures this time, and they all began moving rapidly and in random order. It was difficult to tell them apart as they moved, but I was in awe once Arthur started the course.

The shadow creatures misted when the arrow struck their bodies. Arthur moved in a fluid motion, drawing arrow after arrow until the last few started launching themselves towards him. Arthur ducked, aiming above his head and striking one right in the chest. My jaw dropped. One by one, every lost arrow moved through the grass towards Arthur before a large shadow hand put them back in his quiver for him.

"Your turn," he said abruptly. My eyes widened.

"I can't do that!" I protested, and he chuckled softly.

"I couldn't either when my father taught me, but you can learn, Kymra."

"I didn't know your father taught you this," I replied as he kissed my cheek.

I had heard very little of his past, and I held my breath, wondering if he'd tell me more.

"He did when I was young. Now scoot. I don't have long before I need to run an errand, and I want to see you try it."

I sighed. "Okay... I'm going. Just take it easy on me, okay?"

He grinned, twirling his fingers at me, and I rolled my eyes. I drew an arrow and got in my stance.

"I can do this," I whispered to myself.

Ten creatures appeared once more, and they began moving in the same pattern as before, just slower. Even with the slower speed, it was difficult keeping up with his shadow monsters as they moved sporadically through the trees. I spun my arms around wildly, trying to get a lock on one of them, but I was too afraid to let my arrow fly. Suddenly, one dove for me, and I ducked just barely in time to watch them pass above my head.

"Focus, Kymra. Move with them!" Arthur shouted from behind.

I groaned. *He made it look so easy!* I tried to move with the creatures, and fired an arrow, missing entirely. It was close, but my timing was off, and I gritted my teeth. I fired again, hitting it's shoulder this time and ran towards the next creature.

I spent the next twenty minutes firing at the moving targets, hitting four out of the ten marks. *Not great, but it was something.* Still, my shoulders slumped in defeat.

Arthur grinned before pulling me close again. He wrapped his arm around my waist saying, "Kymra, you did so well!"

"Thank you," I replied, letting him drag me back to the castle. "I just want to be better. I finally found something that I enjoy, and I don't want to be awful at it. Do we have to go inside now? Can we keep practicing?"

Arthur slowly rocked his head back and forth, debating my request. He looked back at the woods and then to the castle. Finally, he sighed and grabbed a small piece of wood and rope that was laying out in the back. He hung it from the closest tree to the castle.

"My errand won't be far, but I can't have you going through the woods today. I might be too drained to rescue you, so you need to stay close enough to run back to the safety of the castle. Can you stay right here while I'm out?" he asked, studying me closely.

"Of course, Arthur," I answered, "but what are you doing that will drain you so quickly?"

He just kissed my cheek. "Nothing to worry about, Kymra. I'll be back soon," he said, before disappearing into the woods again.

I signed. A part of me hoped he would have asked me to join him, but he still seemed to have his secrets. I couldn't blame him though. *This between us was so new. I couldn't expect him to let me in on everything.* Still, I couldn't help but wonder what he could possibly be up to.

I spent the next couple hours practicing hitting the target. I even practiced firing the bow while running so I could get used to the movement. Some of the arrows fell off the board, but quite a few actually stuck, and I was quite proud of that. It was quickly getting late in the day though, and there were still no signs of Arthur. I was beginning to worry as I stared into the dark forest. *Where could he be?*

I grabbed a fallen arrow when a loud roar sounded off in the distance, and my heart stopped. I turned and darkness flickered in the forest. *Arthur...* My feet were moving before my head could stop me. My chest burned badly now, and I just knew it was because of Arthur. *He needed me.*

I followed the trees as they guided me through the Forbidden Woods, following the continued snarls and viscous roars. I pushed passed a thick oak tree, when my eyes went wide. Arthur stood before me, with his arms raised and blood trickling out of his nose in front of two Bloodhounds. Fear gripped my heart, and I drew an arrow. *They were going to kill him...* But they didn't move right away. Instead, their bodies shook violently, and then they began moving unnaturally, like something was *forcing* them forward. They went from walking to running before they clashed against one another. They began to shake again, and one of them roared in agony *in pain.*

Arthur snarled in frustration as the Bloodhound twisted about. It opened it's mouth, and black shadows leaked out. The creature relaxed, his body less rigid, and my eyes widened when Arthur twisted his hand and forced them back down the throat of the Bloodhound.

Oh my God... he was controlling them.

My hand covered my mouth as I stared in shocked. *It just seemed cruel to control them like this.* Arthur's arms shook slightly from the pressure. *He was wearing out... But why would he do this?*

Suddenly, a third Bloodhound flew into the clearing next to me and charged. I screamed, and Arthur's gaze snapped to mine. He dropped his hold on the two and launched a knife out of his right hand, hitting the Bloodhound in the chest. It collapsed at my feet, and Arthur was at my side in seconds before he covered us in shadows, and we disappeared back to the castle. He spat me out of the shadow veil, and I landed hard on the floor. I was back in my room once more, and I turned to look at him. His eyes were completely black, and he crossed his arms, blocking the exit.

"What did I tell you to do, Kymra?! It was one simple request! Why did you follow me into the woods like that?! You could have been killed!" he bellowed, but I scurried to my feet, ignoring any rational thought telling me to stay away from the angry man who could kill me in a blink of an eye.

"What were you doing to the Bloodhounds, Arthur?"

His eyes narrowed before he spoke. "It's none of your concern, Kymra. I asked you for *one thing* today to protect you!"

Arthur was beyond upset with me, but I wasn't exactly happy with him at the moment either. I didn't want to be his excuse to do terrible things. "What does controlling the Bloodhounds have to do with my safety? I thought the whole point was to avoid those creatures!"

"For you, yes! But I need them, Kymra!"

"Why?! You are already the worst monster out here, Arthur! Why do you need them?"

"BECAUSE YOU ARE A LIGHTSPARK, AND I NEED TO KEEP YOU SAFE!"

I took a step backwards as he screamed at me. My brows furrowed, and I shook my head. *I was what now? No, he was wrong... He had to be. I wasn't a Lightspark. I couldn't heal people or the land!* I thought as I rubbed my face. I looked back at him as his eyes softened, returning to their normal stunning blue. *He actually seemed to believe this crazy theory of his...* I shook my head in disbelief. *He believes it, and he's hurting those creatures because of it.*

CHAPTER 18

"Look, I had meant to tell you in a different way."

"You're wrong."

He stared at me blankly. "I am *not* wrong, Kymra. Your powers may not be fully woke, but it's in your blood. I've seen it! Why do you think you healed so fast the other day?"

I shook my head in disbelief. "I've bled before Arthur, and nothing has ever come of it. Don't you think I would have known something as important as being the Lightspark? Wouldn't I have healed the land by now if I was? I'm not the Lightspark."

Arthur sighed as he took another step towards me. "You are, Kymra. It's why we are drawn to one another. You are my other half, and I am yours. *You keep me balanced inside, from losing my mind to the darkness completely. It took me awhile to figure it out, but I'm better when I am with you. Don't you see?"

I staggered backwards, putting much needed space between us. These last few weeks have been a whirlwind as it was, but *this* was too much. *How could he think that I was the Lightspark?* I would have known something like that. He's using me as a way to justify doing awful things as the Nightlocke, and I wouldn't stand for it. *I didn't want to be apart of hurting others.*

"No, I don't!" I shouted back, clenching my fists at my side. "You're out in the woods controlling the Bloodhounds, which looked painful for them by the way! You won't tell me who attacked the other day, nor will you say what you even did to stop them! You steal from the King and the kingdom, who are suffering enough as it is. I'm not balancing you out at all! You're *still* behaving like the Nightlocke, and I won't be your excuse to be wicked!"

Arthur flinched. I immediately regretted my words as he looked like I struck him. Guilt ate me up inside, and his eyes darkened once more. He had put the mask back on, closing himself off to me again, and my heart shattered.

"Arthur, I didn't..."

"Stop, Kymra. You've said quite enough. For your information, it was Thomas and his army that invaded my home *looking* for you. Care to know why? It's because the King has figured out what you are and is on the hunt now. He promised Thomas your hand in marriage in exchange for him finding you, but he has no intentions of letting you out of that cell once he throws you in. The King will drain the blood from your body to cultivate his land, and I won't allow it! I sent Thomas running back to his father with a message to stay away from you, but I don't think it will be enough. I need those Bloodhounds to rid the world of your precious royal family!"

I blinked. *Thomas. He was trying to find me?* I slumped down to my bed in shock. *Arthur was just going to kill the King and both Princes because he thought they'd just lock me away and hurt me?* I thought, and my head began to throb. *No, they would never hurt me like that!* This was all wrong. He didn't know them like I did, and I wouldn't allow their deaths to be on my hands over a mistake.

"You are wrong, Arthur. The King would never do that to me, and I'm not the Lightspark. I've never been able to do any of the things they can do, and you're going to kill innocent people for nothing. I won't stand for it!" I said, my voice shaking.

"I am telling you the truth, Kymra! I know I've made plenty of mistakes when it comes to you, but I've never lied. Thomas wasn't even kind to you! Why are you defending him like this?" he bellowed, pacing the room before me. "Do you want to know the truth about that man? He's a coward! I watched him throw one of his *own* men into the arms of a Bloodhound, just so he could escape. None of the royal family are good, but I am trying to be! I've figured out why the Nightlocke even exist, Kymra. The dark and wicked shadows that fill me to my very core is on this planet to protect *you*. The Lightspark. I have the ability to do what needs to be done to ensure your safety, so you can save everyone else. Sometimes a necessary evil *must* take place for the good of all! I'm even here to balance you so you don't let others take advantage of you, while you keep me sane and my morals in check! I haven't even plagued the kingdom since you've come here. I am changing, Kymra, whether you see it or not."

I covered my mouth to keep a sob from escaping my lips. I cared so deeply for Arthur. I *loved* him, but I did not agree to this plan. *This was my own fault,* I thought as my heart broke in two. I had fallen in love with the villain, and now I was suddenly having issues with the way he behaved. I loved everything

CHAPTER 18

about this man, expect the violent streak he had, but I didn't know what to do. The idea of him doing such awful acts in my name *sickened* me. *I wasn't a Lightspark, and he was making a huge mistake.*

Despite the horrible words Thomas said to me, I didn't believe Thomas would do something as awful and cruel as throwing one of his own men to their deaths just to save himself either. He honored his men, just like Liam and King Alexander. The royal family would never throw me in a cell. They would never hurt me. *I grew up with them,* I thought, thinking back to my childhood and the good memories I had. I *knew* them, and they weren't bad people.

"Say something!" Arthur shouted, startling me.

A single tear fell down my cheek as I replied, "I won't let you kill them, Arthur. You are *wrong* about me. I'm not special, and what you're doing is a mistake."

Arthur's face fell. He stared at me, breaking my heart into tiny pieces with that one devastating look. Suddenly, his face twisted into a violent rage, and he stalked towards me. He hauled me to my feet, tossing my bed aside to grab the pages I stole from his journal. *I had forgotten about them,* I thought as my eyes widened. I had meant to destroy them, but I had *forgotten them*. Arthur's eyes blackened as he glared at me. *Oh God, he must think....*

"I see you've been busy," he snarled at me.

"It's not what you think..."

"Really? Because I think you stole pages from a private journal that contained knowledge on how to actually kill me and steal my powers! What were you planning to do with these, Kymra? Get me to trust you, make me *fall in love* with you, only to figure out my secret and take it back to your precious King!" he spat out as tears fell down my cheek.

"Wait, you know what's on those pages?" I asked in disbelief. He snarled again, and I flinched. I took a step backwards and stammered, "I swear, Arthur! I would never betray you like that! I didn't..."

"I don't believe you," he growled, crushing the pages in his hands. My shoulders fell. "I only pretended I couldn't read so I had an excuse to be close to you, and what a fool I've been! I cannot believe I *ever* trusted you! I've tried to be the man you deserved! But all you see is the Nightlocke. If that's what you want, then that's what you'll get."

My heart shattered into a million pieces then. *He was ending everything,* I thought as anxiety rippled through me. *I could hear it in his tone.* Panic flooded my brain as I watched him step further from me. *I may not want him killing in my name, but I would never betray him like that.*

"Arthur..."

Arthur shook his head. "Just stop. I'll make sure these are properly disposed of."

He stomped to my door and swung it opened. It clattered against the wall as Arthur stood rigid. He slowly turned to me and another tear fell down my face. "I'm done, Kymra. I should have never trusted you to begin with but..." his voice trailed off as he looked to the floor. Pain rippled on his face briefly before he glared again. "I won't betray you like you were planning to with me. I understand why we were made so differently now. It's because I have the stomach to do what is necessary. I will kill the royal family to ensure your safety, and then you can go home. I'll make sure you stay alive, but I promise I'll stay *forever* out of your sight."

Arthur slammed the door, and I rushed towards it. I yanked on the handle as heavy boots stomped away, but it wouldn't give. A sob burst from my lips as I shouted his name. I begged him to let me out, to come back to me so I could explain myself, but he never came back. I slid down to the ground bawling.

How do I fix this?

I hurt him deeply. While he was wrong about me and the royal family, I never meant to hurt him like that. I cringed, thinking over my harsh words, and for being so stupid in taking those pages in the first place. I stole them to protect him because I thought he had no idea the dangerous information that was on them. Never once did I plan to take them to the King. *He said he was done with me,* I thought as pain gripped my heart. *Arthur wanted me to go home and to never see him again.*

I laid my head in my arms and fell apart. I didn't want that. I *needed* him. I forced myself to sit up, wiping my eyes as I got control of myself. *I refuse*

CHAPTER 18

to accept that. I loved him even with all his flaws. I'd make this up to him. Somehow I'd fix this, and then I'll show how much he means to me. My chest burned again, and I took that as a good sign. Now all I needed was a plan. First and foremost, I had to stop this crazy plan of his. He won't listen to me until I show him the truth. Arthur would calm down, and maybe we could negotiate a peace treaty between the two. The King would be thrilled to have the Nightlocke leave his kingdom, and I could show Arthur that not everything called for violence. *Maybe then he could give up being the Nightlocke? He didn't have to stay the villain because to me he was so much more.*

I just needed to get to the King to explain everything. Once the King understood that I was not in danger, I'd call Arthur through the shadows and then clear everything up. Then I'd spend the rest of my life trying to make it up to Arthur. I had to because I needed him.

I loved him.

I got to my feet as the plan formed in my head and went straight to the windows. *Arthur may have locked my door, but I doubt he locked them all,* I thought as I stepped onto the balcony. I stepped over the rail, trying not to look down at the possible looming death and hopped over to the other balcony. It led to another dusty bedroom, and I went into the hall, finding what was keeping me locked in. There was a chair wedged under my handle, and I sighed. I had to fix this. I refused to let a night pass without making amends with Arthur.

I left the castle and ran through the forest. The trees to my right were dark and menacing so I ran forward. I refused to let my legs stop, and soon a bright clearing appeared just ahead. But then suddenly, I heard a sickening screech.

A Wraith.

I dove into the thick bush, pushing my body against the tree, praying it didn't see me. I held my breath, afraid to even move and bring destruction upon my own self. I had never seen a Wraith up close before, but this creature was *not* what I was expecting. A large floating man hovered above me, and my breath caught in my chest. My eyes widened in terror as it sniffed the air, opening it's chest cavity ever so slightly to show an intense darkness inside. Then it wailed in the air and flew off.

I released the breath I had been holding, listening to it's wails get quieter and quieter before I carefully left my hiding place. My heart thundered in my chest, and I cursed myself for leaving my bow back at the castle. There was nothing to do about it now. I shot through the tree line, taking in my kingdom for the first time in months. I ignored the looks I got from the other villagers, running straight towards home. The kingdom murmured as I ran faster. *My father would know how to help me.*

I barreled into my home, startling my family.

"Oh my God, Kymra!" my sister shouted as my family plowed into me. My sister burst into tears as Dad kissed my forehead.

"He let you go? Oh, I thought I'd never see you again!" my father shouted, and I gently pushed them back.

"No, I left on my own, but that's besides the point. I need help Dad and..." I stammered, when I finally took in the room. My eyes widened. A stock pile of food, spices, and wine sat in the corner. Multiple bags were on the table. It looked like my family was dividing it out, and I stood there in disbelief.

"How?" I asked. "Did the King send this?"

My dad gave me a funny look. "The King didn't even send word you were taken. We found out from one of the servant girls there. Some girl named Sarah informed us of what happened, but I thought this was a request made by you. The Nightlocke has been giving it to us on almost a nightly basis since... Well shortly after you disappeared with him. Didn't you know?"

Arthur did this?!

I shook my head as guilt slammed into me. *I accused him of not changing his ways, yet Arthur has been feeding my family since I've been gone,* I thought to myself. *And the King did nothing for them...* I was beginning to question everything, when someone started pounding on the door.

My father gave me a questioning look, but before he could answer it, the door slammed open. A large shadow filled the doorway, and I half thought it was Arthur at first, but then a knight stepped through, and the hairs on the back of my neck stood.

"Kymra Fields, you are being summoned by the King. Failure to come will result in your arrest," the guard bellowed as he stalked over to me. *They were going to arrest me?!*

I took a small step back. "I was planning to come see the King myself, but I just needed a moment with my father. I will..."

The guard pushed my dad out of the way, grabbing my arm harshly. "He wants you now!"

He tossed me roughly to the other guard and fear began to creep up inside me. *The guards have never treated me this way before. Why was this happening?!*

"Take her!"

"Wait, you can't just..."

The guard decked my father, and I screamed. My father was forced to the floor by the knight's boot and panic rippled through me.

"Stop it!" I shouted as I thrashed against the knight. "You don't have to do this!"

"They have an abundance of food here. Take it all, by order of the King!" the guard shouted as the rest started ransacking the place.

"You can't do that! They'll starve!" I shouted. "This isn't against the law!"

"Actually, it is! Stock piling is not permitted in the Kingdom of Odemark. If you need assistance, then you are required to join the rations program, which reminds me. *You* are still a slave and have failed to do your duties. That's grounds for arrest. Now, let's move boys!"

A stock piling law? I had never heard of such a thing! But none of that mattered when the knight tossed me over his shoulders.

"Dad!" I shouted. My fingers just missed the wall where the shadows lie, and I was quickly yanked outside into the sunlight. My heart raced wildly in my chest as the realization hit me like a ton of bricks. The only person that was wrong here... was *me*.

Arthur wasn't lying.

Chapter 19

Arthur

I stormed into the woods absolutely *livid*. My anger and sadness cast a darkness over me unlike anything I had ever felt before, and that was saying something. My shadows swarmed around me and blackened my eyes like a shield trying to protect me, but it was too late. I was already dead inside.

She didn't believe me.

Kymra basically called me a liar, and it was clear she still viewed me as nothing more than the Nightlocke. I would never be good enough for her, and that destroyed me. I was completely pissed for trusting her in the first place. *I don't know why I even bothered! No one could love a monster like me, and honestly no one bothered when I was just Arthur anyways.* If it was my job to protect the Lightspark then I'd do it, but it was clear it didn't mean we were meant to be anything to one another. I just had the stomach to do what was necessary, which is why this job was left to my kind. Tomorrow, I was going to kill the King.

I stormed further into my woods towards the border. This wound in my chest was worse than anything I had ever felt before. I didn't think my heart would ever mend after this. *Maybe I should just fall into the darkness instead of holding on to the balance so fiercely.* Everything hurt, and I was sick of feeling this way anyways.

I decided I needed to hunt.

I took off into the woods, slaughtering anything I could find and sharpening my skills for the attack soon to come. Unlike the previous Nightlocke, *I'd* be ready, and I would get the job done. I had traveled far passed my castle now, nearing the boarder to our two lands. I was covered in blood and breathing heavy, but unable to go home yet. I couldn't bare to hear her screams to be freed from her room. I couldn't hear her criticism or judgment of me again. I just... couldn't.

I just needed to get the job done, so Kymra could finally go home back where she belongs. *Because she doesn't belong here with me,* I told myself. My shadows hissed in protest, but I shrugged them off. Deep down, I knew it wasn't true. I loved that girl, but I couldn't have her. *I was too far gone for someone like her. I've made too many mistakes.*

I collapsed on the ground, resting by one of the large oak trees, my arms feeling like jello. Blood covered my torso from the unfortunate creatures I crossed paths with, and I leaned my head against the bark. The Forbidden Woods was quiet at the moment, and I closed my eyes. Kymra's face appeared before me, and the darkest despair I have ever felt filled my heart. *I hadn't felt this awful since momma...*

Suddenly, I heard a man's scream. I sat up, listening to woods, but it had fallen quiet again. I frowned. *No human should be here,* and *the woods didn't alert me to any danger... Did I miss something in my desperate attempt to get Kymra off my mind?* That thought made me uneasy, and I slowly got to my feet. I took a step, when I heard another scream, and my eyes widened.

Who in the world was here?!

I grabbed my bow and ran. I followed the sound, hearing the familiar screech of a Wraith. I muttered a curse under my breath. *Someone just had a death wish,* I thought as I shoved past the thicket bush. Suddenly, I ground to a halt when I saw Kymra's father swinging a large stick at the Wraith above him. He dove as the Wraith swooped down, it's body opening up to eat him whole, and just narrowly missing him. I cursed again, yanking a different arrow from my quiver and lighting it quickly. The arrow ignited, and I ran towards her father.

The man bolted, his eyes widening when he saw me, and he screamed for help. The Wraith followed, opening it's chest again as it wailed, and I took aim.

"DUCK!" I shouted.

He obeyed, dropping to the ground in an instant. I let my arrow fly, hitting my mark dead center, and the Wraith was instantly engulfed in flames. It roared as it dropped to the ground, writhing in pain. I frowned, Kymra's words from earlier filling my mind as I watched it suffer. I shook my head and turned to her father.

"What are you doing in my woods?!" I shouted, and he put his hands up defensively.

He had gotten to his knees but was breathing hard. Surprisingly, I gave him a minute to catch his breath, despite being angry I just killed a Wraith because he was where he shouldn't be. Maybe it was respect that he managed to stay alive against a Wraith for as long as he had. Or maybe it was just because he was Kymra's father that I was calming myself down. I shifted nervously on my feet, when Kymra's father finally stood, taking one last look at the dead Wraith on the ground.

"Thank you, Nightlocke! It was chasing me awhile. Listen, I know you don't want me here, but I need your help. The royal guard forcefully took Kymra from my home today. They *arrested* her. She looked terrified..."

I gripped his shirt tightly, pulling him close, and his eyes widened. "What do you mean they *took* Kymra!?"

"Just what I said! They arrested Kymra this afternoon! Something very wrong is going on, Nightlocke, and I *need* your help to get her back."

My heart stopped as I staggered backwards. *No... This can't be happening!* I thought as I released my shadows. *He must be lying!* I engulfed the two of us in darkness and used the veil to travel to my castle as fast as I could go. *I left Kymra safe inside my castle walls. She was just there!*

Her father gasped for breath as I dropped him outside in the hall and kicked the chair from the door. I slammed into the door, finding her room empty. *She's gone. Kymra's just... gone.* I dug my hands in my hair as what was left in my heart *shattered* completely. Fear wrapped so fiercely around me, in such a way that I hadn't felt since Momma was sick.

I failed. I failed her... Just like I failed my mother.

"Nightlocke, please!" her father shouted behind me. "I'm terrified for her. They won't even let me through the gate to see her. This isn't the way the

King has *ever* acted towards us before. We used to be friends almost but…"

I couldn't breathe. My shadows shook violently within me, and my eyes darkened in a way I've never felt before as I stared at her empty bedroom. Her father talked incessantly, but all I could think was this *my* fault?

"Look, you fed us *and* kept my daughter safe this whole time when you could have made her a slave or killed her. I know you must care in some way because Kymra was healthy and clearly well fed. I could see that when she came to the house. She looked so different, confident even, but now she's been taken! Please, help me!"

I gripped my bow so tightly that it nearly snapped in two. He had no idea the terror I was about to unleash on the Kingdom for taking what was *mine*. I slowly turned to her father, feeling resolved in what I must do. I calmed the shadows within as I said, "I will save our girl. I promise you that, but you must remain in the safety of your home until I send for you. The army at my command may not recognize friend from foe, understand? I will not take that chance with you. I will take you home, but *do not leave.*"

His eyes widened.

"You said *our* girl," he replied quietly.

"I did. Kymra is a Lightspark, and it is the job of the Nightlocke to protect her. She is my balance, my sanity… and my *whole* world. I will stop at nothing to bring her home safely."

Kymra's father thought for a moment before asking me a question I didn't expect.

"Do you love her?"

"More than anything sir," I replied confidently.

"When do we start, son?"

My blue eyes returned, surprised by how quickly he just accepted my declaration of love to his daughter. I was the monster in their lives, yet he didn't seem to bat an eye over my claim to Kymra. I was prepared for defiance and hostility, not sincerity and understanding. My brows furrowed as I thought about that for a moment, but I quickly shook myself from my thoughts as grabbed his hand.

"Now."

We moved through the veil, and I pulled him out as gently as I could this time. We were inside his house, and Kymra's sister nearly screamed at the sight of us. I released my shadows abruptly, slamming over her mouth and silencing her scream. I cocked my head to the side, warning her to stay quiet. She looked terrified, and while I didn't mean to be harsh, she seriously needed to shut up.

"Amarna, quiet please! I got us help," Kymra's father said as he rushed over to her.

The girl shook as her father wrapped his arms around her. "Dad, he's the Nightlocke! Why is he here?!"

"Because he loves your sister, and right now, he is the only one that can rescue her," he replied, and I gave him a grateful nod before peeking out the windows. Knights were stationed everywhere, and there were even guards I did not recognize. *The King called in reinforcements, it seems.*

"That's not possible," she protested.

"Amarna think back to your childhood. Remember your mother always said Kymra was too good for this world. The Nightlocke has figured out why, and I'm starting to think the King knows it too. He says Kymra is a Lightspark."

Amarna sunk further into her chair. "But she showed no signs, Dad."

"I think she has in her own way, and maybe the rest is yet to come. I don't know, but it makes sense. If the King knew, then he would keep her hidden at his castle like he did with the last one," Kymra's father stated.

I narrowed my eyes. "You knew about the last Lightspark?"

He nodded solemnly. "I did. I met her only once, although it was purely by accident, let me tell you. The King did not let her move about the castle hardly ever, but she was the reason why the castle grounds always flourished. Back then, I was so busy working at the castle, I never paid much mind to those outside those walls. It was foolish really. They always said ignorance was bliss, and I guess I was so grateful my children were taken care of that I never questioned much else."

He looked shameful, and I pursed my lips together, not really knowing what to say. I finally replied, "Not much you would have been able to do about it anyways."

CHAPTER 19

"I still should have tried harder. The King and I had become friends over the years, but he is not the same man he used to be, and now Kymra's just... gone," her dad said quietly, and I moved towards the two.

"Sir?"

"Uriah, please," he said.

"Uriah then. Tell me *exactly* what happened."

"Kymra came barreling in here, looking entirely stressed and worried over something. She needed to tell us something, but never got the chance. She was completely floored by the food you brought us too. I just assumed she knew about it, but before she could explain anything to us, the Knights were at the door. They basically arrested her for failing to complete her assigned duties, and then confiscated all our food. They even gave me a fine for breaking a stock piling law!"

I gritted my teeth angrily as I listened to him speak. *She left on her own then. She left me.* I quickly shook myself from those dark thoughts. I'm the one responsible for everything, and I basically told her I wanted her to go home. I shouldn't have yelled at her and been so cruel to her, but it was too late. Thomas and the King had her, and I needed to get her back.

"Anything else?" I asked gruffly.

"The King has announced her engagement to Thomas. The whole kingdom is invited tomorrow night for the wedding. It happened while you were gone," Amarna chimed in, and my shadows roared inside me.

"Marriage!?" Uriah asked horrified.

"It's just another way to ensure she remains at the castle with them," I gritted through my teeth. "They will *never* let her go voluntarily. The King believes he owns her, but he is about to find out how wrong he is. It will cost him his life. Do not attend that wedding!"

Their eyes widened, and Amarna protested, "It is mandatory! The knights will escort us tomorrow, Nightlocke!"

"Arthur," I said quietly, checking the windows again.

"What?" she asked.

"My name is Arthur. Stay away from the King's men, and I will have my shadows protect you the best I can. Do you own a sword or a knife?"

He shook his head no, and I gave him two of my daggers.

"Hide them, and keep it close. Whatever you do, stay together and *away* from the creatures you will see. Promise me."

They both nodded, and I filled the room with my shadows. Amarna stood well away from them, but Uriah seemed in awe almost. I let them see they were not always as harmful as they could be before I said my goodbyes.

"I promise, I will save our girl," I said gruffly, disappearing from them altogether. It was time to awaken my army and call upon the beasts of the Forbidden Woods. Thomas and the King took something of mine, and I *wanted* it back.

Chapter 20

Kymra

    I was carried all the way to the castle and couldn't shake the feeling in the pit of my stomach that I had just made a very critical mistake. *Why are they treating me this way?! Surely, there was a reasonable explanation for all this. A misunderstanding, maybe?* I was going to explain *everything* to the King to make things better between them and Arthur, but they didn't need to do this! I'm trying to save lives and prevent a war. *Didn't they understand that?*

    My mind ran amuck as we moved quickly through the castle, and we went straight to the King's private office. Warning bells went off inside my head. *Whatever was about to happen was intended to stay private,* I thought as anxiety rolled in my stomach. The knight set me down abruptly inside the room and promptly tied my wrists together tightly.

    "Stop that! Why are you cuffing me?" I shouted angrily, when the doors opened behind us.

    "Kymra!" Thomas shouted as he slammed into me. He wrapped his arms around me, hugging me tight. I looked into his pale eyes, remembering the hurtful words he said about me. I frowned when he kissed my cheek.

    "I've been looking all over for you! I'm so glad you're okay! I was terrified when you were taken by that vile monster," he said, holding me close again.

    I pulled away. "He isn't a monster, Thomas. I was wrong about him... We all were. He's made mistakes but everyone has. Isn't that right, Thomas?"

    Thomas's eyes flashed with emotion as he frowned. "Kymra, what I said about you is nothing compared to all the suffering the Nightlocke has brought upon this kingdom."

I blinked. *Did he really just say that?* Thomas didn't even apologize for the things he said about me and seemed almost annoyed that I defended the Nightlocke in the first place. The door clattered open, and the King walked in followed by Liam. He was the only one who looked genuinely relieved to see me.

"Kymra! You're alive!" Liam shouted as he crossed the room to greet me. His father blocked his path, and I frowned. *Why could Liam greet me?*

King Alexander gave me a small smile. "It is good to see you alive and well, child. Now that you are safe where you belong, I promise that devil will never hurt you again!"

My heart hurt at the thought of never seeing Arthur again, and I stepped past Thomas. *I had to try and fix this. The King would help make peace,* I thought, shoving my doubt aside. *He just had too!*

"Your Highness, *please* hear me out. I came to help make amends between you and the Nightlocke! He isn't what we thought!"

The King scoffed before plopping down in his chair. "You've been with him for some time, Kymra. I think your vision is a little skewed."

I shook my head confidently. "No, sir! In my time spent with him, I learned a great deal about him, your Majesty. The Nightlocke is actually a kind man, who has endured a tremendous amount of pain and suffering. The Nightlocke is different now, and we can mend the rift that divides us! I believe he will agree to leave the kingdom alone, if we stay out of his woods. We must hurry though! He has this crazy idea, and I fear war will happen if I cannot get control of the situation and show him the truth, your Highness."

The King's eyes furrowed as he sat forward. "And what idea would that be?"

I shifted nervously on my feet. *I was afraid to actually say the words out loud.* Something in my gut told me to stay quiet, and I decided to listen to it.

"It doesn't matter, but he thinks you are a threat to me. I *know* you're not, your Highness. If you would just let me go, I can show him that he's wrong about you. We can sign a treaty between you and him, saving us *all* from war."

The King slowly sat backwards as Thomas stomp over to his father in frustration. No one spoke for a few minutes, and I stood there in disbelief. I expected him to be overjoyed. *Relieved* that this nightmare would finally be over, but he just watched me intently. To the point it made my stomach churn.

Liam pursed his lips together then. "I think we can lose the ropes, don't you think? This is Kymra after all."

I sighed in relief, ready to get these stupid things off, when the King tossed his hand up and halted the guards.

"Not quite yet. This is a lot to process, Kymra. I am not too inclined to believe that the Nightlocke is a kind man, but I do appreciate the heads up that he is planning to go to war. I am more concerned on how you seem to feel about him though. It isn't natural to care for such a man. Bring in the equipment, please."

My eyes narrowed as a few servants, including Sarah, came in now. Her eyes went wide, and I couldn't keep the fear from trickling in. *This wasn't the family I grew up around. This wasn't the King I remembered.*

"Your Highness, please..."

"Father? Maybe we should hear her out. It would be better to prevent..." Liam spoke before his father cut him off.

"Hush. You see the Nightlocke isn't the only one with *theories*, so we are going to do a little experiment, Kymra. If you pass, I promise you a life of luxury with a marriage to my son Thomas. That would greatly increase your station and keep your family well fed. Wonderful, right? However, *if* you fail, you will have to return to your station as a servant girl. You've signed an agreement already, and my son will marry another. Am I clear?"

"And what if I want neither option, your Highness?" I asked boldly, and Thomas looked bewildered. The King however turned cross.

"It's insulting, your lack of gratitude, Kymra. My, my, has your mind been twisted by the Nightlocke. Nothing my son cannot fix though, I'm sure. You servant! Give me the knife!"

"Father!" Liam shouted, but it fell on deaf ears.

My eyes widened, and I tried to retreat, but the knights forced me to the table. *Were they going to kill me?!* Arthur said the King thought I was a

Lightspark and was looking for me. He told me I was promised to Thomas in marriage. *Everything he said was coming true.*

Thomas crossed his arms angrily, while his father stomped over to me with the knife. The King yanked on my arm, extending it to the point I thought he'd snap the bone. I screamed when he sliced my arm and a steady stream of blood began to pour out. My arm throbbed, burning in agony as the blood dripped to the floor. I looked to the brothers I once called friends. Liam had the decency to look bothered by what was happening, but Thomas watched me bleed with excitement in his eyes. *How could he allow his father to hurt me like this?*

"Bring the dirt!" the King said, and the servants carried a heavy bucket over to us. I tried to yank my arm away, but he held me with such a dead grip. To my surprise, the King moved my arm over the bucket of soil. He let my blood soak the pail of earth before wrapping my arm and releasing me. I stumbled backwards, clutching my arm.

"I am not the Lightspark! Arthur was wrong about that too! If you don't listen to me then war will happen!" I pleaded. Thomas glared at me.

"Arthur? Is that the prick's name?" he asked furiously, and I just stared blankly at him. Shame filled my face, and I dropped my gaze. *Arthur's name was private, and now the entire kingdom knew.*

Suddenly, flowers bloomed in the bucket. They burst to life in a brightly colored arraignment, and my heart sank. I stared at the life blooming inside that bucket, feeling utterly wretched. *Arthur was right about everything. I was a Lightspark, and I wouldn't listen to him.* I didn't believe him.

My heart broke even further, remembering all the hurtful things I said to him. I hurt him, sided *against* him, and he was right the whole time. I felt sick to my stomach, staring at the beautiful flowers in front of me. *What have I done?*

The King was absolutely giddy as he shouted, "We have a Lightspark once more! Child, you have passed the test and will wed my son! You will live right here at the castle with us. Our land is saved!"

"Tomorrow night," Thomas snapped, and I turned to face him. "We will wed tomorrow night, father."

CHAPTER 20

The King gave him a questioning look but waved his hand away. "Whatever you want. You need not worry about the Nightlocke though. We have ways to keep him away from her after all."

My eyes widened as fear gripped my heart. "Keep me away from him? I did not agree to this wedding. I do not accept! I will help heal the land, your Highness, but I wish to return to Arthur."

Thomas slammed his hands on the table. "You will marry *me*, Kymra! The vile man will not..."

"Calm yourself, son. Kymra, I think there has been a misunderstanding here, so let me clear this up. The marriage is nonnegotiable, and I cannot let you leave the castle. Someone else will take you, and I will not risk the chance of you just deciding not to return. Do you not understand how much power I gain with the other rulers in this world by having a Lightspark at my side? You see, it's best you remain here where I can keep an eye on you. I will not lose *another* Lightspark."

This wasn't happening, I thought to myself as I stood there frozen in disbelief. *I risked everything for these people, and they were turning out exactly as Arthur said they would.* I felt so stupid. I sentenced myself by returning here. I hurt the man I loved all because I refused to believe that I was wrong. I was so confident that the King and the Princes weren't awful people, but they weren't here to help us. I thought back to the first Nightlocke. He tried to save her from the King, and I stupidly assumed she was here on her own accord.

"Are we sure this is wise? The Nightlocke will surely come for her," Liam spoke, pulling me from my thoughts. I gave him a grateful look, but his family was none too pleased.

"Oh, grow a pair brother," Thomas snapped to Liam, who just looked frustrated.

"This is for the best, son. We've correct things since last time. Take her to the innermost cell, please. It's coated in Nightshade already," the King stated, and my eyes widened. *They knew Arthur's secret...*

"No, you cannot do this! Let me go! PLEASE!" I bellowed, but it didn't matter. They were carrying me towards a cell, *just like* Arthur said they would. I reached for the dark shadows on the wall but stopped myself. *Arthur warned me of this, and not only did I not listen, I insulted him,* I thought angrily. *I chose the royal family over him, so why should I call for his help now?* He wanted me gone, and now I was. My lot in life was my own fault, and I didn't deserve his rescue. I didn't deserve for him to risk his life to save me. *I don't deserve him.* I slowly pulled my hand back and was carried further into the castle to a place I had never been before.

Tears filled my eyes, when I was tossed into a cell with only a small bed in the corner. There were no windows, only walls and the cell door. The entire room smelled sour, and it was grimy to the touch. My eyes widened when I recognized the smell. Deadly Nightshade. I quickly scurried to my feet and wiped my hands on my shirt. I didn't want the toxins on my skin. Tears fell down my face as I realized that everything I touched in my cell would make me toxic to Arthur. I'd kill him, even if he did come to my rescue. I'm sure the bed was filled with the stuff as well, and I couldn't even sit because the floors has a thick film on them. *How long did the first Lightspark last before she finally collapsed from exhaustion?*

I paced the floor, tears filling my eyes as the day's event replayed in my head. *How could the King do something like this?* I thought back over the years, and while the kingdom had always been in disarray, I had never seen him be this harsh before. Arthur's words came to mind. *He really wasn't a nice man. He had the Lightspark all that time, but he never helped his kingdom. Only the castle grounds.* As a kid, I never paid any attention to it, and I don't know why I didn't see it before. When we moved into the kingdom, I just assumed everyone fell on hard times. But I was wrong.

I felt foolish. My memories were distorted from the truth. I thought back to the incredible amount of food we'd prepare for the royal family to eat, and I always chalked it up as normal because of their station. They had so much, yet the rest of the kingdom had nothing. It was just the King's way to keep his palace full of servants and slaves, and I don't know how I never saw it that way before.

All I wanted to see was my two long-lost friends, and the memories of the life I used to have with them. I only thought of the crush I had for years on Thomas, and when he began to give me attention once I began working at

CHAPTER 20

the castle, I stopped seeing everything around me. I was lost in him, and it ruined me.

My legs ached from standing so long, but I was too afraid to move or touch anything. It wasn't long before I heard steps out in the hall. Thomas appeared at the door, and he leaned against the bars, staring hard at me with his brows furrowed.

"You have become a thing of pride for me, Kymra. I don't like to lose, although you probably remember that from when we were kids, don't you?"

I glared at him but refused to answer. I had nothing more to say to this man. He was not the person I always thought him to be, and the longer I was around him, the worst he became.

Thomas snorted. "I will not lose to a prick like the Nightlocke. Did you know he tormented my mind while you were gone?"

My brows furrowed.

A sly grin appeared on his face. "He showed me all the things I'm sure he wanted to do to you, but now he will get to actually watch it happen with me. You are *mine*, and I will do as I please with you, Kymra. Get that through your head real quick and life won't be so bad for you."

My eyes widened. I gritted my teeth, clenching my hands into tight fists as I glared at Thomas.

"Says the man who's already lost the crown to his own brother. Arthur has treated me far better than I even deserve, while you have been nothing more than a cruel, cowardly prince. I pity the poor girl that ends up being your wife."

Thomas hit the bars hard, causing me to jump. "Oh, you have no idea what's coming, Kymra. I have plans of my own, you see, and I will not fail! Enjoy your night, *wife*. I'll be back to fetch you before the ceremony. This will be your room, unless I require your services."

Thomas winked at me, leaving me in peace finally. I crouched down, careful not to touch the floor, and bawled.

I was so stupid.

I missed Arthur.

I should have listen to him. Trusted him.

I *never* should have left.

Chapter 21

Arthur

I watched the castle from afar, hoping to catch a glimpse of Kymra, but I knew I never would. That would be too easy, and she was probably deep within the castle, far from reach. I sent my shadows out and called her name, but my vision blurred and became downright painful when they found her general location. I couldn't pin point it exactly, but something was blocking me. And I knew exactly what it was.

Nightshade.

This was what the first Nightlocke mentioned with Julianna, I thought as I scanned his journals again. *She was just out of reach, trapped, and untouchable.* It was *pissing* me off. I was going to have to wait until they pulled her out into the open. I watched the place while scanning the journals once more, hoping I missed something the first time around.

The servants meandered outside, setting up the wedding in the main courtyard just past the gardens, which was great for me, but it also put me on high alert. Something wasn't right, but I had yet to figure out what they were up to. Our world's connected on this side with only a wall dividing us, but that would be no problem for the Bloodhounds. Just past their ridiculous wall was their fake gardens, and looking at the spot where I first saw my girl tugged at my heart. I forced myself to look away, focusing on the task at hand.

The Bloodhounds could easily destroy the concrete wall, I thought as I scanned for weak spots. *But I'd only be able to hold them for so long before I'd have to let them loose.* I wished I knew how to control the Wraiths, but that wasn't something I thought I could handle at the moment. I was going to have to fight myself, and I didn't want to be so drained from controlling them that I couldn't manage.

A part of me was scared about using the creatures of the forest though. I didn't want to throw Kymra or the villagers in harms way by letting all these vile creatures loose, but I didn't want to come up short either. I had *one* shot to save her and kill the King and his vile sons. It was just a risk I was going to have to take. *Thomas had better not touch my girl.*

I snarled, thinking about him holding Kymra or kissing her. I forced it out of my mind, otherwise I was going to lose it, and I'd never see her again if I made a stupid mistake such as losing my temper. *Again.*

I needed more though. The King had a large army as it was, and more and more were coming in from some neighboring country. I scratched my head, trying to figure out what to do. I had been planning this kingdom's demise for the last few years now, but I was waiting until my army of changed ones were so large that nothing could stop them. I wanted to do this *effortlessly*, and I was enjoying torturing them in the meantime. Plus, it takes a lot out of me to change a person into a creature of the forest, so it's been slow to say the least. I didn't have that kind of time now, and I needed everything to go right.

I spotted Liam strolling the courtyard with a princess I did not recognize. *All these new knights were from her kingdom.* I rolled my eyes, watching him dote on the girl. She had a hideous laugh, and my nose scrunched watching them. *What in the world did Liam see in her?* Suddenly, a brilliant idea came to me, and I smiled wickedly. I scanned the gardens they were entering for the best place to do this. Tall hedges stood off to the left, and my smile grew wider.

The two walked with guards through the garden. Either the King was extremely cocky, assuming I wouldn't retaliate, or there was more at play here. *Either way, I wasn't passing this opportunity up.* I had never attacked in broad daylight before, but there's a first time for everything. I rubbed my hands together, warming them up to snatch a Prince.

I laid on the ground, digging my fingers into the dirt before I released my shadows. They traveled silently on the ground towards the four of them on

CHAPTER 21

the other side of the wall. Within seconds, my shadows shot up the bodies of the knights behind the Prince and Princess. I forced my shadows straight into their mouths before they even had a chance to scream. *If it worked on Bloodhounds, then it should have no problem with these weak-minded fools.*

The knights shook subtly as I took control, and Liam turned to face them. He merely shook his head and continued on with his lady, seeing nothing but their bulky masks and heavy armor. It took me a second as I felt myself connect to the knights, and I pushed their memories and thoughts aside. As if I had a cage inside their mind, I threw them inside and took all control away from them. I pushed further into the mind of one of the guards, telling him what to say.

"Sir?"

Our voice blended together in a dark raspy voice, and I hoped Liam wouldn't notice. I could hear everything through the mind of my victim, and I smiled, pleased with my new found ability.

This was *cool.*

Liam turned again.

"Yes? What do you need?"

"This area is not secure. I must insist we move to a better location for you and your Highness," we said together, and I watched Liam frown as he scanned the area.

"It looks alright to me. My father has this place secure, and the Nightlocke cannot step out into the daylight."

I nearly laughed out loud. *They thought what now?*

"Please, sir. We would rather be safe than sorry," we spoke, and I motioned the knight's hand up and towards where the hedges were. *Easy for snatching,* I thought wickedly to myself.

"Let's just listen, Liam. We can't be too sure, not with a monster like the Nightlocke hanging around," the lady said, and Liam sighed in frustration.

"Very well. Lead the way," he said, and I winced.

Now was the tricky part, I thought. *Walking.* I moved my guards forward, albeit a little rough, but I honestly did fairly well for only learning this ability recently. The moment Liam and the Princess stepped behind the hedges,

I released the guards and used those shadows to engulf them all. They disappeared without a trace or a sound, and I smiled proudly of how easy it was to steal a prince.

Should have done this years ago, I chastised myself before sliding out of view and disappearing to my own castle. I could hear the lady's scream before I had even emerged from my shadows. My eyes drifted to the cell I put Kymra in months ago, and I forced myself to look away, darkening my eyes before stepping into their view.

"Welcome, welcome, welcome! *Welcome* to my lovely home!" I bellowed, raising my arms up in a mocking bow.

Liam held the girl tightly in his arms with his two guards standing in front. They had their swords drawn, ready for a fight, even though we *all* knew it was pointless. Annoyed, I shot my hands out, slamming my shadows into them, and they hit the back wall with a loud thump. They fell unconscious in heap on the floor, and the girl screamed again. I rolled my eyes, seriously done with this girl's antics, and clamped a shadow hand over her mouth. She lost it the minute my shadows touched her face.

"Either control her or I will knock her out as well! I only *need* one of you!" I bellowed again as Liam tried to silence her. He gripped the sides of her head, forcing the girl to slow down her breathing. He surprisingly managed to calm her some, and I released my hold over her mouth.

"Now let's get down to business, shall we?" I said, rubbing my hands together. I was going to enjoy *every* second of their fear before I delivered the punishment this Prince so rightfully deserved. *The poor Princess sadly just got in the way.* I stepped closer as my shadows merged with my voice. "You all took something that belongs to me. Did you assume I would not retaliate?"

Liam glared at me. "If you think an exchange will work then I'm here to tell you that you are wrong. My father cares more for the Lightspark than for me."

I cocked my head to the side curiously. "I actually wanted information, but maybe I should try to ransom the both of you? Yes... That may work as well."

"Did you not hear me? My father won't exchange Kymra for me! He has Thomas to rule after him, even if I am the favorite. He doesn't care as long as he has the Lightspark!"

"But her father might?" I replied, and Liam's face fell. Fear had finally filled his eyes, and I grinned wickedly. *Now I was getting somewhere.* "When I offer you up in exchange for Kymra and your father rejects, I will have no choice but to kill you in front of the entire kingdom. Then that leaves her in my arms. What do you think her father will do once he sees your head roll? Hmm? I doubt he'd offer his men in support to dear ole Dad then."

The young lady paled, and Liam looked to his feet.

"It wasn't my idea to take her you know," he said quietly.

"Oh, I know. I was there that night when you and your family plotted to steal what belongs to me. Either way, you did nothing to stop it, and here we are."

Liam eyes widened, and he gritted his teeth. "What happens now?"

"Now you tell me where Kymra is in that castle and how tonight will go. I want every detail, and I swear to you, Liam, if anything you say isn't true, then I will skin this one alive and feed her to the Wraiths that live in these woods. Are we clear?" I asked, filling the room with my shadows. He paled as she cried quietly in his arms. Liam pulled the girl close, trying to shield her from my shadows. My brows furrowed as I watched. *Liam seemed to genuinely care for the girl.* I assumed it was an arranged marriage, but it didn't matter. It only worked to my advantage.

Liam looked to the girl, kissing her forehead before turning back to me. "Kymra is in the innermost cell that's in the center of the castle, deep beneath the grounds. My father has the room coated in Nightshade, so you will never find her."

"Why is this wedding happening?" I asked, crossing my arms.

"It was a deal made with Thomas. I don't know much more than that though. I believe my father just wants to pacify Thomas because the throne will go to me, and he wants to keep Kymra under his thumb at all times. I am already engaged to Agatha, so Thomas is the next best choice."

"When will Kymra emerge?"

"After dark."

I cocked my head to the side. "If you all believe I never come out in the daylight then why risk the dark?"

Liam stared hard at me. "That was Thomas's choice. I don't know why he chose it this way, but my father has allowed it. Be warned though, my father has Nightshade on every sword, arrow, and knife. He has the stuff planted all around the alter as well as two armies at the ready. This is their way of showing everyone, *especially you*, where the Lightspark belongs, but I believe there is more to it than just that. It would not surprise me if they try to kill you when you come for her."

I gritted my teeth in anger. *This was going to be trickier than I had hoped.*

"Thank you for your assistance. I'll be back to fetch you in time for the wedding," I finally spoke as the girl cried harder.

"Nightlocke!" Liam shouted, and I hesitated by the bars. "I know you won't believe me, but I *never* wanted to do this to Kymra. No one would listen to me when I warned about your retaliation. For what it's worth, I wanted you to know at least."

I stayed quiet as I processed what he said. I wasn't sure if I should believe him, but he seemed sincere. I opened the cell door to leave, when Liam's voice stopped me again.

"Are you going to kill my father and brother?"

"Wouldn't you?"

Liam dropped his head, and I vanished. Liam was at least smarter than his younger brother, and Kymra's word about the royal family rattled around in my head. *Was I wrong about all of them?* Clearly King Alexander and Thomas were vile, disgusting men that deserved what they had coming to them, but Liam seemed different. *Did he really try to stop them from harming Kymra or was he lying to save himself and his girl?*

He seemed to accept his fate though, and it honestly made my stomach churn a little. *I wonder how it really felt to know your own father wouldn't do everything in his power to save you from a death like the one I planned to give Liam.* He was resigned and willingly gave up the information I needed, knowing his fate was sealed, and that I was going after his family. *Was Kymra honestly right?*

I leaned against the wall, frustrated with everything. I listened to Liam

CHAPTER 21

console the girl from the other side of the wall, and suddenly the idea of killing them just made me sick. She seemed to put her faith in him, even though the odds were not in their favor right now. I sighed. I had to get my head in the game and rely on my shadows and the dark to keep me going. I needed to be smart about how I went about saving her. *I couldn't make the same mistakes the previous Nightlocke made.*

While I had a formidable army below my own castle, I wasn't sure they would be enough to take on one army, let alone two. If every weapon is dipped in Nightshade than I couldn't get hit once, and neither could my army, since my shadows lived inside them. If I died, the power would be lost to another. *One the King could control.* I shuddered at that thought. I sighed, knowing I had to try. I would never forgive myself if something happened to Kymra. *If I had just been honest with her when I first discovered what she was and gently showed her the truth, none of this would have happened.* But no. I had to be a coward only to lose my temper with her and force her to flee.

I tapped the back of my head against the wall, trying to figure out my next step, when I suddenly remembered something. I bolted to my room now, searching for that stupid book. I had burned the pages Kymra stole already, but the rest of the journal was around here somewhere. I tore my room apart, and I found it under my chair of all places. I searched through it quickly, trying to find the part about the forest.

There!

"The forest belongs to the Nightlocke. Whoever owns the power, owns the forest. The Nightlocke is the heart, it's center, and everything dark and evil is connected to each other. I have yet to find out how this works, but it makes sense why I am always the only person that walks this land. It is my home, and will remain my home until the next chosen to take the power as I am alone in this race."

Whoever owns the power owns the forest. I rattled that around in my head, trying to make sense of it. *How in the world did I own the forest? Is this literal or figurative? Why couldn't the Nightlocke before me just explain things plainly, instead of these awful riddles!?* My head hurt, knowing I didn't have a lot of time to figure this out. I disappeared outside, willing to try anything at this point. If I could control the creatures in these woods a different way than using my shadows, then I'd have far more power to attack the castle with. I wouldn't struggle, and I could focus solely on reaching Kymra.

I dug my hand in the earth, having no idea what I was even doing. *Maybe just by touching the ground I could connect to everything at once.* It was probably a stupid idea, but I was getting desperate. I shot my shadows out, feeling them fill the forest floor.

"I call upon the Wraiths, Bloodhounds, and the Mist that roam my lands. I call for you to take up arms, and protect your King and Queen."

It took a lot out of me to make this call, and I didn't even know if I did this right. I waited for some time with nothing but silence to keep me company. The forest was silent. The creatures were *silent*, and I shook my head in frustration. I stomped back towards the castle, ready to grab those I did have at my disposal. It was time to make my way to the castle and get my girl. Whether I survived or not, I was saving her. She was going to be free.

I yanked the door open when I heard a sound that froze me in my tracks.

A screeching wail.

Chapter 22

Kymra

I stayed hunched on my ankles for hours as they burned in agony. I just needed to hang on a little longer. As badly as I wanted Arthur to come, I prayed he'd stay far away from me. I would never forgive myself if I got him killed trying to rescue me. But my ankles burned, and my eyes were heavy with exhaustion. I wouldn't last much longer.

The awful stench from the Nightshade made my head throb, and I just wanted to run. But I put myself into this situation in the first place. I was stubborn, and now I would just have to deal. I was in agony though. I missed the dark. I missed the Forbidden Woods even, but most of all I missed Arthur. Sometime in the middle of the night, I heard footsteps approach. To my surprise, it was Sarah.

"Here," she whispered, tossing me a blanket through the bars. I opened my eyes wide as I caught it in the air. I quickly spread it on the ground and nearly sobbed in relief as I sat down on the blanket, letting my ankles and feet finally rest.

"The toxins will seep through eventually, but you can get some rest at least. I am so sorry, Kymra. I tried to come sooner!"

"Thank you, Sarah. It means a lot," I whispered softly. Sarah stayed still against the bars, and I turned to look back at her again. *I half expected her to bolt already.*

"Is the Nightlocke really a good man?" she finally asked.

"One of the best, Sarah."

"Thomas said he loves you. Is that true?" she asked again, and my heart hurt.

"I messed up, Sarah. I don't know if he loves me anymore, but I think he did."

She stayed quiet for a moment as tears fell down my face.

"Do you love him?"

A sob escaped my lips. "More than anything."

"Hang in there, Kymra. The Nightlocke will come for you, I just know it, but stay on guard. Thomas is plotting something, I believe. Even hiding it from the King. I don't know anymore than that, I apologize. I must go, but be careful, Kymra."

Sarah left me in the light then. For the first time in my life, I craved the dark, but somehow I managed to fall asleep on the hard ground.

***

"Kymra... Did someone bring you that blanket?" Thomas bellowed, startling me awake.

"I got it from the bed," I lied, rubbing my eyes as my head continued to throb. *God, I felt miserable.*

He grunted, opening the cell doors. "Let's go, wife."

"I am not your wife, Thomas," I snapped as I left the bright cell. Thomas grabbed my arm harshly before slamming me against the wall and kissing me hard. I had always dreamed of what this would feel like. To feel Thomas's lips against mine and to have him hold me like he was right now. The reality was so much worse though. Thomas taste vile. Like scotch and cigars mixed harshly together, it made me gag, and I tried to shove him off. My heart didn't flutter like it had with Arthur. Arthur was gentle and kind. He made me feel like I *mattered*, but Thomas would never look at me like that. He would never care about me. I shoved him again, and Thomas stumbled backwards, looking disgusted.

"What happened to you, Kymra!? You used to worship the ground I walked on, and a few months with a foul beast and this happens? This is what you

CHAPTER 22

wanted! There are plenty of girls that would kill to be in your shoes, you know that?"

"Well, then take one of them," I bellowed, and his eyes widened. "Oh that's right, you've already taken them all! You're nothing but a whore, Thomas, and I won't be another notch on your belt! I won't scratch an itch for you. I found someone who truly loves me. Who sees me! He does *everything* for me because he just wants to make me happy, even though lately I haven't deserved any of it."

My chest heaved by the end of my little rant, and for once, something I said made a difference. Thomas looked startled, his eyes flashing with hurt before turning to rage. He was at my throat in seconds, squeezing the life out of me, and I scrambled to remove his hand.

"See, what I think is that you are a lot like me. Yes... I think we are one in the same, Kymra. We *both* are attracted to power, and once I have *his* power, you will be begging to spread those pretty little legs for me. Everyone in Odemark will respect me then. Even my dad would have to see me for who I am, and then that throne will be mine! So, I suggest you stay quiet by my side or you'll spend the rest of your life rotting in this cell, while I slowly drain your body dry."

He finally released me, and I fell, gasping for air. My eyes widened. *That's what he wanted? Thomas was going to take Arthur's power?!* The only way to do that was to kill him and steal it from him. My heart stopped, picturing Arthur's fallen body, the shadows leaving his corpse and flowing into Thomas. *No... That can't happen!* I swore to myself. *Thomas cannot become the next Nightlocke.*

Terror shook my body at the thought of him wielding Arthur's power. The destruction he would ultimately bring upon us all. Arthur was walking right into a trap if he tried to rescue me, and I realized that *this* is what the whole marriage was really about. Thomas wanted to draw Arthur out of the woods. He and his father were going to kill him, and they were going to use me to do it. There was only one way to even accomplish something like this, and that was with Nightshade. *I was about to get Arthur killed.*

"He's immortal, Thomas," I whispered softly. My heart was breaking because there was nothing I could do to save my Arthur. I was a helpless, useless pathetic girl who got herself into this horrid mess.

"Well, he obviously killed the first one somehow so there must be a way. I figured I'd take my chance with the Nightshade since it weakens him anyways. If that fails, I can always throw him into your cell until I figure out how to steal those shadows," he said as he yanked me to my feet. We started walking to the stairs now before Thomas suddenly pushed me against the wall again. "You keep this between us or I'll make his death a slow one, got that? That includes your father and sister."

"I hate you," I whispered to Thomas, my throat sore and raw.

"I really don't care," he replied, and he dragged me up the stairs to his bedroom. Sarah and another maid were waiting for the two of us already, and Thomas pushed me into them.

"Get her ready. Ceremony is in an hour," he demanded, and they quickly ushered me into the dressing room.

"Hurry, Kymra. Thomas has been in a bad mood all day. He won't leave until you are ready," Sarah said quietly as she tugged off my shirt.

"No! Please! Don't take it. It's all I have left of him," I cried out, reaching for my shirt back.

Sarah looked heartbroken, but the other maid glared at the two of us.

"I'm not getting Thomas's wrath over this. Remove your pants or I will do it for you!" she cried out, and my eyes widened.

"Clarice!" Sarah hissed.

"No! Thomas wants this dress on her, and he's threatened the two of us to do it right! Now move it, Kymra."

Sarah's eyes softened. "I'm so sorry, Kymra."

I gave her a small nod, grateful she was willing to help me before I slipped off my beloved outfit. I put on the dreadfully heavy white dress, and my brows furrowed in disgust. *It looked ridiculous! Just full of feathers and fluff.* It would *never* be something I'd ever chose for myself, and it required a incredibly tight corset to wear. I gritted my teeth in anger as Sarah helped me with my hair and added on the face powder that all the Princesses wore. I barely recognized myself when I finally looked in the mirror. While I was pretty, it wasn't me.

I missed the way I looked before.

I used to look like Arthur, but with this gaudy thing on, I just looked ridiculous. Tears filled my eyes, and we walked into the other room where Thomas waited. He was dressed and ready for tonight as well, giving me a dashing smile.

"Now don't you look beautiful, Kymra," he said, reaching for my hand. I held my breath, glaring at him. I didn't want to marry him, and I didn't care that his smile had fallen. I didn't care that rage had filled his eyes or that he looked at me like he wanted to kill me. *Let me stand in front of the entire village with a black eye for all I cared. Let the people see that I did not want this!*

"Excuse us, ladies," he said coldly.

Sarah whispered an apology as they scurried out of the room. Once the door closed, he took one step before shoving me into the back wall. I hit my shoulder hard as he gripped the sides of my face. *The boy I knew was gone. How did I not see the man he had become? How did I miss this?*

"Do you not understand the situation you are in? You will marry me, and you will put on a pretty smile for the entire kingdom to see! Got that? Otherwise, I'll have your father and sister arrested, and you will never see them again!"

My eyes widened as fear gripped my heart. I couldn't be the cause for all this pain and suffering. *This was my mistake...* Shadows flickered on the wall from the fire, and I stilled. I *could* actually help. *I could warn Arthur,* I thought as my mind raced. *I could save his life, and if I stayed obedient then Thomas and the King wouldn't harm my family. Everyone* would remain safe, and no one else would pay for my mistake. My hand immediately touched the shadows on the wall.

"Arthur is stronger than you realize. Your plan is ludicrous, Thomas. It is impossible to steal the Nightlocke's power, and the *only* way to save yourself is to let me go!"

Thomas placed his arms on either side of my head, pinning me against this wall. His hands grazed the shadows above, and I bit my lower lip to keeping from grinning. *Go ahead and tell Arthur* everything, *you prick.*

"It's not impossible, Kymra. I've had plenty of time to think since he took you, and if he was able to steal that power then so can I. However, I'll know what to do with a power like that, unlike Arthur who just hides away in the forest, messing with people's minds. He is weak! Nothing more than a *coward*, but not me."

"Stealing Arthur's power won't make you brave or give you respect like you think it will. That comes from within. It isn't the power that gives Arthur courage. No, he's just that way naturally, which is why the Nightlocke's power *chose* him all those years ago. You see, it had the chance to pick you, but it skipped right passed you to Arthur. Courage is just something that you will always lack, I'm afraid. I mean I heard about what you did to your own men in the Forbidden Woods. You *are* a coward, and it's why you will never be King."

Thomas's eyes filled with rage before he struck me across the face, and I dropped to the floor. My vision blurred as my cheek pulsed in agony, but the pain never came close to how I felt inside. *At least Arthur will be safe,* I thought as I carefully rolled to my side. I placed my hand on the shadows whispering, "I'm so sorry, Arthur. Stay far away from me. I love you."

Thomas yanked me up by my hair, and I screamed.

"Keep testing my patience and watch how fast I kill your father! Now move your feet, Kymra! I have a trap to set," he snarled, and I glared at him. *I can't believe I ever found him attractive in the first place.*

As we walked down the hall, my face throbbing, I thought of Arthur. I hated the last thing I ever said to him I accused him of not being good enough. Of still being the violent man I thought he was. *Arthur wasn't a bad man. No... Deep down he was good.* He was right when he said that sometimes a necessary evil needs to happen for the greater good. Thomas would hurt many people if he stole Arthur's power somehow. Thomas would be ruthless, and he needed to be stopped.

Guilt ate at me as I listened to the sounds of my heels clicking on the pristine tile. *I should have never gotten involved in this.* I should have trusted just Arthur, letting him handle the whole thing or at least worked with him somehow. Instead, I made things worse by running off to handle it myself, and now

CHAPTER 22

Arthur's life hung in the balance, along with my family. My chest burned with the need to save them, but I was afraid to even try. I had made such a mess of things as it was. But this power *wanted* me to fix things, even at my own expense. A single tear fell down my face, realizing the longer I stayed away from Arthur, the less control I'd have over my life. He balanced me like I balanced him.

Thomas guided me outside, squeezing my hand harshly the moment everyone's eyes land on us. He smiled, becoming the lighthearted Prince everyone knew as music played softly in the air. As we walked to the alter, I realized the entire area had Nightshade around it. My eyes widened as we shifted around the vile plant.

He placed me center stage and knights surrounded us. My eyes drifted to the dark woods beyond the massive courtyard. The treeline was empty. *The way it should be.* Thomas leaned in like I was whispering a secret before giving me a sly grin. I narrowed my eyes, frowning when he bopped me on the nose.

"Of course I will help you, my darling!" Thomas said loudly before dropping to his knees. Moving quickly, he lifted my dress, and I felt his cold hands clamp something around my ankle. I jerked my leg back, feeling the heavy chain digging into my skin before I stumbled. Thomas righted me, giving me a *nice try* look before standing tall again. *I'm stuck*, I thought as my heart thundered in my chest. I glared over to him.

"Was that really necessary?" I asked, but he only winked at me before kissing my cheek. There was nowhere for me to go now. I was a prisoner on this grand stage for the entire kingdom to never know. I gritted my teeth as the official crossed the stage to stand before us. The knights returned to their post, and I scanned the crowd, searching for Arthur.

I couldn't help it. While I was relieved he listened and stayed far away, a small part of me hoped to see him hiding amongst everyone. My heart ached in my chest. *God, I missed him...* Suddenly, my eyes landed on my father and sister. My face fell as a knight stood directly behind them in the crowd.

"Welcome Kingdom of Odemark! Tonight is a very special occasion as we are all excited for the union between Prince Thomas, son of King Alexander and late Queen Sophia to Commoner Kymra Fields, daughter of Uriah and

Liliana Fields!"

I rolled my eyes as the crowd cheered excitedly. The kingdom didn't get invited to things like this very often, nor did they eat well. Everyone would go home with full bellies tonight, and I could see that food was the main thing on their minds. *No one was paying me or the bruise on my face much attention.* My chest burned fiercely again. I would hold on as long as I could against the pain and Thomas's wishes, but I knew there was only so much I could do. Eventually, I'd have to give in. I wished more than anything I could go back in time and never leave Arthur's castle in the first place. I wish I never said those things to him.

"Let us begin with the vows! Prince Thomas, you shall go first!"

Thomas gave me yet another dashing smile, but I knew how fake it really was. My mind raced as I scrambled to think of something to stop this. But in the pit of my stomach, I knew there was no hope.

"Do you Thomas Einar take Kymra Fields to be your royal and wedded wife? To have and to hold until death do you part?"

Thomas turned to me. "I do."

"Do you Kymra Fields take Thomas Einar to be your royal and wedded husband? To have and to hold until death do you part?"

I stayed silent as Arthur's face flashed before me. Another tear rolled down my cheek. *This is wrong.* My gaze drifted over the crowd, finding my father shaking his head ever so subtly. Thomas gave a nervous chuckle, squeezing my hand hard in warning, and I turned to him.

"Give her a moment, everyone! She's just shy being around so many people! Don't worry, my love. You will get used to it."

Thomas turned his back to the crowd, scowling at me, but the thought of saying *I do* sickened me. My chest burned again when the knight stepped closer to my father. *They needed help... But I just couldn't do it.* I couldn't bring myself to say those two little words. I looked out to the empty treeline again. *He wasn't coming.*

"Kymra..." Thomas said quietly, and his voice deepened. I knew I'd receive a lashing for this later. I knew the pain that was coming, but despite the fire in my chest, I just couldn't do it. I couldn't betray Arthur, and I would gladly

CHAPTER 22

spend the rest of my life in that cell than marry this man. Feeling resolved in my decision, I stared back at my captor.

"I don't," I said.

The crowd gasped and heat filled Thomas's cheeks. He gave the crowd a sheepish smile before tugging me close. I gasped when his nail dug into my skin while he glared.

"You will..."

A loud wailing sound pierced the night sky, and we all froze. Thomas paled at the sound as he stood behind me then, but my eyes searched the Forbidden Woods. It sounded again, and then suddenly a lone dark figure appeared before us all.

"ARTHUR!" I shouted, recognizing his hood. *He came! He actually came for me!*

Thomas gripped the back of my hair as someone sounded the warning bells. The kingdom panicked, but Arthur had yet to move. It felt like time stood still. I couldn't see his face from this far away, but I *felt* our eyes meet. Guilt lay heavy on my chest as I stared at the man I loved so fiercely. He came for me... Despite everything I said to him, he came *for me.*

"You stole from me, Thomas Einar! I've come for *my girl!*" Arthur bellowed across the courtyard. The crowd froze.

My heart melted, hearing his outright claim over me. *He still cares for me... He still* cares. I barely held back my sob as I followed the pull I felt towards the Nightlocke. The chain clattered against my leg, when Thomas grabbed my waist and stuck a knife against my back.

"Move one more step, and I'll kill you where you stand," he snarled. "I need him closer!"

Fear gripped my heart, and I turned back to Arthur. *He was still plotting, and I needed to stop it. I won't let him harm Arthur.* My eyes drifted to the bow on one of the knight's shoulders. *If only I could get my hands on that.*

Arthur yelled again, "Release Kymra or sacrifice your kingdom! I'll shred you all, starting with these two!"

A thick shadow appeared to his left, and when it faded, we saw Liam and Agatha suddenly appear. They were bound by their hands and mouth, and everyone gasped. My eyes widened. *I didn't even realize they weren't here.* In all the commotion with such a sudden wedding, no one else noticed it either.

Thomas snarled, and the King stormed across the stage. For the first time, I saw fear in Alexander's eyes as he searched the royal seats for his son.

"Thomas, I warned you of this! I said having the wedding outside was dangerous, but you said you had everything under control! You told me you knew how to defeat the Nightlocke!"

"I do, father!" Thomas hissed.

"This is not under control!" Alexander snarled. "He has my son, our future King!"

"You have two sons, father! I have a plan, and if Liam was dumb enough to get caught, then he shouldn't lead in the first place! Besides the Nightlocke is bluffing! Why would he kill his only bargaining chip?!"

The King struck Thomas across the face, and Thomas stumbled. He righted himself, wiping the blood off his lip as he looked to his father with such hate and malice, it *scared* me. *I knew the first person he'd go after if he managed to steal the Nightlocke's power.*

"Your mother ruined you," King Alexander growled. "You have killed your brother with this foolish plan of yours, and I should have *never* listened to you."

The King turned to face Arthur again. I wished more than anything that I could slip into the shadows and be at his side again.

"We cannot make a trade, Nightlocke! Kymra is the Lightspark, and she is too important to us all. My son understands that. It would be wise to let him go peacefully or face my wrath and meet your end!" the King shouted, and my eyes widened.

The King was risking his own son's life just to keep me prisoner. My stomach churned. Liam merely dropped his head as if *he knew* this would happen, and my heart shattered for him. Liam was the only one who ever tried to speak against what was happening to me. I shook my head, hoping Arthur was watching me. *This was wrong. Please don't do this, Arthur!*

Arthur shouted, "WRONG ANSWER!"

He drew his sword, striking Liam in his neck in one swift motion. Agatha

CHAPTER 22

screamed, collapsing in a crumpled heap as Liam's head rolled off his body into the grass below. Bile rose to the back of my throat as his body fell forward, and the crowd screamed at the sight before them. My body began to shake as I looked back to Arthur. His eyes were still on mine, watching my reaction, I suppose. *I had doubted him once before, and I would not do it again. He must have a reason, and I would not abandon him.*

The King roared in agony, while Thomas merely stared at his fallen brother. No emotion, no grief, just a blank stare, and rage burned through my veins. *This was your brother!* My hands clenched at my sides. Grief filled my own heart, and I could not stop the tears from falling.

Arthur bellowed again, "SHALL I CONTINUE?!"

The King shook with emotion before howling, "ATTACK! Bring me the Nightlocke's head!"

"Alexander! Do not risk my daughter!" Agatha's father shouted angrily, but Alexander shoved him aside and drew his sword.

Screams filled the air when Arthur raised his hands, and the horrible wailing sound returned. The creatures that gave this kingdom nightmares poured out of the forest. My heart stopped, watching them run *around* Arthur. He wasn't afraid, and the creatures weren't attacking him. My eyes widened when I realized he was calling them.

The Bloodhounds slammed into the stone wall, crushing it in seconds, while the Wraiths flew overhead. Everyone screamed as chaos filled the courtyards, and it was all I could do to take my eyes off the sight. Thomas ducked behind me as a Wraith flew over us, eating a guard nearby. I glared at him and forcefully shook him off my arm.

"Give me the key!" I demanded, but he just glared back at me. He gave a sharp whistle, calling his personal guards, when a loud sound of clashing metal pulled my attention.

The Bloodhounds had finally reached the knights, and they loudly clashed together. My eyes widened as I watched them shred the King's armies, and that's when I heard Arthur whistle. The earth shook beneath us, and I held my breath. *What in the world is this?* Suddenly, black creatures ran out of the woods followed by the thick green Mist. My body *trembled* as creatures I had never seen before ran inhumanly fast towards the army. And Arthur was controlling of them all.

"PROTECT YOUR KING!" a guard shouted as they formed a tight circle around King Alexander.

I scrambled to release my foot from the chain, when I realized Thomas had disappeared in the crowd. I gritted my teeth in anger. *He was probably running away.* I stole a glance towards the battle. The gruesome looking creatures had bodies that looked human, but they ran on all fours like a wild animal. Their teeth were long and sharp, much like the way Arthur's shadow creatures were. In fact they reminded me an awful lot of his shadow creatures. They had no eyes or ears, and they screeched loudly like Wraiths. Their skin oozed a thick black goo, and my stomach threatened to empty itself as I watched them shred their victim's skin with their teeth. They tore through the knight's armor like it was nothing.

Arthur had begun running towards us now, and to my amazement he ran right through the Mist. It didn't hurt him, but it dropped the others it touched. I couldn't see my father or my sister anymore, and I started to tug on the chain that bound me to the stage, snapping out of my trance.

One of the King's archers screamed as a Wraith picked him up, and he disappeared inside. I could hear it tear the flesh from his bones, consuming his body entirely before dumping him in front of me. All that remained was a pile of bones, mutilated chain-mail, and the archer's longbow. I slung the bow over my shoulder as I searched the archer's mangled remains for anything that could free me from this wretched chain around my ankle.

This was once a person. Those words rattled my head *repeatedly*, and bile rose to the back of my throat as I pushed the bones away. I needed something to help me escape, and I knew all the King's knights carried a dagger with them. My heart soared when I found it, and I began slamming the blunt end of it on the chain. It wasn't budging, and I snarled in frustration.

I looked forward, and Arthur wasn't far from me now. He was fighting with such skill and precision that it was mesmerizing to watch. I went back to work, doing everything I could to get free, but when I glanced back to Arthur, my heart *stopped*. Thomas was moving quickly through the crowd now with a dagger in hand. The royal guard surrounded him, sacrificing their own lives to repel the ruthless onslaught of unholy creatures that sought to tear this cowardly Prince limb from limb. Thomas raced towards Arthur, with determination in his eyes, and I couldn't breathe. *Thomas's half-cocked plan was about to become a success.* Arthur was overwhelmed, and I scrambled to remove this blasted chain.

"No, no, no!" I slammed the dagger down again, when my father raced towards me. He carried a key with him!

"Dad!"

He quickly turned the lock, releasing me from the chain. He reached for me, but I pushed him away.

"I'm sorry! There's no time!" I shouted, grabbing the bow and quiver. I took off to the end of the platform, finding Arthur once more. There were so many knights between us. *I would never reach him in time.* My eyes searched for Thomas.

Suddenly, Arthur gasped when a knight sliced him. He clutched his side where the knight's blade had struck him and proceeded to return the favor, plunging his blade through the knight's chest and swiftly kicking his lifeless body to the ground. I scrambled to think of something, when my eyes found Thomas. He was *right* behind Arthur, and I drew my bow.

I took a deep breath.

"Sometimes a necessary evil must take place for the good of all," I whispered, letting my arrow fly.

Thomas lunged with his dagger raised as Arthur turned to face him. I saw Arthur's eyes widen briefly before my arrow pierced Thomas's neck.

Chapter 23

Arthur

My heart stopped, seeing that prick mere inches from me. Thanks to Kymra, I knew what his plan was and *somehow* it nearly happened. But an arrow shot through his neck with deadly precision, stopping him from stabbing me in the chest. Thomas's eyes went wide as blood bubbled forth from his mouth, and then he dropped. My own eyes widened on the lone figure standing behind him with her bow raised. Kymra.

She killed him.

I felt sick knowing this was *all* my fault. Kymra was good, pure, and kind. *She was supposed to save the world and... I corrupted her.*

A knight advanced again, and I barely brought my own sword up in time to meet his. We clashed, and I quickly disposed of him. I needed to reach Kymra, who was now lost in the crowd. My mind was reeling as panic surged through me. *Where was she?!* I raised my hands, sending my shadow out and snapping the necks of four knights standing in my way. I bolted forward, when a loud voice stopped me. The King had Kymra with a knife to her neck.

"Stop your army, Nightlocke!"

I gritted my teeth in anger, but I raised my fist and whistled sharply. Everything stopped, and another line was drawn. The wound on my side had begun to ache, but there was nothing I could do for it now. I could already feel the poison trickling in, and I wasn't sure if it was a death sentence.

"For too long, you have plague our lands, and now look at us! You have slaughtered half my people already, but I will not let you kill the Lightspark, Nightlocke! Not again!"

CHAPTER 23

What was left of the crowd began shouting angrily at me. I held my ground and restrained my army from gutting every last unfortunate soul in this courtyard. *They had no idea what they were doing.* I showed restraint and held my temper back.

"I would never kill her! You cannot keep her prisoner like you did with the last one! Kymra *belongs* to me! We balance one another, and if you really wanted to save your land, then you will let her go!"

"Never! This is my land, and you will not ruin us further! The last person she'd ever belong to would be you."

I glared at him before turning to Kymra. She gave me a small nod, and I released my shadows. Everyone backed up, looking to their King for guidance, but he foolishly pressed his blade into Kymra's neck even further.

"The only one threatening the Lightspark and your people is you, Alexander. Whether you believe it or not, the Lightspark belongs to me, and you are not the only King that can keep her safe," I snarled, making him laugh.

"What you?! You are not a King, Nightlocke, nor are you fit to even stand in the company of me and the Lightspark!"

"I beg to differ!" I said, raising my arms. The creatures I brought all roared in agreement, and I gave the King a wicked smile. "I am the Nightlocke, *King* of the Forbidden Woods, and you have declared war on my Kingdom when you stole my Queen! According to my law, that is an offense punishable by death!"

My shadows had reached the two of them now, and the moment I declared judgment on King Alexander, I grabbed him. He fell into the veil of darkness, and I pulled him right to me. The King was disoriented and struggling to breathe from traveling through the veil, and I grabbed his neck.

"Death to you, *King*."

I covered his face with my hand as I shoved the darkness down his throat, letting my shadows wreak havoc on him from the inside out. He convulsed, limbs twisting and snapping as I pulverized his bones. Blood poured from his nose and eyes before I twisted my hand, snapping his neck and finally ending his misery. He dropped to the ground as his liquefied entrails began to drain from his mouth in a murky puddle of blood and what used to be organs. Nobody dared to move, but I didn't care about the rest of them. My eyes searched for the only person that mattered to me in this world.

Kymra shot through the crowd as I rushed towards her. Relief washed over me that she was alive. Alive and well and within reach, but she slowed just in front of me, hesitating slightly. Fear trickled in that she still saw me as nothing more than a monster after what I had done, but she gently raised her hand towards me. She looked relieved to see me too, and suddenly I had hope.

"Arthur?" she said quietly as tears filled her eyes.

I let go of the breath I'd been holding as her hand gently touched my cheek. *She was finally back where she belonged,* I thought as the dark shadows hummed happily inside. I hated the things I said to her, and I was going to spend the rest of my life making sure she knew exactly where her place is. I never wanted her to leave me again. She will forever be at my side as Queen, and I was going to make sure she felt loved and cherished every day.

"Kymra," I said softly, opening my arms to embrace her, when I was suddenly thrown backwards by powerful force.

Kymra screamed as I hit the ground in a tremendous amount of pain. The last thing I saw was a spear sticking out of my chest before my eyes rolled in the back of my head, and I fell into darkness.

Chapter 24

Kymra

I screamed as Arthur was thrown backwards with a spear protruding from his chest. A spear that surely had Nightshade on it. I drew my arrow without hesitation as shadows began to slowly leave Arthur's body. I followed them to a guard, who was running away from them, completely afraid and lost to what he had just done. I let my arrow fly, dropping him, and the shadows started to dissipate in the night sky. I ran towards Arthur, whose shadows were slowly leaving him. His breathing was very labored and tears filled my eyes.

He was dying.

"DAD!" I shouted. *I can save him,* I thought as fear gripped my heart. *I just had to be smart. I've helped my father a thousand times before. I can do this.* I yanked on the poisonous spear, trying to get it out of his chest, but it was so freaking heavy. I couldn't get it to budge, and I turned to the crowd.

"SOMEONE HELP! Please!" I begged, but everyone stood frozen as they watched. The people were afraid, and soon the unholy creatures started to drop. They lay unmoving as the other creatures fled back to the safety of the woods. Tears ran down my face as I tugged harder.

No, this can't be happening!

My father and sister were the only ones that came to my aid. My dad helped me pull the spear from Arthur's body, but the look on his face when he saw the wound broke my heart.

"Do something!" I shouted, trying to stop the bleeding.

"I don't know how to treat this, Kymra! This isn't a normal wound."

"Try anyways! Please, Dad," I begged, looking at the man who risked everything to save me. *The man I was madly in love with.* "I can't lose him."

My dad's face soften, and he began to shout orders at those standing near us. He bellowed again, when they still didn't move and some finally started to help.

"Why should we help?" someone shouted in the back of the crowd, and I saw *red*.

I stood to face everyone, glaring at the crowd, despite the aching burn in my chest to return to Arthur. "This man saved you all, and you have no idea! The King has been keeping you all starving and poor for years. He has plenty of food in his castle, even without a Lightspark, and don't you all remember the last time the Lightspark was even here!? She never set foot outside the Castle walls!"

"But the Nightlocke is the reason the Lightspark died!"

"And he has tormented us for years!" someone else shouted.

"The previous Lightspark was a prisoner! It was a horrible accident when the first Nightlocke tried to save her! God, you people don't get it! The Lightspark is the Nightlocke's other half! The shadows consume him when he's left alone for too long, and none of you have any room to talk! This Nightlocke is Arthur Drakos. You," I shouted, pointing my finger at the villagers, "you all shunned him, refused to help him and his mother when they desperately needed it, and you brought the torment on yourselves for your own despicable behavior!"

Someone had brought my dad a bucket of water and the few supplies he needed. Dad started working on the wound, and I prayed Arthur would be okay.

"Haven't you all realized the moment my sister disappeared, the town stopped seeing the effects of the Nightlocke? Not like any of you even *once* offered to go look for her! No, everyone cowered away, pretending it didn't happen, even when we started giving you food. My father and I have been giving you all food for some time, have we not? Well, take a wild guess where it all came from because it sure wasn't from the King, I can tell you that!" Amarna shouted boldly. She stood at my side proudly, and I gave her a grateful smile, while the crowd dropped their heads in shame.

"Kymra!" Dad shouted, and I dropped back to his side.

"What's going on?"

My father shook his head. "I can try to stop the bleeding, but it struck his chest and lungs, narrowly missing his heart. There's this black substance here too, but I don't know if it's poison or if this is just apart of him. I don't know what I'm doing here, and he's fading fast! You've spent the most time with him, and you say you're his other half. I think... I think it's up to you, Kymra. You are the Lightspark after all."

A sob escaped my lips as I stared down at Arthur. "But I don't know how to use my powers, Dad. My blood spilled, and the ground flourished, that was it!"

"Kymra, calm yourself. You can figure this out. I know if you just trust yourself and focus on him, you can do this. You were meant for great things, my child. Now save him!" he shouted.

Arthur looked so pale and fear rippled through my body. I ran my fingers through his hair as the tears flowed freely. *What if I couldn't figure this out in time?* I put my hands over his wound, willing something to happen. *Anything* at this point. I tried to copy what Arthur did when he used his powers. His shadows were apart of him so if I'm his other half, then mine should work the same too, I thought, trying to convince myself at least.

"I am the Lightspark," I muttered as I stared into the wound on Arthur's chest. I tried to picture it closing as tears fell down my face.

"C'mon... Please work!"

Suddenly, a power erupted in my chest, and I gasped as it surged to the surface. My hands began to glow with a bright white light, traveling slowly up my right arm, burning as it went. I *felt* the toxins in Arthur's body. I could *see* the gaping hole in his lungs. I pulled out the toxins and forced his cells to stitch themselves together again. His shadows slammed back into his body and hope filled my heart. *I could heal the land and make things grow. I could heal wounds and save lives. I was the Lightspark, and Arthur will not die today!*

The light burst, striking everyone who stood and watched. My body felt entirely drained as I collapsed against Arthur's chest. I could barely lift my head and felt nothing but the burning sensation left on my arm. Arthur's chest didn't move, and another tear rolled down my cheek.

"Please, Arthur... Please come back," I whispered.

I needed him more than I needed air. This dark, quiet and brooding, dangerous man. With his temper and flaws. With his loving kindness and honesty. I loved this man, shadows and all. *Please come back to me*, I begged.

Suddenly, Arthur sharply inhaled before groaning loudly. I forced myself to sit up, finding his piercing blue eyes searching for mine.

"Kymra?" he whispered, and I lost it. I collapsed against his chest again, sobbing hysterically. His arms wrapped around me, and he pulled me entirely on his lap before slowly sitting the two of us up together. I sat in his lap, tucking my face in his neck. *I couldn't believe it... He was alive!* Arthur was alive and here with me. I *saved* him.

"Kymra," he said quietly again. He carefully pushed my hair from my face before running his fingers under my jawline, gripping my chin gently. "You saved me."

Tears fell even harder as he kissed me. I melted into his embrace as I wrapped my arms around him. I clung to him as he did with me. I couldn't get enough of him, and I was desperate for his touch. When we finally broke apart, he cupped my face in his hands, wiping my fallen tears with his thumb before resting his head against mine.

"I am so sorry, Arthur. You were right about everything and I..."

"No, Kymra. I was harsh with you. I was jealous, and it is me who should be sorry. I don't want you to ever leave me. My home is your home, and I need you with me. Always," he said.

"Arthur, I never want you to feel like I don't see the wonderful man that you are. I love you, and I never want to leave your side either."

He smiled wickedly. "Good. Otherwise, I'll be forced to kidnap you again."

I laughed, kissing him again before my father cleared his throat. He knelt down to us both, and I realized we still had an audience. I blushed, forgetting everyone staring at us.

"It's good to see you well, son, but we have made a mess of things here. The kingdom has no King, and your... um... monsters are waking up. It's scaring

CHAPTER 24

the people," my father said, shaking Arthur's hand. I blinked in surprise. *The two seemed to know one another...*

Arthur and I stood tall, but he yanked me back towards him when I went to take a step forward.

"I wasn't leaving," I whispered as the corners of my mouth rose.

"Right now, you need to stay *exactly* where you are. I'm not ready to let you go any further, understand?" he asked, and I nodded my head when his eyes darkened.

"I have no desire to leave you either," I replied quietly, when his gaze dropped to my arm. His eyes cleared, and he pulled my right arm forward. I looked down, and my own eyes widened. Tattoos ran up and down my arm, and I turned back to Arthur.

"What does this mean?" I asked. *They looked just like Arthur's.* He turned my face around to inspect my head and neck before gesturing to my legs.

"Let me see, please," he asked quietly, and I gently pulled the awful dress up, and sure enough, my right leg had tattoos as well. *I didn't even feel the pain on my leg when everything happened.*

"It stops at your shoulder, it seems. They match mine," he said softly, and the corners of my mouth rose. The only difference was the color. Mine was white, while his were black.

"I like matching you," I whispered, and he grinned.

"Me too," he said.

"Guys... Focus. You started this, and you need to end it. There is no King now," he said, and I blushed again. *It was easy to get lost in Arthur now that I had him back.*

"There is still a King, Uriah," Arthur said, and my brows rose.

"Hear me, citizens of Odemark! The return of the Lightspark has begun to restore balance in... Well, me. Kymra has shown me that compassion and selflessness are what is needed to bring prosperity and happiness to our embittered and divided kingdoms. I was wrong before... I realize that now. The Nightlocke was created, not to be a monster that terrorizes others, but to protect the Lightspark at all costs. Without her, I am lost to the darkness, but those days are past. From this day forth, my Realm of Darkness and the great Kingdom of Odemark will enter into a new time of peace and prosperity. I think it's time for you to meet your rightful King."

Arthur raised his hand to the woods, blackening his eyes as he summoned something deep within the forest. I could feel it this time somehow, and my eyes went wide when I watched black shadows bolt from the woods.

Who was coming?

Chapter 25

Arthur

I summoned my shadows with ease, noticing it was easier to use my powers at a greater distance than before. I even felt like the depth of my power had grown, and moving two people through the veil without being present was surprisingly easy. *It must be because Kymra had finally unlocked her Lightspark abilities.* She made me stronger, better than I ever could be on my own, and I was so ready to disappear with her once more. But first, I had to reveal the last trick I will *ever* play on the Kingdom of Odemark. I vowed right then and there that I would *never* trick or torment this kingdom again.

As my shadows grew near, I prepared to catch the two that would struggle once they finally emerged from the veil. My shadows swirled in front of me, dumping Liam and Agatha to the floor, and the kingdom gasped. Liam stood tall and helped his bride to her feet. His head was still very much attached to his body, and he was most certainly alive. Liam's eyes found his father's body right away, and then slowly drifted over to his brother's.

"I'm sorry," I said to Liam, genuinely meaning it, and he slowly nodded.

"I heard everything through the projection. Was it you?"

Kymra stiffened, and I stood in front, trying to protect her again.

"Yes," I replied, taking the fall for Thomas too. I had always planned on killing him anyways, and I hated that my lack of morals rubbed off on Kymra somewhat. *She should have never been in a position to take his life in the first place, and if I had not yelled at her back at my castle, then she would have never run off.* This was all on me, and I was okay taking the blame.

But Kymra had other ideas as she stepped passed me. "Liam, he is lying.

While he killed your father, it was I that killed your brother. I am sorry it came to this, but I am so happy to see you alive."

Liam's eyes furrowed at her revelation, and he gave her a slow nod as well. I gripped her waist, pulling her back to my side, waiting to see Liam's reaction. He was alone now. No family left, and I knew that feeling all too well. Agatha's family finally forced their way through the crowd, and he let her go to greet them. They were ecstatic, and I was surprised when her father gave me a small appreciative nod.

"It's alright, Kymra. They had become corrupt and wicked when they started mistreating the citizens of Odemark long ago. Although much to my surprise, they treated you far worse. My father made a deal with Thomas, and from that day on, I was kept in the dark as to what their true plans and intentions were. It would seem they both had an agenda of their own. I, however, will *never* treat you as they have, and I apologize for their cruel and inexcusable behavior," Liam said to her, and I exhaled a sigh of relief.

I can take the heat over what I did, but I didn't know how she'd handle it. Taking a life, even one as wicked as Thomas's, was going to effect her whether she realized it or not, and I planned to help her through it.

"I still want to help the people, Liam," she replied, taking my hand. "Just at Arthur's side."

My cheeks heated slightly, and I couldn't keep the grin off my face. I turned to her father, who gave me an approving nod. An overwhelming feeling hit me then, not fully expecting what his approval would honestly mean to me. Kymra had no idea, but I seriously respected that man. Uriah was incredibly brave, and I knew *exactly* whom Kymra took after. Liam stepped towards me, offering me his hand, pulling me from my thoughts.

"We have neighboring kingdoms, Arthur, and the Kingdom of Odemark hereby recognizes yours with you as King. I propose a truce and an alliance between our kingdoms," Liam said, and I blinked in surprise.

"You want to remain friends?" I asked, studying him carefully.

"No," he said, "more like family. You stuck your neck out for me when you had every reason to kill me and my bride for the actions of my family and my kingdom. You *chose* to spare my life, when my father wouldn't even negotiate

CHAPTER 25

for me. In my eyes, you are my brother, more than Thomas ever had been. I always knew I'd have to sleep with one eye open once I became King, and this is somewhat fitting because Kymra was always like a little sister to me anyways."

Kymra beamed up at him before turning to me with wide eyes. I had barely accepted the fact that I was a King as it was, but here she was looking at me with those big green eyes, pleading with me to accept. I turned back to Liam and shook his hand. I'd accept if it made her happy, even though the only person I ever needed in my life was her. *Maybe this wouldn't be so bad?*

"I accept," I replied.

"Everyone, I promise you that as King, I will fix the problems my father created! Our land will flourish, and we will be prosperous again!"

Everyone cheered as Liam went straight to Agatha. He held out her hand, and she ran to him. *I take it she's choosing to stay by his side after everything.* I looked down to my own girl, kissing her forehead.

"Let's go home, Arthur," she said, and I gave her a smile.

"As you wish."

Epilogue

Kymra

Three years had passed since I first met the scary Nightlocke, and now everything was very different than what it used to be. I married Arthur the minute he saved me from Thomas and wicked King Alexander, and we've stayed together ever since. We kept our alliance with the Kingdom of Odemark along with their new King and Queen.

Liam married Princess Agatha very quickly after his coronation, and he has really come into his own since then. Unlike his father, he's a fair and kind ruler. I always thought Liam was quiet and passive, but really he was just trying to survive living in the castle with his father and brother. They have a little one of their own now, a beautiful girl named Zoey.

With the help of Arthur, I've have found balance in my own life. I am able to cultivate the land, without spilling any blood, and he helps me along the way as I learn more and more about my strengths and abilities. I no longer give when I have nothing left, and he makes sure I have everything I could ever want to be happy and healthy. I am content and happy, and my chest no longer burns in a desperate need to help others.

Arthur is still his dark and brooding old self, but he has lost his temper since that fateful day at the castle. Our kingdom is different than most as his subjects are the dark creatures in these woods. He protects them fiercely now, and he keeps out those who think themselves brave if they can bring down a Wraith or Bloodhound. Other than specific people, *no one* is allowed in our land. It's much safer that way, and quite frankly, that's how we prefer it. I love these woods, and I feel more at home here than I ever did in the kingdom.

While our woods remains dark, gloomy, and ominous, the Kingdom of Odemark is beautiful now. Lush green grass cover the fields, wildflowers bloom nearly year round, and it's brought back a wide variety of wildlife. Not just around the castle too, but the entire kingdom is thriving again. It took a tremendous amount of work on my part, but it was definitely worth it. We had so much food that the kingdom has nearly tripled in size, becoming a trade and commerce center of sorts. Arthur and I try to stay out of sight for the most part, letting Liam run his kingdom as he deems fit. I come in every so often to revitalize the earth and help anyway I can, but Arthur insists we travel at night. He gets uptight with others seeing me, especially now since the kingdom's gotten so much bigger. There are constantly Kings and Queens visiting here, hoping to form an alliance, and the first thing they ask Liam is if he owns a Lightspark.

Liam always tells them he has no idea what they're talking about, and I have become somewhat forgotten, with those who know keeping my secret. Arthur says it's safer this way, and I trust him.

Liam has only ever called upon Arthur once, when another King threatened war against his throne. I had taught Liam how to use the shadows to speak to my husband, and when Arthur heard the call, he was genuinely shocked. I had to beg him to let me come and watch, and I ended up in the safety of the dark, watching my husband fill the room with his shadows before appearing directly behind the pompous King. He was just a young arrogant King trying to expand his tiny kingdom and had no idea who Liam called his brother.

The poor guy wet himself, and we never saw him again.

It quickly became known that the Nightlocke and King Liam were ruling together, and no one has dared to go against either of them. Liam has his own army of highly skilled knights, where Arthur still controlled the Forbidden Woods. My husband still has his elite army that he released the day he saved me, although he has refused to convert anymore. Arthur has never told me what it even entailed or what they were, but just said it was the old him, and that he would never do it again. I was proud of him, but I still stayed far away from those scary creatures.

Amarna received a massive dowry like I always knew she would, and it was for her bravery in defending my husband that caught the eye of general's son. She and her new husband are happily living on the castle grounds as he is currently training to command his own regiment for King Liam. I was happy for her, and my father was tremendously proud. He had become head physician in the royal house once more, so I got to see him often at the castle. Marge apparently has had her eye on him for some time, although he tries hard not to lead her on. I think it's funny.

Today, however, was a very special day. I had been trying to figure out the best way to go about it all morning. I finally confirmed my suspicions yesterday, and I could not contain my joy any longer.

I had to tell Arthur.

I was in the kitchen, lost in thought as I prepared dinner for the two of us. It was just a typical night here at home, but I wanted to make everything special. I was recreating the very first meal I had ever made Arthur, when he was just the Nightlocke to me. It had become his favorite, and I had even spent the morning making a cake for the special occasion. I loved getting to bake again but hiding the cake was a whole other story. I somehow managed to do it, and honestly, I was more proud of that fact than the cake itself.

Arthur came in from outside, hanging his bow on the hook before setting two very dead chickens and a hare on the counter. I paled at the sight. The smell churned my stomach almost immediately.

"Are you alright, Kymra? You're looking a little green, love," Arthur said as he began to skin and dress the animals. My eyes were stuck on the critters though. I was trying desperately not to lose the contents of my stomach, but I was losing this battle. I bolted from the room and barely made it outside before I tossed everything left in my belly.

"Kymra, what in the world?" Arthur cried out before grinding to a halt behind me. I couldn't stop though, and he wisely kept his distance.

When I finally stopped puking my guts out, I wiped my mouth clear. I was thoroughly embarrassed as I had never gotten sick in front of Arthur before. *I was planning on spending the rest of my life letting Arthur believe I never got sick or even went to the bathroom, but I guess that was officially out the window.*

Arthur finally approached me and put his hand on my forehead.

"You don't feel warm. Have you been feeling sick, Kymra?" he asked, his eyes full of concern.

"Well no... But something is going on that we need to talk about. I wanted to tell you in a special way, but then you brought in the kill from your hunt and well... Yeah."

Arthur narrowed his eyes, and I knew I was blundering this. He gently lifted my chin asking, "Kymra, are you sick? Do you need your father? We can go right now..."

I put my finger to his lips, silencing his ramble. "Arthur, I'm not sick. I'm pregnant."

Arthur's eyes widened, and he stood there entirely rigid. *My husband, the cool, collected, quiet man who never feared anything, was standing here looking absolutely petrified.* I pursed my lips together.

"Arthur?"

I reached for his hand, but he was lost. I gave him a gentle squeeze before finally waving my hand in front of his face, and I still got no reaction. *This was bad. Definitely not the reaction I was hoping for.* My face fell then. *What if he didn't want children? Maybe this was something he never wanted and now was forced upon him?*

Suddenly, he snapped out of his trance and yanked me into the shadow veil. He spit us out in the middle of Liam's castle and began shouting loudly.

"URIAH!" he bellowed down the halls, dragging me behind him. I was struggling to keep up with his long strides though. It took me three steps to his one, and I was quickly getting out of breath.

"Arthur... Wait!"

My husband turned, gritting his teeth before he hauled me up into his arms. *This wasn't what I meant.*

"Arthur..."

"URIAH!" Arthur shouted again as every servant and Lord near us began to stumble into the hall. Liam appeared amongst them, looking alarmed.

"Arthur... Kymra. What is going on?" he asked, worry spreading across his face.

Heat filled my cheeks as Arthur answered, "I need Uriah *now*."

Liam looked to me. He nodded and ushered us forward as my face turned an entirely new shade of red. *They all must think something horrible was going on with me.* Arthur had this determined look on his face. Nothing was changing his mind now, and I would have to see my father before I could get my husband to settle down enough to listen.

Liam took us to his private room, where Agatha was with baby Zoey. I barely got a glimpse at the newborn before Arthur whisked me straight to the massive bed. He set me down promptly before tossing his shadows out to shut the door on the many faces watching from the hall. My father walked in shortly after and came right to my side.

"What is wrong? Are you hurt?" he asked as his brows knitted together in concern. I buried my face in my hands *completely* embarrassed.

"No, this is all blown out of proportion, Dad. I'm fine, really. It's just that..."

"She's pregnant, and I need to know that they are healthy. *Both* of them," Arthur demanded. My father's eyes widened when he turned back to me, and his lip quivered ever so slightly.

"Is this true? Am I to be a granddad?"

I gave him a small nod, and he hugged me tightly.

"Congratulations, my dear," he whispered, and I replied with a thank you. Liam patted Arthur on the back, who still looked stressed.

"See, Arthur? We celebrate first, then visit the doctor," I said chuckling, but he just looked exasperated by me. He rubbed his face harshly. His stress was clearly not going away, and my dad chuckled.

"Oh, leave the boy be. All Dads stress for their first baby. It just means he's going to be an amazing father," my Dad said before grabbing his medical equipment. Arthur gave my father a grateful look before sticking his tongue out at me. My jaw dropped, turning into a playful grin as I shook my head. *He has never done that before. I liked seeing his playful side.*

"Well, now that the whole castle is in an uproar seeing you screech about and carrying Kymra through the halls, I think we should go inform everyone that there is no danger. Our Nightlocke and Lightspark are perfectly safe.

Come, my love. Let them have this moment to themselves," Liam said, reaching for his Queen. Agatha congratulated us before taking Liam's hand.

I gave my friends a grateful nod as my father began listening in on my stomach. He smiled, looking at us both as Arthur joined me by my side.

"It's beautiful, you two. Listen," he said, giving Arthur the headset first.

Arthur put it to his ears as my father placed the other end on my belly once more. After a moment, Arthur smiled wide, looking between my father and I. He was beaming, and it made my heart burst with joy.

"It's there, Kymra. I can hear our child's heart beat, and it's strong," he said ecstatically.

"So, you're happy, Arthur? Are you really okay with this?" I asked as tears filled my eyes, and my father stood up.

"I'll give you some privacy, but do not leave without finding me again," he said before leaving the two of us alone, and Arthur gently grabbed my chin, commanding my attention.

"I'll be honest, Kymra. The idea of being a father *scares* me half to death, but I know you will be a fantastic mother. I am happy, more than happy my love. I am sorry if I didn't seem like it before. It's just my job to protect you, well both of you, and it hard to stop that from taking over."

I leaned into his embrace, feeling his warmth and kindness.

"I love you, Arthur," I whispered.

"I love you too," he replied.

Bonus Chapter

"Khalan!"

My son halted in his tracks, turning to face his mother, whose hands were on her hips.

"What do you have to say for yourself?" Kymra demanded, raising an eyebrow. I bit my lower lip to keep from laughing. Khalan rocked back and forth on his feet, giving her a sheepish grin.

"I don't know," he answered softly.

The doors to the castle's kitchen open and out walked two boys covered in some chocolate goo with the steward behind them. He gave Khalan a look before looking to me.

"I'll handle it," I said quietly, and he gave me a grateful nod. The two boys glared at my son, and I cleared my throat. Red coated their cheeks, and they looked to the floor as they walked by.

"Khalan..."

"Oh c'mon, mom!" Khalan protested. "They were being jerks and..."

"It does not give you the right to do something like that!" Kymra scolded, and Khalan sighed. "I'm sure the kitchen staff will not be happy to know their hard work was ruined like that, and those boys didn't deserve that either. We have to get along with our kingdom's..."

"They're not our kingdom," my son interrupted. His shadows swirled in his eyes so dark that I blinked, wondering if I was noticing it correctly. I've sensed his shadows since birth, but now at the right age of five, Khalan's shadow abilities have come in full swing. They always trickled out whenever his emotions got the better of him, but lately he's been *creative* with them. *A natural really, but a pain in the butt to discipline.*

"Let's take a walk, son," I said firmly. The gray in his eyes receded, and he looked to the floor. Kymra sighed, patting me on the shoulder before heading in the directions those chocolate covered boys went.

I walked towards my son, when I noticed movement out of the corner of my eye. I turned, finding Zoey hiding behind the door with her eyes wide. She jumped when I caught her and promptly shut the door and ran. The corners of my mouth rose. *I should have known...*

"Let's go, Khalan," I said, chuckling to myself. I released my shadows, taking his hand and stepping into the veil. As my vision cleared, a large familiar oak tree came into view. I knew every notch in this tree, and I ran my hand over it like I had a thousand times. My gaze drifted to momma's headstone before I sat down against her tree and patted the dirt next to me.

Khalan sighed but obeyed. He laid his head in his arms, tucking his knees close to his chest. I inhaled slowly, breathing in the comforting forest air of my Forbidden Woods and noticed he had done the same.

After a few moments, I asked, "Do you want to talk about it?"

Khalan raised his head. I couldn't contain my smirk at the frustrated look he gave me. *God, he was just like me.*

"Ben and Finnick are just stupid," he said finally. I gave him another moment, knowing there was more weighing on his chest, and he finally caved. "They called me a freak. They said I shouldn't be allowed at King Liam's castle because I was dangerous."

I frowned. My shadows reacted to my anger, and they swirled between my fingers, eager to be released.

"You are not a freak, Khalan," I said firmly, "nor are you dangerous."

"Aren't I though?" he asked, looking at me. His big eyes searching my own. He held out his hand and gray shadows poured from his finger tips. My eyes widened when he began to create shapes. "I can do things no one else can."

"Doesn't make you a freak," I said in a calm tone as I watched him move the shadows he was born with. *His control over his shadows was incredible. The color puzzled me too.*

"It makes you different, Khalan," I said, shaking myself from those thoughts. "People don't like different."

Khalan pulled the shadows back and rest his head on his knees again. "What if I hurt someone?"

I sighed heavily. *This was a conversation I'd expect to have when he was older, but Khalan's never been much of a kid, I suppose.* He was so observant and quiet. It was easy to forget how young he really was.

"You got mad today," I said softly, and he slowly looked to me, "didn't you? You reacted before you even realized, right?"

His eyes widened, and he quickly dropped his head. I patted his shoulders before pulling him towards me.

"Khalan, I did the same thing when I was young," I said, leaving out the gruesome details of my mistakes. "You will learn self-control and discipline over your shadows as you grow up, but you are not dangerous. People like Ben and Finnick are just jealous. Jealous and afraid of the gifts we posses. So they try to bring you down to their level, but we are Nightlocke, son. We will *never* be at their level."

Khalan's brows furrowed as he thought about what I said. Worry flashed across his face, and I waited for him to say what else was wrong. He always did in the end, and I was more than happy to give him the time he needed.

"Ben said his dad thought you shouldn't be in King Liam's court," he said quietly. "He said Liam should drive you out of the Kingdom and back to the dark where we belong."

My eyes darkened. *That prick...*

"George doesn't know what he's talking about," I said, irritation lacing my words. "You don't worry about what anyone says, Khalan. No one will harm our family."

His little lips pursed together, and I sighed, pulling my shadows back. I gently poked his chest and asked, "What do your shadows tell you when you hear a threat like that?"

Khalan took a deep breath, and his eyes turned gray. Pride swelled in my chest when he said, "They want to stop it."

I smiled. "Exactly. Listen to your shadows, Khalan. They will always be there for you. Now, we're going back so you can apologize."

His shoulders slumped forward. "But Dad!"

"No buts, Khalan," I said, standing. "Your mother will tan your hide *and* mine if we do not own up to our mistakes. We're going."

He groaned as he got to his feet. "Fine."

We drifted through the shadow veil towards the beacon of light that was always there to me. Kymra. Others gasped as we stepped through, but not my Kymra. *Never my Kymra.* The parents of the two boys were there along with Liam and his wife, Agatha.

"Love," I said, kissing her cheek. "Khalan has something to say."

I gently pushed my son forward, and the boy dragged his feet to the other two about his age.

"I'm sorry," he muttered. His gray shadows swirled around his fingers, but he kept them close. Kymra narrowed her eyes, but I shook my head. *Not now.*

The two boys grumbled something foul, and my anger flared. *George wouldn't correct it so I will.* I took a step forward. "He said sorry, Benjamin."

The kid's eyes widened, and he quickly stammered, "It's fine."

"It's not really," George said, stepping towards me. "Your son could have seriously injured mine."

"With chocolate?" I quipped, and his face flushed.

"With those shadows of yours!" he hollered. "It's not safe…"

"Choose your words *carefully*," I said, stilling the room. My shadows filled the room, spreading fear across everyone's face. George and I have had issues since I joined Liam's court, but this time his disrespect had gone too far.

"Arthur…"

Kymra's soft voice was the only one who dared to speak. I sucked in a breath and pulled my shadows back, despite their protest. *For her. Only for her.*

"Everyone out," I commanded, "except George and King Liam, please."

The children bolted, but I was proud of Khalan, who held back and waited for Zoey to catch up. He took her hand and off the two went. Kymra gave me a firm look before leaving with Agatha. I understood her warning. *Don't kill George.* I was willing to do my best with her wishes, but I made no promises. I crossed my arms the second the door closed.

"What's going on?" Liam asked as he stepped closer. He looked to me and then George. "Is this about the kids?"

"I've heard what you've said about me and my family," I said, stepping closer to George, "and I'd like you to tell *your* King."

George paled. "I have no idea what you're talking about."

Liam narrowed his eyes as I snorted.

"Of course, you don't," I said. "Not when you actually have to say it to my face and his."

"George?"

George's eyes darted back and forth between the two of us. "I don't know, your Highness!"

Liam sighed, pinching the bridge of his nose. "*Someone* tell me what is going on."

Shadows poured from my fingers, wrapping around the man, who looked ready to pass out already. His pale skin felt clammy against my dark shadows, and I could feel his rapid heart rate continue to increase.

"I am not going anywhere," I said firmly, my voice changing with the darkness, "and you best get use to seeing me and my family around. Do not fill *anyone's* mind with nonsense about how dangerous we are."

I stepped closer, and my shadows reached his face. They wrapped around his neck, tightening ever so slightly, while the man shook before me. "I'm only dangerous to my enemies," I said firmly. "Are *you* my enemy, George?"

He frantically shook his head, and the corners of my mouth rose. "Good. Because I haven't killed anyone since the last King, and I've been itching to reach for the dark again. Don't give me the excuse to."

I pulled my shadows back and stepped away from the man, finding a very pissed off Liam. I stepped aside to look out the window, while George begged for Liam's mercy. Apologizing time and time again for insulting his ally and friend. Not one apology came my way, but I didn't care. Not when the memories of my last battle came to mind. I nearly went to battle alone that day, but the creatures of my forest came to my aid. I am their King, and I would protect them always, but I don't have an army like Liam's or even like George's. I had nobody in my kingdom other than my wife and son. *We were the last of the Nightlockes.* Suddenly, a sickening thought came to mind. *If anyone came after my throne or family, it would just be me fighting to protect them.* While I wasn't worried about my abilities or doubting the forest coming to my aid again, I can't be in multiple places at once.

"Itching to reach for the dark, eh?"

I turned as Liam approached. He leaned against the desk, giving me a pointed look. "Should I be worried?"

I shrugged. "I was more messing with him than anything. I found out from Khalan what he said, and it pissed me off that he made Khalan worry over it."

Liam slowly nodded. "*That* I understand. I'm not happy with his very vocal opinion of my choices. He will not get away with insulting you. You are my most trusted ally, Arthur."

My mind drifted as I shrugged again. "As long as he stops, I don't care," I muttered.

Liam's eyes narrowed. "You normally enjoy scaring the living daylights out of people. Got something else on your mind?"

I sighed and turned back towards the window. The Forbidden Woods were in directly in front of me, going on and on for what seemed like forever. *It was such a massive kingdom.* I have never truly been over every inch of the place, and maybe that was my problem. *Maybe there was more out there that could help me protect my family?*

"Do you know much about my kingdom?" I asked, my eyes still stuck on my home.

Liam stepped forward. "You know more than I do, brother. We have some records of your kingdom but not much. Why do you ask?"

"I wasn't the first Nightlocke," I said quietly, turning to look him in the eye. "The Nightlocke that killed your mother... He wasn't me. I know next to nothing about my home or where the shadows came from and..." My voice trailed off as I glanced back towards home, "and I am utterly alone in defending it."

Liam's gaze softened as he clasped my shoulder. "You are not alone. You have me and my armies if you ever need. We're more than just allies. We are family, Arthur."

I gave him a grateful smile. "I appreciate that, but I don't want to risk you or your family either. We aren't blood so getting involved in a war..."

"Is my decision," he said, giving me a look. "You know Agatha and I are rooting for Khalan to win Zoey's heart. We are giving our daughter the chance to decide for herself, but we are praying it's with your son. We trust you and Kymra, and if you ever needed help, we will be there."

I pursed my lips together, nodding my head gratefully before clasping my own hand on his shoulder.

"Thank you," I said, smiling. "I am at your disposal if you ever need it too."

He grinned wide. "Oh, I know. I thoroughly enjoy using the Nightlocke card too. It's fun to watch'em squirm in their seat."

He patted my back and walked towards the door.

"Hey, Liam?" I said, and he turned towards me. "Can I see those records anyways?"

Bonus Chapter

I scoured over the documents Liam had in the royal archives. It was a dark dusty old room under the castle, close to the cell they held my Kymra in all those years ago. Liam had the room entirely sealed off, never to be opened again, and for that I was grateful. It still made my skin itch being this close, but nowhere near the pain I felt before.

There wasn't much in here about my Forbidden Woods, other than that it ceased to be part of Odemark's kingdom over a hundred years ago. I wanted the history or even a list of the known creatures found in there, but I found nothing like that. Just invoices and receipts between the King of Odemark and the Morgan family. *They must be the last owners,* I wondered to myself as I skimmed through the papers. The invoices and receipts showed trades happening between the two lands. Food, textiles, livestock... All were listed from Odemark's side of things, and weapons were given in return from the Morgan family.

I leaned back in the sturdy chair as I flipped through the record book. *So much information was kept down here, and I never once thought to look into our history,* I thought, pursing my lips together. *Not really sure what sort of King that made me.* As I turned the page, a brown parchment slid out and onto the floor. I picked it up and unfolded it on the table. My eyes widened.

It was a map of the Forbidden Woods.

My fingers traced over the dark border lines that mapped my kingdom. I found my castle marked clearly, and my finger trailed the lines heading right. *There was a town in my forest. Like an actual town.* Amaru was written near it, and I trailed my thumb across the word. *Was this the town's name?*

I traced the trade routes then, and it didn't seem too far from Odemark. It was just separate from my castle, but I couldn't help but wonder if it was still here. I've never ventured that far east before, and I quickly pocketed the map and stepped into the veil. Blinding sun light pierced my eyes as I looked around. Odemark was bustling today as merchants and vendors alike all had things to sell. Most gave me a wide birth, but I didn't mind. I had things to do, and people would just get in my way. I rolled the shadows between my fingers and strolled to the far end of the Kingdom.

I stopped at the edge and looked around. The large dirt road led straight to Eastern deserts, where the sun was as unbearable as the people who occupied that territory. Their mines were unlike any others though, if you could reach them. The journey alone killed most, and I pulled my attention away. Rahma and the Naiman Deserts were not what I was looking for.

My eyes drifted to the left where Amaru should be. An overgrown dirt path lay before me, and I narrowed my eyes. *This path was overgrown and clearly not used for some time, but this was a road.* I looked behind me and frowned. All Odemark's primary trade routes came from this road or on the opposite side from the ocean kingdoms, but this dirt path led straight into the Forbidden Woods. *It had to be the road to Amaru.*

I followed the road a ways to the edge of my kingdom and slipped into the comforting dark. The forest was especially dark here, and I listened carefully, hearing only my boots crunching on fallen leaves on the ground. My kingdom was so vast, it was hard to maintain, but a small part of me had always been overwhelmed by the sheer size of it. I had been practicing taming the creatures that I grew up with, but as I ventured further into this section, I began to wonder what else lived in my kingdom. *And would they recognize me as their King?* The road curved inward, and I shook myself from those thoughts.

"Arthur, I don't know where you've run off to but find me when you can. We need to discuss our son's behavior," Kymra's voice entered my mind.

I pulled on my shadows to find my wife. She was safely tucked inside Liam's castle still, and I smiled. That diamond nearly cost me an arm and a leg to get, but it was worth it to be able to track my wife. *And she would never know.*

I pushed past a thick bush, when my shadows suddenly hissed. I winced as my head throbbed under their anger and took a second to get my bearings.

What in the world?! My shadows had never reacted this way before, but they seemed to recognize this place. My skin crawled with every step, and suddenly my body started to hurt. *Pain,* I thought. *My shadows were in pain somehow...* I forced my feet to move faster.

I broke out in a run, letting my shadows be my guide. A hint of familiarity filled me as I ran faster through the trees. *I know I've never been here before, but my shadows knew. Somehow they knew this place.* And it was killing them inside.

Light shown just ahead, and I shoved passed the trees into an open field. A cliff's edge lay before me, but I dropped to my knees when I saw what last past it all.

A village. An honest to God, broken *village* was in my woods. *People lived here once,* I thought to myself. *And I never knew.*

My shadows poured out of me. For the first time in a long time, I didn't have control of them, and they raced through the streets and buildings before me. I was seeing too much, too fast and couldn't focus on anything that passed by. I shut my eyes tight as my shadows searched the lands. And all I could feel was pain and sadness. Slowly, they returned defeated, and I took a couple of deep breaths. I stood, feeling sick over what lay before me. *They didn't find what they were looking for...*

I took one step, then another, and before long I made it to the village's edge. To my right, I saw the road I was following before. I must have gotten off course, but I shrugged my shoulders and stepped further inside. The structures were broken and some lay completely ruined. My heart ached with my shadows as I drug my hands against the stone walls. *People lived here. What happened...* I stepped out past the building and stopped dead in my tracks.

Bones. So many human bones lay scattered about the street. I couldn't breathe as I stared long and hard at the bodies I saw. Some were small, and my stomach twisted in knots. *They were children...*

I staggered away, running down another street only to find more. More and more broken bones from fallen bodies, and I couldn't get away fast enough. My shadows were in agony, grating against my skin painfully like they wanted out but couldn't leave. I saw some bodies clutching weapons, while others held onto one another. I shoved down another street and stumbled.

A large skeletal remain lay before me, and my heart stopped. *This was not human remains... These were dragons.*

The beast rested before the large field of wildflowers of all things. Flowers didn't grow in my woods, but the field was full of beautiful color. A three-prong mountain was in breathtaking view far past the field, but my eyes were glued to the beast. He wore a saddle. Its long tail wrapped around a single human remain as if protecting it somehow. *To its dying breath apparently.* I struggled to get my mind off another thought entirely. *The dragons could bond.* They bonded *with people.*

The people who lived in my forest...

My mind reeled at the discovery I found. My shadows twisted angrily inside, and my head was beginning to split in two. I couldn't stay much longer. It was too painful, but it killed me not knowing what happened to these people. *Were they Nightlockes?* I thought, shaking my head as goosebumps traveled up my arm. My body twitched as my shadows sang in fury, and I had to step away from the dragon remains. Nightlockes were *immortal. What in the world happened to my people then?*

I needed to figure this out. If something killed the Nightlockes long ago, then it could come back to kill my family. I stepped into the veil and back onto the cliff, where I could breathe a little easier. I took one step before I turned one last time.

These were my people...

I clenched my fists tightly, knowing I couldn't leave them. *Not like this.* I stepped into the veil again, feeling utter pain when I saw the bones again. Walking slowly, I dropped every body, *every bone,* into the veil. My head pulsed as I held everyone in my shadows, getting worse the closer I got to the mountain. My shadows worked hard, and soon I set everyone beside the dragon.

Sharpening my shadows into a blade, I slammed it into the earth. My mind rattled on impact, but I kept going. I repeated the process until it finally gave way and a hole appeared. I dug deeper and deeper into the earth. Sweat lining my brow as my skin crawled. It became more obvious that these *were* my people by the fact my shadows were in agony just being here. Somehow they knew these bones, but despite the alarm bells ringing in my ears to get away from this place, but I didn't cower to it. I was *the* Nightlocke, and I would give my people a proper burial.

I dropped to my knees, breathing rapidly once the hole was deep enough. Lifting my hand, I dropped the remains into the veil. Dragon and all. I gently laid them in the hole I dug, looking down sorrowfully at the little remains who never got a chance to live.

"I'm sorry," I said, even though I didn't know them. They didn't deserve this, I knew that much. "I am so sorry."

Shadows poured from my fingers, twitching as they went to the pile of dirt besides the grave. They pushed it in, and I sagged in relief once it was done. The sun was setting in the sky by the time I laid everyone to rest. *I needed to go home,* I realized. I didn't know what lurked in this part of the forest at night, and I didn't have the strength to face it if it somehow found me. A loud screech sounded in the distance, telling me it was time to go.

After one last look at the grave, I stepped into the veil once more.

* * *

Kymra eyed me carefully when I came to pick them up. I was late. Oh, so very late, but she didn't question me in front of Liam and Agatha. I knew *that* was coming later. They had eaten with her father already, so I carried them home to our castle, feeling fatigued and weak for the first time in a long time. My bones chilled when I stepped through the veil and into our home. My gaze drifted to the right, knowing full well what lie far in the distance. My heart ached, and I quickly turned and followed my wife inside.

"You ready to tell me where you were all day?" my wife asked as Khalan ran to his room. One of our attendants, who came from Liam's staff, rushed after him, and I shrugged.

"I just had some things to check over," I said softly. I reached for her hand, and she wrapped her dainty fingers around mine. "Nothing to worry about."

Her brows knitted as she studied me. "*You* seem worried, Arthur."

I frowned. Worry wasn't the only emotion I was feeling. Anger, devastation, and fear were swirling around inside my chest so roughly that I struggled to control the shadows answering their call. I gave her a forced smile saying, "I'm fine, my love. Can we spend some time in the library tonight? I miss listening to you read."

Her face softened as we walked up the stairs. "Of course. But Arthur?"

I turned, finding an expression on her face I couldn't quite figure out. My beautiful wife sighed.

"When you sort through whatever's going on with you," she said softly, "promise me, you will talk to me. Okay?"

Guilt ate at me, but I didn't know *how* to tell her what I found out today. I gave a soft nod, choosing to remain silent until I could figure out how to share this. But this was a burden *I* didn't want. I just felt sick inside whenever I thought about all those people dying. All those children... *The shadows weren't enough to save them.* And how could I burden her with this too?

"I'll fetch you dinner and meet you in the library," she said, kissing my cheek.

Kymra made her way to the kitchen then, leaving me a muddled mess. I made my way to the library in search of more information as to what happened. I scanned every row. *Every* shelf for any sort of record. *This had to have been the King's castle before me,* I thought as I moved to another row. *Was the Nightlocke that gifted me the shadows before King? Or did it go back even further?*

I sighed, knowing I didn't have any answer to that question. The shadows held the memory and emotions of their last host, but I had no idea how many hosts were before me. And the Nightlocke before certainly didn't have memories of any dragons.

I sighed, putting my hand on my hips and debated what to do. I didn't see anything of use here, so I walked back towards the main area. My steps slowed when I saw silver tray of cold stew sitting on the reading table with a note. *How long had I been in here?* I wondered, picking up the note. I smiled softly to myself as I read.

You didn't even notice when I entered the room, so I'm going to let you continue on this quest of yours in peace. Come to bed when you're ready, and I will read to you another night. Just remember whatever's going on, trust your shadows. They've yet to let you down.

-Kymra

I set the note down and picked up the spoon. I didn't care that the food had gone cold. Kymra was an amazing cook, and I dug in as my belly grumbled. *I need to make this up to her.*

Suddenly, I stilled. Putting my bowl down, I picked up the note again. *Trust your shadows...*

"God, Kymra..." I muttered softly. "You are brilliant!"

I stood and faced the library again. Shutting my eyes, I released my shadows into the room.

"Find me what I'm looking for," I commanded, and I let them go. The shadows raced through the library, spreading across every inch of the room, and my mind followed the mental picture they gave. Suddenly, they settled on one book. In the far back corner of the room, just below the tapestry, sat an old and weathered book.

My shadows drug it back, and I held the book in my hands. I have never seen this book before. The leather was worn and dusty, and I sat down on the couch again, brushing off the dust. *Kyrell's Guide on Dragon Kind.*

I opened to the first page and began to read.

Only the worthy can bond a dragon. Only the fearless can ride one.

Bonus Chapter

I hadn't noticed the sun rising as I devoured the book. This *Kyrell* was knowledgeable in all things dragon related. Thanks to his bonded dragon, Thanatos, I had a detailed map of their kind. I learned that dragons have a hierarchy amongst themselves, and there are more than one breed of dragon in the world. Different breeds meant different abilities and power, but they all have the common thread of being stubborn and ruthless. That's why only certain ones were chosen to bond, and once the bond happened, it was *for life*.

Kyrell never once mention whether he was Nightlocke though. He kept the text purely about the dragons, which was great in knowing how to properly care for them, but I had to actually *have* a dragon before I could take care of it. *Speaking of that; where did they all go? No one's seen a dragon in decades. I thought they were extinct.* As I neared the end of the book, my heart plummeted because he still had yet to explain what happened to them. I tapped my foot anxiously as I scanned the last couple pages. I *needed* a dragon. I needed to protect my family at all costs. It couldn't just be me.

Dragons are insanely protective of their hatching grounds. Rarely do they let in a bonded rider even. I have only ever been once. The eggs are delicate yet powerful. Thanatos explained the power of the dragon lies within the shell, feeding the dragon as it grows inside. The hatchlings grow to adolescents, and then finally becoming full-fledged adults. The power or fire a dragon receives at birth emerges at the adolescent stage...

I skimmed through the section, hoping he'd mention the hatching grounds again. If they still existed, then maybe I could convince one to bond with me. He goes on about how each dragon breed has their own powers and abilities, but ultimately one Alpha will rule each breeding grounds. Great stuff for when I find them, but I was beginning to worry I never would. Finally, in the *last* paragraph, Kyrell writes about them.

The hatching grounds are sacred. No human is permitted to visit unless guided by a dragon, and even then, approval must be given. The red, green, and brown dragons, who typically carry dagger tails or club tails, hail from the island of Dangeni. Their hatching grounds are somewhere deep on the island, but they have no issues flying the continent with their increased speed.

However, Thanatos is a large Blue Morningstar dragon. The Alpha of his grounds. He hatched...

The passage stops. I flip through the empty pages and groan. *Kyrell never finished the book...* I thought to myself. I bit my lower lip as I wonder if *he* was one of the ones I buried.

"Good morning, love," Kymra said, startling me. She laughed when I jumped hard, dropping the book to the floor. I reached for the book, but she beat me to it, collapsing next to me on the sofa.

"Kyrell's Guide on Dragon Kind. This looks old," she said, flipping through the pages.

I rested my elbows on my knees. "It is."

"Is this what kept you up all night?" she asked quietly. Her eyes studied me closely, and I sighed. *She was smart,* I thought to myself. *She'd sniff out any lie I'd tell her, even if it was just to protect her.*

"Yes," I answered solemnly. "I made a discovery in our kingdom yesterday."

Her eyes widened. "What sort of discovery?"

I stood, making my way to the massive window overlooking the dark forest as the pain of what happened rippled through me again. "An unpleasant one. I need to leave for a little while, Kymra. I have to know if they still exist."

Kymra's eyes dropped to the book in her hands as she asked, "They?"

My lips pursed together as she looked back to me. Her cheeks drained of color as it all suddenly clicked together for her.

"Should we even try to find them?" she asked in a hushed tone. As if one of the servants would hear her and start blabbing to everyone I was interested in those beasts. "They're dangerous, Arthur."

"I know they can be tamed," I said, walking towards her. I pulled the book from her hands, setting it down on the table before I tucked her soft hands in mine. "I *have* to know, my love. If they are the difference between keeping you and Khalan safe or losing my kingdom, then I must try."

She slumped in her seat utterly lost in thought. "I worry about this."

"I know," I said softly, "but this could be a good thing. You and Khalan will stay with Liam while I go look."

Kymra sighed before she shot to her feet and paced before me. "But what if you find yourself against one that can't be tamed? What then, Arthur?!"

Worry etched her brow, and I sighed as I stood. My shadows slithered out from my feet, pulling Kymra back into my arms. I held her close, breathing in her lavender scent from the soap we bought at the Market, and after a moment her rapid heart began to slow. A slow smile spread across my face. *I got lucky when I met her.*

"I will only look," I said softly. "The second things get hairy, I'll slip through the veil and come home."

"Promise?" she asked quietly. So quiet that I barely heard her, but fear and trepidation were in her tone, and I never wanted that to be there.

"Promise," I replied, kissing her on the top of her head. "Now, go get you and Khalan packed. It might take me some time for me to get where I need to go."

She sighed as she pulled away. "You better come back to me in once piece, Arthur Drakos. *One* piece."

I grinned. "As you wish."

Bonus Chapter

Getting to the harbor near Oceanus, no problem.

Securing a boat, easy.

Finding this stupid island in the middle of monster infested waters... Eh, not so much.

I secured a small one man boat that could handle the massive waves on the seas and took off alone. I didn't know what lay before me, and I didn't want to risk needless lives if I actually found the place. I also wanted no one else to know what I was up to. It had been a week already though, and I was beginning to lose hope.

I opened up my supply bag and grabbed the last apple. I was nearly out of supplies, and the idea of slipping through the veil to grab more made me nervous. Getting back to a market, no big deal. Getting back to the boat in the middle of the ocean that would more than likely drift while I was away... That would be trickier. I didn't plan this as well as I thought.

I turned the boat towards the setting sun. The freaking island was not easy to find. No one in the harbor was any help either. It was like the dragons simply wrote themselves off the map somehow or whoever left those bones did it for them. This was a mystery island, and I was merely going off the advice of one old fisherman who explained a section of waters he and his family avoided. He said dark forces were at work in that area, and that was what I was searching for now. But no matter where I cast my shadows, I found nothing.

I tried not to shudder when I thought about the lost people at the village in the Forbidden Woods. *Who could be powerful enough to kill off my entire kind?* I wondered. The endless ideas stressed me and my shadows out, but every minute out in this God awful sea was worth it if I could find the dragons. I just had to keep trying.

Kymra and Khalan sent me many messages throughout my time on the boat. It was entertaining to hear the stories they had to share. I was missing an awful lot, which only made me feel worse, but this was important. At least that's what I kept telling myself. It was still nice to hear their voices through the shadows though.

I leaned over the wheel as I ate my apple, watching the waters before me. Luckily, I haven't run into any monsters, but I knew better than to trust dumb luck. I kept one eye on the dark waters just in case. There was no way I wanted to fight *any* of the rumored creatures that lived here.

Suddenly, I saw something just ahead, and I squinted my eyes to see better. I held my hand up to block some of the setting sun as I chewed on the piece of apple in my mouth. *What in the heck was that?* I wondered, cocking my head to the side as I tried to figure out what that solid white cloud was. It looked just like a massive wall of white cloud that stretched over a large circumference. *It looked like my shadows honestly,* I thought to myself. *Only white... But shadows weren't white.* This white mist blocked everything though. You couldn't even *see* passed it. *It must be some sort of smoke.* Even though that thought still seemed ridiculous. *Maybe I could pass through it?*

I adjusted the boat and headed straight for the white wall. *This has to be it,* I thought. I've searched all over these waters, and this was the general location that fisherman gave me. The map I purchased at the harbor had nothing marked in this area either. *Things were looking up.*

My boat neared the wall, and I braced myself to pass through the mist. What I did *not* expect was to bounce off the stupid thing. The boat lurched forward, and I barely caught myself in time before I face-planted on the deck. My eyes narrowed as I searched the front end. The boat was intact at least, but it was stuck somehow. I frowned as I approached the bow. The white wall was exactly how it looked. White smoke-like shadows trapped in some sort of invisible wall. I looked on either side and the wall went on for miles. Placing my hands on my hips, I studied the white wall. It went as high and as far as I could see. *It must wrap around the entire island.*

I slowly extended my hand, wondering if my shadows would be enough to let me through. My hand touched the wall, feeling an oddly familiar power flow through the mist. It was strong, but solid as can be, and I definitely wasn't getting through. *All this effort only to be stopped at the door? Maybe I just needed to give a little more?* My shadows pulled from my core, slamming into the white wall before me. The blast was enough to shove me back, but still not enough to open the door. I groaned, dropping to the deck floor in a frustrated heap. *Well, what do I do now?*

I watched the sun continue to set before me as I debated what to do now. Not a sound came from the other side of the wall, and no other boat drew near. I had no idea if this was even the island of Dangeni, and no real way to find out. Everything was a guess at this point. Suddenly, an angelic voice entered my mind.

"I miss you."

My heart ached when I heard Kymra's voice. Those three little words meant the absolute world to me. *I missed my family.* This was the longest I had been gone from them, and I hated every second I was away. Kymra gave me an update everyday so I knew they were okay, but I hated not being there to protect them myself. Plus, I just missed them. I missed the way Khalan grumbled every morning because he hated porridge or whatever breakfast Kymra and the staff made. I adored listening to Kymra snore slightly and the way she'd sleep with her hands above her head. I missed the gentle kisses she'd give after a long day of work or the way Khalan would run to me when something in the forest frightened him.

I missed *them*.

I stood, turning the white wall once more. *Maybe this was for the best. Maybe dragons weren't the answer I was looking for.* Guilt twisted at my core. I had been gone away from my family for too long. Anything could have happened to them too, but I wouldn't know because I wasted my time chasing extinct creatures. It was clear the dragons weren't an option for me. Not right now at least.

My shadows pulled at my feet, and with one last sigh, I stepped through the veil. Laughter and unrelenting chatter filled my ears as I emerged into Liam's massive ballroom. The people around gasped as my shadows filled the room, and I ignored the hesitation the people still felt towards me.

"Dad!"

My gaze turned to find Khalan and Zoey running towards me. The corners of my mouth rose, and I knelt down to scoop up my son.

"I've missed you, son," I said as he wrapped his arms around me, patting Zoey on the head, "and you, Miss Zoey."

"Hello, King Arthur," she said softly. Her bright red curls swayed as she bounced on her tiny feet. I loved that she wasn't afraid of me, and I released my shadows around her. She smiled wide, giggling as they playfully tugged on her curls and swished around her feet.

"Arthur!" Liam shouted across the room. He stood at his table, waving with Kymra and Agatha. My heart melted when my eyes met my wife's, and I grabbed Zoey with my shadows and lifted her in the air. She squealed loudly, and I chuckled as I wrapped my arm around her. With both children in my arms, I crossed the room, ignoring the ones who stared. Setting the kids down to play, I wrapped my arms around my wife and pulled her in. My lips found hers immediately, and I breathed in the lavender scent that was her.

"Welcome home, my love."

Her voice was heavenly, and I felt better about my decision to return home. My quest was a dead end, and I was sick of leaving my family in someone else's care.

"I missed you too," I said softly.

"How was your quest?" George cut in, and I turned to the table. My eyes narrowed on him, and he shifted nervously in his seat.

"What?" he said defensively. "We *all* know you left on some urgent quest, and I just wanted an update. We're all allies after all."

I gave a pointed look to Liam. *I didn't realize what I was doing was getting broad-casted to the Lords and Dukes already.*

"I believe what I informed the council was that Arthur would be unavailable for some time, and we should welcome his family in with loving arms," Liam corrected firmly. "We do not need an update from King Arthur as this mission was not commissioned by my Kingdom, George. Should Arthur need allied support then that would be another matter. For now, let's let him settle in and eat. He's been away from his family long enough."

I gave my friend a grateful nod, who returned it promptly.

"*We're family, Arthur,*" he said through the veil before moving his foot off the shadows. *And how true those words were.* Kymra pulled me away from a brooding George to the back where a banquet of food lie. She began to fill my plate, and I was never more grateful to this girl.

"You will tell *me* all about your mission though," she said softly. "Right?"

My mouth rose to a soft smile. "Of course, my love. It was a fruitless endeavor anyways."

Her brow rose, and I shrugged my shoulders.

"It might be better to just drop it like you said," I told her quietly. We stood together on the side as the room chattered on and danced about. I remember spying on nights like this long ago. *Funny how things work out.*

"Did something happen to make you change your mind?" she asked, worry etching her brow.

"In a way," I answered with a sigh. *More like the lack of anything happening really.* "This whole excursion just got me thinking. Maybe it is better we stay quiet and out of sight. Maybe I don't need..."

My voice trailed off, and I scanned the room. Maybe it was nerves getting the better of me, but I couldn't bring myself to say the word. Not with so many people around. If word got out I was searching for dragons... I shook my head. "What we have going for us is a good thing. We just need to focus on our family and our kingdom. Nothing more."

Kymra gave me a smile, standing on her tiptoes to kiss my cheek. "I think that is the right call too. Besides, while you may doubt your abilities in protecting our kingdom and our family, I *never* have."

Color stained my cheeks, and I dropped my head, letting the hood on my shirt cover me in darkness. *God, this woman...* I thought to myself. *She doesn't know what she does to me, but I don't deserve her.*

"Come," she said, pulling me back to the table. "You've had a long day of travel, and I've missed my husband. Take me home and tell me everything."

And I did just that.

About the Author

M. L. White is a Fantasy and Shifter writer primarily as she is obsessed with wolves and all things fantasy or dragon related. She loves to read, and actively seeks out books that suck her in and make her feel like that world is better than reality, so she is determined to spread that same joy to others with her writing. Her books are like a movie in your head with characters you can't help but fall in love with.

When M. L. White is not writing, she's chasing after her three children and taking care of her wonderful husband. They're her whole world so she's pretty busy spending as much time with them as possible. You can find her walking the trails with her two dogs or gaming with her husband and son in her free time as well!

You can connect with me on:
- https://www.authormlwhite.com
- https://x.com/Author_MLWhite
- https://www.tiktok.com/@author_mlwhite
- https://www.instagram.com/author_mlwhite

Subscribe to my newsletter:
- https://dashboard.mailerlite.com/forms/1169872/137001126070322601/share

www.ingramcontent.com/pod-product-compliance
Lightning Source LLC
LaVergne TN
LVHW041919070526
838199LV00051BA/2665